A CASE OF
ROYAL
BLACKMAIL

A CASE OF ROYAL BLACKMAIL

by
SHERLOCK HOLMES

MEDIA A

THE
CONAN DOYLE ESTATE

Published by Affable Media Ltd
Beaulieu, Hampshire, UK

ISBN 978-1-91349-142-0

Printed in the UK by Jellyfish print solutions

Contents

CHAPTER I

Oscar Wilde

EVERY CRIME MUST have a motive, that much is clear. The motive behind my crime against the English language in writing this account is that I have just completed a case that may be of some significance to historians in years to come. The case lasted for just one month, the whole of July 1879. The opportunity to write it is occasioned by spare hours during the Christmas and New Year celebrations, when as usual Brother Mycroft and I find ourselves here in the East Riding of Yorkshire spending time with our parents. I am also aware that events just five months old are still fresh in my mind, that the many case notes kept during that time are still decipherable, and so with time to write and recall, and with paper and ink to spare, my crime shall commence.

It is tempting to start at what seems to be the beginning, the invitation to a meeting with the royal solicitor George Lewis to help him untangle a blackmail case arising out of the Prince of Wales's abundant romantic endeavours. I shall explain how that came about presently. However, the case really began with something that at the time seemed to be completely unconnected, a visit to my Montague Street rooms by an unknown poet, Oscar Wilde.

I was feeling unusually melancholy on that uncomfortably hot and airless morning of 1 July. I had spent most of the morning in the Reading Room at the British Museum researching the subject of bees with which I have a growing fascination, and from whom I am increasingly taking instruction. Another reader had left a glass door open and the way the light fell I saw a reflection of myself in it, too clearly. I saw a rather gaunt-looking 24-year-old man, too tall for many, too thin for most, with prospects that amounted to a dream, with rooms that amounted to the barely adequate, with friends that amounted to the far between, with clients as sparsely scattered as friends and with habits shared only by the antisocial. I am usually content with my lot, a lot I had after all chosen for myself. Maybe the unusual melancholy was spurred on by the long spell of summer heat, the air stuck and lifeless in the great domed room, the habitués stretching the Reading Room's 'Rules of Attire' with loosened ties, rolled-up sleeves and even, out of sight, kicked-off boots.

The first sign of trouble came at eleven o'clock as I was about to leave to keep the appointment with Mr Wilde. All the doors and windows were wide open in a vain attempt to let the air circulate, when the noise of a voice amplified by a megaphone struck up in the near distance. Inquisitive, I hastened to leave. This sound outside became louder as I neared the main door, and outside on the steps was a man with his back to me standing on a half-yard box rabblerousing a crowd of about a hundred malcontents arranged in a loose semicircle in front of him. They held banners and placards, all proclaiming the bearers to be members of the Marylebone Anarcho-Syndicalists Union. Now the speaker's words became clearer.

'...we ever see this so-called "Majesty"? No, we don't. Do we want to see her? No, we don't. Do we need to see her or her kind ever again? No, brothers and sisters, no we don't. And why don't we ever see her? Because she's cosseted away in one of her luxury palaces paid for by the skin off your knuckles and the blisters on your feet, that's why we don't see her. Flunkies attend her every wish, why, I don't suppose she even has to wipe her own royal arse. Parasites, feeding off your blood, every one of them. Now this dwarf queen is bad enough, but you know the worst of them all? Her fat pig of a son Edward, calls himself Bertie, the Prince of [foul word] Wales. Never even thought about doing an honest day's work, let alone done one. Leech number one, mark my words brothers and sisters and – Hello, hello, comrades...what have we here?' I was aware that all eyes were now looking at me. 'Leech number two, by the look of this particular specimen of a bourgeois running dog!'

Now others started abusing me.

'Shame!' cried one.

'Swine!' shouted another.

'Monarchist lackey!' yelled yet another.

I grant that compared to the rabble I was cleanly dressed and the satchel full of papers may have given an un-anarchic impression. I turned to confront my accuser. Instantly I recognised him: Frank Connell, a well-known confidence trickster and illegal bookmaker who had featured in the May edition of the *Illustrated Police News*.

I strode straight up to him and could sense the crowd

closing in around us. 'Frank Connell, I know who you are, and these fine people should know too. Give me that megaphone this instant!' I had the considerable advantage of height over him, even standing on his box, and as I strode up advanced, in shock he stumbled backwards. I grabbed the megaphone, took his place on the crate and addressed the throng:

'Good anarchists of Marylebone, you have been misled. Your speaker is a well-known fraud, Frank Connell. He is no more the anarcho-syndicalist than I am. His usual twist is Bible-bashing, quackery, or scratch-bookmaking. Why, I can see his colleague passing with a hat among you now. Give these rogues not a penny.'

'How do you know?' a shout came back from the crowd.

'Because I'm a consulting detective, and it's my job to know. This man is no stranger to the police or the press.'

Behind me a scuffle between Connell and one of the mob broke out. I skipped down from the box and made my way out through the crowd.

'Oy, not so fast. Who are you?' A large man of military bearing stood in my way. He wore the black badge of anarchy and the red badge of communism and stank of un-wash. I said: 'My name is Holmes, Sherlock Holmes. Now please, let me through.'

'You look like a toff to me.'

'I assure you, sir, I am no toff. Look out!' I pointed to the sky. As he looked up, I brought my heel down hard on his toes and as he took to one leg, I barged myself a gap in the horde, made my excuses, was rewarded only by more foul oaths and abuse, and left.

Back at my rooms in Montague Street I prepared for my visitor with a swift tidy-up. I looked again at the card he had hand-delivered two days ago. The address at the top read: '13 Salisbury Street, London, WC2'. I knew the road, just off the Strand backing down to the River Thames, hard by Waterloo Bridge. I read the message aloud: 'Mr S. Holmes, I am, sir, indebted to our mutual friend Victor Trevor, Esq., for recommending I consult with you about a theft, in the hope of recovery thereof. Unless you inform me otherwise, I intend to visit you on Thursday at noon. Yours in the keenest of anticipations, Oscar Wilde.'

What to make of it? The handwriting was neat, right-handed, symmetrical, generously looped, carefully crossed and forward-facing – and reminded me that the new science, some say false science, of graphology was on my list of subjects to study. From what minima I knew of graphology at that time, his card yielded little in the way of clues beyond pointing to a warm-hearted and generous personality. Salisbury Street is not particularly residential, being mostly clerical offices and Number 13 meant nothing to me. I imagined the rent would be low, the convenience middling and depending where it was on the street, the river view variable. Neither a smart nor disreputable address, but certainly an unusual residential one. To start the note with 'Mr S. Holmes' shows a lack of formality, whether on purpose or out of ignorance was hard to tell. Presuming that he had actually met my friend Victor Trevor, that must have been in Norfolk as Victor is a home bird given the choice. Unless of course they met at Oxford for some reason. Then there is 'consult with' which hints at an Irish, or even an American author. The middle sentence is finely balanced, suggesting someone with an eye or ear for literature. 'Yours in the keenest anticipations' is not a recognised complimentary close, far from it, indicating a creative, extrovert streak in my visitor. Musing thus, I was grateful for my alarm clock sounding at 11.55am, its five-minute warning bell a habit I have developed to remind myself of immediate events.

Twenty-one minutes later the doorbell rang and I greeted Wilde at the front door and invited him to follow me up to the first-floor rooms. We both had to clamber over and around a gang of plumbers installing hot water pipes for the new boiler, with my landlady and cousin Sara Holmes overseeing manoeuvres. He was tall, as tall as me but considerably more heavily built. The two of us made fine use of the small front room. His hair was chestnut brown and fashionably long, his soft face unfashionably close-shaven and noticeably pale, made more so by stray freckles, great green eyes and perfectly arched eyebrows. His smile showed slightly green teeth, probably caused by mercury, possibly taken as a cure for syphilis, but that would be to prejudge him. He wore no hat, in itself singular, even at this time of year. The large black frock coat was silk-trimmed and cross-sewn, and carried over his arm in a concession to the heat of the day. He still wore a brightly flowered waistcoat covering a black silk shirt, ending in harp-motif amethyst cufflinks, and a silk cravat, black with white lilies, held in place by a ruby tie-pin. His trousers were pale brown, the socks hidden, and the brown brogue shoes dusty from a long walk in London's streets. He was out of breath, surely not caused by the short flight of stairs, as well as sixteen minutes late.

I poured tea; he took one sugar and no milk.

'Where did you meet our mutual friend Victor Trevor?' I asked.

'At Oxford,' he replied, sitting down. 'We were all three there together as it happens, different colleges of course. You left a year before your time. Trevor and I were both members of Apollo Lodge and we stayed in touch. Last week was the Lodge reunion and he mentioned your genius at detection. The mystery of the good ship *Gloria Scott.*' His voice was loud and soft at the same time, his speech perfectly rhythmical, a combination I had never heard before.

'And what needs detecting?' I asked.

'The very devil,' he said, standing up, 'someone has stolen my tie-pin. Normally I would be merely annoyed, but like Beelzebub rising from an undiscovered circle, my mothership Lady Wilde is visiting me next week. Annoyance would be a mercy compared to her ladyship noticing the vanishment of the tie-pin.'

'It was a present from her?'

'Worse, it's a family heirloom. The unkind would posit *the* family heirloom.'

'Intaglio amethyst, 28-carat?'

'How did you know that?' he asked, almost accusingly.

'From the motifs on the cufflinks you are wearing now.

Clearly part of an incomplete set. The jeweller I presume was Carragher's of Dublin?'

'Yes,' he said. He seemed a bit put out. 'And I suppose you know the value?'

'About two hundred pounds.' He didn't disagree. 'I notice that you have just arrived by boat from Ireland,' I asked.

'I didn't say that,' he said.

'You didn't have to,' I replied. 'Your frock coat is cross-sewn in the Irish style. Your accent is almost perfectly English, except for the smallest lilt on the elongated "a" vowel; an Irish or West Country denominator. You said you were at Oxford, but there was no need; your cravat has the Magdalen crest and Magdalen arranges with Trinity College Dublin. The dock strike in Dublin only ended last weekend, so you have either been here a few days or more than a month. You still have the faintest trace of the passenger's exit stamp on your left wrist, so the former. And the missing tie-pin is just that, a simple pin without a clasp or catch?

'Yes, straight in and out.'

'You couldn't have been pickpocketed or mug-handed as the tie-pin is five feet three inches off the ground and right in front of your eyes. It must have been taken when you were sitting down and almost certainly asleep. Have you been on public transport or in a club recently?'

'I never go on public transport, the seats are too sordid and the passengers too variable. And the germs, insufferable. But yes, I was in the Arts Club in Dover Street three lunches ago, my first day back, and did fall asleep in an armchair after a particularly famous lunch.'

'And who were you lunching with?'

'Algy Swinburne, if you must know. Are you suggesting – ?'

'No, not at all. I am merely calculating that it's not impossible for anyone in the club at the time, members, guests or staff, to easily have removed it when you were asleep. It's a wide field. When did you notice it missing?'

'In my rooms at Thames House, when I was disrobing.'

'Thames House?'

'It's what we fondly call 13 Salisbury Street. On account of the view. If you lean out of the top floor window and someone hangs on to your ankles, you can just glimpse the odd putrid ripple on the river. Look, Holmes, here's my idea. Why don't you come round and see if there's been a burglary? To put my mind at rest. The alternative is that I've lost it. I could of course never live with myself, although equally I will have to do so. We are having an art-and-tea party Sunday afternoon, why don't you join us?'

I explained that there was no point, as the tie-pin had certainly been stolen when he was asleep in an armchair at the Arts Club. But he insisted, and I am, I suppose, a man for hire. At this point we agreed upon my fee, a guinea a day plus incidentals to run for ten days if needed. On his insistence on my attending Thames House, I asked what an art-and-tea party was.

'Just that, a tea party with art,' he replied. 'You've heard of Frank Miles, I suppose?'

'I regret not.'

'He is an artist, of society portraits, largely. Very largely in his case, as you will see. He has the second floor and I have the first. We entertain on the third. Jimmy Whistler will be painting Lillie Langtry. Probably. Millais will be there, possibly, if we are lucky. Rosa Corder, usually. Prince Leopold or Princess Louise may be present too, if they are lucky. It's a cast of plenty and a moving feast. Art and tea, and a party too, you see.'

'Are you an artist too?' I asked.

'I am a poet,' he replied. 'Life is my art.'

And so we agreed to meet again on Sunday afternoon at Thames House. On seeing him out I saw a fresh envelope on the mat. Inside was a card from George Lewis of Lewis & Lewis & Co. To say I was surprised would be to underestimate my reaction, and not just because it was made on one of these new type-writers. It was to some extent like a royal summons; he was after all the royal solicitor and his wife Elizabeth was reported to keep one of the liveliest salons in London in their Portland Place house. Or so I had read in my favourite penny dreadful scandal sheet *Vanity Fair*. The summons was quite specific: *meet me in the Strangers Room at the Diogenes Club at noon tomorrow.* From no clients to two new clients on one cold and foggy morning: prospects were brightening up.

Chapter 2

A Royal Case of Blackmail

Before the second day of writing here in Yorkshire I thought I would take an early morning walk, three miles over to the nearest hamlet, Foggathorpe, and back. It would be impossible for anyone who lives hereabouts all the time, or any other country dweller who never visits one of our great cities, to imagine what this still, cool, clear, quiet and bright morning here would be like in London. A light mist rests like a wraith over the East Riding, waiting for the sun to rise enough to vanish it away. The only sound is birdsong and the occasional stone moving underfoot.

In London now, and this last summer to when my story relates, with the high-pressure air sitting steady overhead, the coal smoke rises from the locomotives and factories into something the cab-men call by a good old-fashioned Anglo-Saxon word: clag. There is not even a cab-man's word for the colour of the air, a kind of grey-brown, perhaps like faded hessian. Neither is there a term for the smell; acrid-acid is the nearest I can find. The eyes smart, the mouth feels clammy, the throat itchy. Much like the gardener longs for rain, the Londoner longs for wind to come back and blow the clag away.

And then there's the noise. The two-wheeled hansom cabs, the four-wheeled growlers, the six- or eight-wheeled omnibuses, all with steel-shod wheels rumbling over the cobblestones accompanied by three hundred thousand horses and their hoofs, light carts pushed along by hawkers and mongers selling their wares, shoe-blacks and street doctors touting and shouting; a Yorkshireman from here wouldn't so much see London, the air alone would make sure of that, as hear it.

Far from these dales, it was on such an unpleasant morning just over six months ago that I left 24 Montague Street, passed the Museum Tavern, turned left onto Duke Street and down Shaftesbury Avenue, over Cambridge and Piccadilly Circuses, cut through St James's Church, walked through St James's Square and onto Pall Mall. The War Office stood to attention opposite and left, the Oxford & Cambridge Club opposite and right, the Army & Navy Club on my right, the Junior Carlton Club to the left and just beyond lay the Diogenes Club. My pocket watch told the tale: 11.57am: 21 minutes for 1.2 miles; just as I had expected.

The Diogenes Club is my regular West End staging post. Luckily Brother Mycroft was one of the co-founders and I soon found myself near the top of the small waiting list for membership. There is only one rule: no talking. This Trappist existence is fine between members, in fact it is the very purpose of the place, but was sometimes vexing when members could not communicate with the staff. A form of semaphore soon evolved. On arrival, the hall porter (I think his name is Jenkins, but we have never said hello), tapped his left shoulder twice and pointed upstairs: my visitor had arrived and was in the one place where conversing was allowed, the Strangers Room.

George Lewis is middle height, middle weight and middle-aged. Most people passing him in the street wouldn't look twice in his direction. Not that he is non-descript: his clothes are expensively, rather than exquisitely, tailored, his shoes handmade, his cane silver-topped with the hallmark on display and his moustache carefully tended. His only remarkable feature is his eyes: onyx green, darting, full of life and inquisitiveness. I had certainly noticed him at the Diogenes before.

'Good morning, Mr Lewis,' I said, introducing myself. 'I've seen you here on other occasions, but as a member or a guest?'

'As a guest, usually accompanying your brother Mycroft. That's how I learned about it. The most discreet place in London. But it's you I want to meet today. Sit down there. Order us some coffee, will you? You have come to our attention recently.'

'Favourably, I trust, and not just because of my brother?'

I pulled the summons cord. Even in the Strangers Room the staff are not allowed to talk so I made the accepted signs for two Turkish coffees, two glasses of water and a plate of tack biscuits.

'Yes, very favourably. After all, you have recovered the lost gold crown of England. Tell me about that.'

He was talking about my most recent case. I explained to Lewis how an old college friend, Reginald Musgrave of the Manor House of Hurlestone, had found his man Brunton up to no good with what transpired to be an obscure family ritual. Fortunately, with the help of the maid Rachel Howells I was able to unravel his plot to steal the gold crown of King Charles I; unfortunately, Brunton died and so was unable to stand trial. Howells escaped.

'Most impressive,' said Lewis. 'Now, I have a new case for you. You are at the start of your career and still relatively unknown, if you will allow, so would be the ideal person to help me unravel the third most heinous crime of all.'

'So not murder, nor kidnapping, but blackmail?'

'Quite so. Take a look at this,' he said handing me a buff office envelope with a smaller, pale one inside it and inside that a sheet of plain writing paper.

It was a blackmail note written in marine blue ink, and clearly scrawled either left-handed by a right-handed author, or vice versa. It read:

> I have in my possession the Prince of Wales's notebook. His lady-loves are in code. By now I know the code. His entries on Ireland are scandalous too. My price is 1 gold bar, deposited with Rahn+Bodmer Co. Zurich, London account 8006. You have one month to pay or Reynolds News will print. Once paid, the notebook is burnt or sent to the Jew.

Taking the lens from my inside pocket I examined it from all the angles and with all the light available.

'It's addressed to you at your office and marked private,' I remarked. 'Is that a guarantee that it wouldn't be opened by anyone else?'

'Yes.'

'It hasn't been steamed and resealed, so you're the only person who's seen it, who knows about it?'

'Apart from you, yes.'

'And it arrived yesterday? So, written then or the day before, probably?'

'Probably. As you can see there's no stamp, so it must have been hand-delivered. Certainly after the office closes at six.'

'And it was sent to you because you are the Prince's solicitor. Are you the only one?'

'Look, I will be frank, and you will be discreet, I'm sure we can agree.' I nodded; he went on: 'I am the only one who deals with his private affairs. Aspects of his private affairs are of course his private affairs. There have been a number over the years, of course, as is well known. My job is to keep the private affairs private. He doesn't exactly help me, so in this case the word "private" means not widely reported.'

'The first question is how seriously to take it,' I replied. 'The notebook may not exist. The note is rather scant and an expected part of a blackmail note is missing.'

'Oh, take it seriously. He *has* lost his notebook, he told me so last week, asked if I had picked it up by mistake or he'd left it behind. The mistresses are bad enough, but at least everyone in his circle knows about them. I'm more worried about the Ireland entries. Bertie's views on the Irish are not likely to be charitable. The epithet "bog" may well feature, frequently. It could be more than embarrassing.'

'My first thought is that if he's told you he's lost his notebook, he's told other people in his circle. So we know the notebook exists, but we don't know where it is or who has it.'

'True, and you said something in the note was missing. What do you mean?' he asked.

'Whoever is behind it left us no means of contacting them. In other cases I have studied, for instance the Zanoni blackmail in Calabria or the von Püelm child kidnapping in Munich, or the recent O'Dyer blackmail in Chicago, there has always been a contact method. Not here. We could take the initiative and place a coded announcement in *The Times*. See if they reply.'

'Maybe,' said Lewis. 'Let's see what else you can discover from the note first. Any obvious clues?'

'I need to find out the type of ink and the type of paper the blackmailer has used. The author is clearly not writing with their natural hand. The study of graphology is new but of interest. But first, I wonder why is the wording in the first sentence so verbose? Why "I have in my possession" not just "I have"? Surely someone writing with the wrong hand would want to be as succinct as possible. What do you know about the notebook itself?'

'He carries it with him from time to time. About six inches by four, fits any pocket, nothing unusual,' he said.

'And who could have taken it?'

'That's a large part of the problem. He lives in Marlborough House and it might have been almost anyone who lives or works there. That's a few dozen people there and then. The Marlborough House staff with access to his dressing room and study, in fact any of the Marlborough House staff. Or two of them colluding. I'd say it was unlikely to have been any of the mistresses stealing it when he was asleep, or first thing next morning he'd have realised it could only be her, but it would have been easy enough for them otherwise. Apart from Marlborough House, he goes to so many functions, every time someone takes his coat and hangs it up another guest, or a pickpocket, or one of the host's staff could have taken it.'

'Yes, I see the problem. Then the "lady-loves" is archaic, but could be written like this as a bluff. And "the code", any idea what that means?'

'I can only think it is a code for his sexual encounters, maybe the type or the frequency. Or both. I'm guessing. As for being able to break the code, as the blackmailer claims to have done, I can only imagine it's not too difficult, having seen a number of them. The Prince is no Archimedes.'

'I'm sure you are right,' I said. 'Then, who would have a Swiss bank account? It's not too difficult to open one, most Swiss banks have London offices and it's the no names no pack drill, but equally it's not that usual. The gold bar could be deposited in their London office just as well as in Zurich. Takes it away from being a chambermaid or footman for instance, in fact pretty much anyone in service. If they were acting alone, of course.'

'And a gold bar doesn't seem like a servant's form of currency. Surely they'd want ready cash?' he suggested.

'I agree. Also, why the plus sign rather than the ampersand between the bankers' names?'

'Speed and ease, I suppose. As you say, whoever it was wrote with the wrong hand.'

'Maybe. Then "burnt" and not burned. Burnt is the American usage for the verb form, doesn't sit well with the archaic "lady-loves". Again that could be a blind. Are there any Americans in his circle?'

'Not in his circle but in his orbit. In other words, he meets people from all over the world, and again at a function any one of them could have taken his notebook.'

'And then "sent to the jew", without a capital J. Any idea who that might be?'

'Yes, me. At least I presume it's me, but I don't know for sure, only that it was sent to me. The person who sent it evidently doesn't like Jews. Unfortunately, that doesn't much narrow the field.'

'Is it widely known that you're Jewish?'

'I make no attempt to hide it or promote it. To me it's totally irrelevant. I never go to the synagogue unless I have to. I couldn't say that it's either helped or hindered me, but one way or another I am the most successful divorce lawyer in London and for those on the losing side it's an easy way to blame my success against them in court. But widely known? I don't know how to answer that.'

I looked again at the blackmail note. '*Reynolds News* is an interesting choice; why not *Vanity Fair* or *Truth* or *Sketch* or *Sphere* or any of the others? I must confess to reading them all,' I said, 'and penny dreadful novels too, the more sensational the better. I suppose *Reynolds News* is slightly more respectable, coming out every Sunday, whereas the others come out as scandal demands.'

'So, tell me, Holmes, how will you go about this?'

'I'm going to need your help as I don't know any of the likely suspects, the people in the Prince's orbit. But let's start with the likeliest candidates. First, I rule out the impossible, for example anyone who was physically absent, so out of town or abroad; or incapable, so anyone illiterate, or anyone without the wherewithal to commit the crime. Whoever remains, however unlikely, is a suspect. A suspect must have a motive, for no one commits a crime without a reason. Then I exclude those suspects without a motive and whomsoever remains is a – or usually the – prime suspect. It's just a logical process of elimination and deduction. Given time. Let's start with his mistresses.'

'That's why we are in the most discreet location in London,' Lewis laughed, looking round to check that no one had slipped in without us noticing. 'In no particular order: Agnes Keyser; Daisy Maynard; Jennie Spencer-Churchill, that's Lady Randolph; Lillie Langtry; Patsy Cornwallis-West; Lady Edith Denison. Edith, Countess Aylesford of course, she's one whose name got out in earlier days before my time. Lady Susan Vane-Tempest. Those are the steadier ones. The overnighters, if I may describe them thus, are less likely candidates, perhaps, with so much else of obvious value to steal.'

'And their spouses? Are they worth considering?' I asked.

'It's possible they might be in cahoots. Rather embarrassing, I'd think, but as you say not impossible. Ned Langtry is always broke, as of course is Lillie. William Cornwallis-West is too high and mighty to be involved in something like this would be my guess. Edith Denison is not married, closest would be her father Lord Londesborough. Lord Randolph Churchill, unlikely to the point of impossibility, I'd say. Jennie is American, by the way, you mentioned burnt not burned. Who's left? Agnes is alone and rich, too rich for this. Daisy is engaged, about to become Countess of Warwick, so no. Susan's a widow, quite a merry one too. Not her style. Don't you take notes?'

'I reserve a part of my brain for memory and I'm selective in its storage. What about opportunity? I'm presuming the book was stolen recently. Which of them would have seen him in the last month?'

'In the last month I'd say Lillie Langtry for sure, also Patsy Cornwallis-West as they're always together. Ah, I forgot Gwladys Herbert, now Lady Lonsdale. Sister of Lord Pembroke, you've heard of him, no doubt. And Gwladys with a double-u is now Gladys without a double-u. Not a mistress, but she is part of a trio with Patsy and Lillie and has certainly seen the Prince recently. Also, he would have met Edith; the Lady Denison one, not the Countess Aylesford one; that was a long time ago. Also, Lady Susan Vane-Tempest in the last week, but socially.'

'Lady Lonsdale, if it were she, has she a motive?'

'Just married to the fourth Earl, but they live apart. He's

always away hunting, shooting or catching something. No obvious motive, but she's trouble. Mischievous.'

'And the Prince's friends, if we can call the blackmailer a friend?'

'He is friends with Lonsdale, but more sports than social. His best friend is Christopher Sykes. They're always together. Sykes was once richer than he is now, mainly because he spends so much money entertaining Bertie. There aren't too many other people he can count as best friends. The fact is, he prefers female lovers to male friends. He knows dozens of people, of course, but not as friends.'

'Christopher Sykes is my local MP, in Yorkshire not London. He is nominally of the Conservative persuasion, but not known to have any interest in politics at all. What else do you know about him?'

'He's the second son of Sir Tatton Sykes, the famous horse breeder, which is the connection with the royal family. His main job is being Bertie's best friend, probably only friend in the sense that the rest of us have friends. That he is totally loyal and discreet, but just by keeping Bertie's company he must know about skeletons in cupboards that even I don't know about. Alix, that is Alexandra, the Princess of Wales is fond of Sykes too and often invites him to her parties to make up the numbers. He entertains the Waleses at his house in Berkeley Square and his Yorkshire pile, Brantingham Thorpe. What else? Rosa Corder is painting Sykes's portrait.'

I remembered Wilde mentioning her name in connection with the forthcoming tea-and-art party.

'And at Marlborough House, who are the main people there?'

'The ones whom I've met are Francis Knollys, his private secretary. He has a deputy, William McLeod and an equerry, Major John Lavery. The Earl of Gifford is Master of the Royal Household at Marlborough House. Princess Alix has just her private secretary, Commander Stephen Sandeman and her lady-in-waiting, Alice, the Countess of Derby. Alix and she are inseparable. She is also close to the royal nanny Valentina Kasperskaya, who was her childhood nanny. She's an old woman now, of course. But Francis Knollys is the principal player. Everything turns around him.

'A suspect?' I asked.

Lewis's clear eyes looked away, down and left, and he said thoughtfully, 'No, well, probably no. I suppose that means maybe yes. He's not rich, nor well paid, but lives in style, of course. I always think he is Queen Victoria's spy, but I have no proof of that. I'm sure you've heard that the Queen and the Prince fight like cat and dog. Once or twice I have thought, how can she possibly know that? He is loyal but untrustworthy, if that tallies.'

'Who's the cat and who's the dog?' I asked.

'Well, she is king of the castle to muddy the metaphorical waters. Ultimately, she controls the purse strings and she knows where every penny of his lavish life is spent. For his sake, and mine come to that, I really prefer she didn't find out about this missing notebook. One of the reasons I'm hoping for a quick result. She's the first to take the moral high ground on any personal issues and as for Ireland, heaven knows what he's written about that benighted isle. And then there's a whole other group of people that the Prince, and my wife come to that, know quite well, artists and their clique. He's not as close to them as his own Marlborough House set, but he does know them socially.'

'Anyone I might have heard of?'

'Jimmy Whistler is the most famous. He's gone bust. You heard about his court case?'

I said I had. I could hardly not have heard of it, reading the type of papers I read. The critic John Ruskin, talking of James McNeill Whistler, had said he'd never expect to hear a coxcomb asking two hundred guineas for flinging a pot of paint in the public's face. I must say I could see Ruskin's point, but it's not really my field. Whistler took Ruskin to court for libel and had won and lost. He won a farthing damages but no costs, and so lost every penny he had.

'Then there's Sir John Millais, another from my wife's salon. But it's just not his style, and I'm not saying that because of her. There's Rosa Corder, one of Whistler's models, a beautiful woman, a *belle dame sans merci* if ever there was one. She's a good artist too. Millais told my wife she forges Rossettis.'

'That's an interesting thought,' I said. 'That the entries could be forged.'

'I would consider that differently. I know there is *a* notebook, because I've seen it and he says he has lost it. The question is, does the blackmailer actually have *the* notebook or not?

Also, you know it is just exactly the kind of thing Bertie

would do, boast about his conquests. And we don't know what else is in there. I mean on top of Ireland. Private thoughts about Disraeli and Gladstone, foreign royalty, ambassadors. The Queen. It could be a catastrophe.'

The Thames House invitation was becoming increasingly relevant. 'Are there any others in this artists' clique he knows?' I asked.

'There's Frank Miles. He owns Thames House and many of the women meet there too, Patsy Cornwallis-West, Lillie Langtry and Gladys Lonsdale. And Oscar Wilde, a poet; he lives there too.'

I told Lewis I had met him, but not why.

'And George Reynolds of *Reynolds News*, now, that's an interesting connection,' he added.

'It is,' I said. 'May I keep the blackmail note? Also the envelope? I need to work on the paper and ink. And handwriting. And look for fingerprints.'

'Fingerprints?'

'Yes, it's early days but could be highly significant. I've been corresponding with Henry Faulds, a Scottish surgeon, who is working on a paper now. Each one of us has his own unique prints. I'm sure you can see the value, but I fear paper is not a good recorder.'

'Of course you must keep it,' he said. 'I've noted the contents. Oh, and one other member of the sets. Langdale Pike.'

'Now him I know,' I said. 'We were at school together. He gave me lunch at the Savage Club two months ago. He gossips non-stop. Now you mention him he'll be my starting point, I think.'

'Unless he's the blackmailer,' said Lewis. 'Be careful. And I don't exist, so we've never met.'

'Indeed we haven't,' I said, pulling the summons cord again to sign the chit. 'The announcement in *The Times*, I think we should do it. How about:

Edward's lost notebook. Reward given if sample page seen by George.

'Very well,' said Lewis. 'At least then we'll know if the blackmailer has the lost notebook or not. It sounds suitably obscure to everyone but our culprit. Why don't you put it in *Reynolds News* too? Seems to be their organ of choice.'

'By the way,' I asked, 'does Mycroft know about this?'

'Not in any detail. I had to vet you, though. In case anything went wrong later.'

'He would be to blame.'

'That's about the size of it, yes. But in fairness Mycroft is worried. As am I. The monarchy is unpopular as you know and this is the type of scandal that could easily spill over and excite the republicans. Not to mention the anarchists and communists.'

'Or the anarcho-syndicalists,' I added. 'Well, we'd better get to the bottom of it, and quickly.'

We exchanged cards and went our ways. I knew the exact shelves in the British Museum Reading Room where I could swot up on past cases of blackmail, and it was to these very shelves that I repaired for the rest of the day.

CHAPTER 3

A Tea-and-Art Party

IT IS A commonplace among Londoners that, every day, horses expel a thousand fresh tons of dung on to its streets. It is also accepted that every day only half of it is swept up. So to walk from Montague Street to Salisbury Street, to keep my appointment with Oscar Wilde and his art-and-tea party, is more pleasantly undertaken on lesser streets and alleys, unfrequented by horses and donkeys and their cabs and carts. But there is unpleasantness on the backstreets too: barely controlled high-wheeler bicyclists themselves avoiding the main streets, and the menace of crime. Not the interesting type of crime to which I intend to devote my life's endeavours, but the petty and violent crime carried out by snarlers and mug-hunters, as well as the ever-present crime, unseen until too late: pickpocketing.

I am tall, young and fit, an accomplished amateur pugilist and stride briskly with a swordstick, so I often venture where others might be more cautious. Thus, on this Friday afternoon, rather than endure he filth and odour of the more direct Drury Lane route, I planned to add a tenth of a mile to my walk, taking me along Bloomsbury Street, Endell Street, Bow Street and Wellington Street, and then over the Strand to my destination.

The footpads were waiting for me in Martlett Court off Bow Street. Three of them: one much more elderly than the others; one clearly drunk and one who looked quite capable. This latter would be my target, but first I must wait for their move.

'Yer oof from yer pockets!' snarled the older one, rushing towards me. I sidestepped and tripped him as he stumbled past. He fell flat on his face. While the other two were gawping at their sprawling comrade, in an instant I unsheathed the sword from my cane and thrust the point into the thigh of the capable one. He crouched over in shock and pain and took a blow on the temple from the knob on the cane for his troubles. The drunken one was easily despatched with an uppercut. He fell poleaxed on the pavement. I re-established my equilibrium and strolled on south to Salisbury Street, arriving at 4.31pm. Eight-tenths of a mile in fifteen minutes; a minute over schedule caused by the inconvenience en route.

Number 13 is at the Strand end of Salisbury Street and it does indeed have a narrow view of the river, especially if standing on the pavement looking south outside the entrance. I took a while to survey the house from the other side of the road to see how a burglar might enter, if one had done so, to steal Oscar Wilde's amethyst tie-pin, or indeed anything else that might have gone missing. It was a typical early-century town house. There were five floors; a semi-basement, a higher ground floor and three equal ones above it. I knew that Wilde lived on the first floor, Frank Miles on the second and the third, the lightest, was an open studio. All windows were identical and sashed. There were no balconies to the higher floors.

Even if Wilde had left his windows wide open, only a burglar with a ladder could have entered his flat from the exterior to the front of the building. Either someone had managed to enter through the main door, with a key or the help of someone already inside, or entry was from the back, almost certainly by way of the fire escape.

Even before I had climbed the steps to ring the bell the front door opened. An empire wife stood cross-gaited across the top step. She said she had seen me survey the house from across the road and wanted to know what I wanted to know. Once assured my visit was social and not governmental, we parleyed pleasantly enough in the entrance hall. Mrs Carr was a spinster, living there with her elderly parents, and was the landlady of the whole house. She said she should have been a gossip writer, with the comings and goings that went on upstairs. Royalty, Prince Leopold and Princess Louise. 'Professional beauties' whose photographs were in all the shops; Lillie Langtry, Patsy Cornwallis-West, Lady Lonsdale. Artists, she didn't know one from the other, but there were lots – and their friends too. And Oscar Wilde, now he's a poet. She particularly liked her Oscar, so witty, so charming. There was a whole group of them upstairs at this very moment, she said. Terrible mess they'd make, she assured me; she did all the cleaning for Mr Miles and Mr Wilde. I bade her a good afternoon and went upstairs to join them. One thing was sure: Mrs Carr was not the burglar, nor did she help anyone else to burgle.

The stairs were uncovered and creaked, dust was

everywhere: ideal for clue collecting but I had a feeling none would be needed. There was no reply from Wilde's door and party noises came from the third floor, so I climbed and entered.

Oscar Wilde came bounding over to greet me. With a hand on each of my shoulders and turning towards the room, he clapped his hands a few times and shouted, 'Everyone, this is Mr Sherlock Holmes! He is the consulting detective I was telling you about.' Everyone looked over at me and almost everyone immediately carried on conversing as before. All except one. I recognised him from the recent court-case photographs, the American artist James McNeill Whistler.

'In my country we have private detectives. What's the difference between a private detective and a consulting detective?' he asked.

'About a guinea a day,' said Wilde.

'Os, you know how useful a guinea would be right now,' Whistler replied. 'But seriously, Holmes, I would like to know?'

I replied: 'A private detective investigates matters too wearisome for the police to bother with, whereas a consulting detective is called upon by the police or a government department when they have exhausted all their own resources.'

'So he's helping me find my amethyst tie-pin. Far too important a matter to leave to the police, or the government,' Wilde explained.

'I give up,' said Whistler, then to me: 'Frank over there

has just won the Turner Medal at the Royal Academy for his *An Ocean Wave*. That's the canvas.' He gestured to the painting on an easel in the centre of the room.

'What do you think of it?' I asked.

'Oh, I wasn't entered this year,' Whistler replied. 'There's no point with all those Jews judging. There's another winner over there.' He nodded towards the far wall where Poynter's portrait of Lillie Langtry hang.

'Poynter the painter doesn't begin to capture her,' suggested Wilde as an aside to me, 'not like Jimmy here did. Jimmy spent as much time capturing "The Lily" in bed as on the easel. Come and meet Millais. He and Lillie are both Channel Islanders.'

Millais was charming and most polite to this new-coming intruder with the unusual profession and he introduced me around. Frank Miles was sketching Gladys Lonsdale, six feet tall and dressed as flamboyantly as her reputation decreed. He waved hello with his pencilled hand without taking his eyes off her; she was as still as a rock in a yellow, silk-embroidered gown with a full draped bustle, white gloves and a magnificent, jewelled comb adorning her braided hair. She managed a smile and a mouthed hello. Then Millais introduced me to Patsy Cornwallis-West, Lillie Langtry and Princess Louise, who were in deep conversation about keeping diaries, of all things. The first two were indeed extraordinarily beautiful women, Cornwallis-West in a pink flounced floral dress decorated with lace and Langtry in a striped blue ensemble trimmed with ribbons; Cornwallis-West outgoing and engaging, Langtry more reserved and formal. My thoughts turned to the Prince and these two wonders of womankind. No doubt he was spared the complications, the distractions of dealing with the female part of life's equation. The complications were left to those like George Lewis and now me to smooth away; the distractions were only caused by the Prince having nothing meaningful in his life to be distracted from.

As Mrs Langtry was finishing talking to me, she said loudly so everyone could hear, 'By the way, as you are a detective, are you able to find my husband in a compromising position? I need to hurry up my divorce.' The room laughed and looked at me. I thought about it for the briefest of moments: a good way to reach inside the blackmail case on the one hand, but my career plans didn't involve being known as a mere hawkshaw. I declined apologetically; she returned a smile to question the most obstinate bachelor's resolve.

'Holmes, we have a burglar to catch. Come.' It was Wilde at my elbow guiding me towards the door. 'Au reservoir from Oscar's detective, everyone!' he shouted into the room.

'Au reservoir, Oscar's detective!' half the room called back.

It didn't take me long to determine that Oscar Wilde hadn't been burgled. All the seals and jambs were sound and there was no sign of a forced entry, and I'd already ruled out Mrs Carr who he said had the only other key. The sitting-room ran along the entire front of the house and the bedrooms, a double and a single, ran across the back, with a tiny kitchen and bathroom – with a fixed bath – respectively at either end. The main room was fantastically decorated: the wood panels had all been painted white, better to show off the pieces of blue china, individual Moorish tiles and oriental rugs and hangings. One vase was fanned out with peacock feathers; another sunflowers; another lilies. On one white panel were signatures of visitors: besides those of the Bohemians upstairs there were other scrawls that Wilde proudly deciphered: Rossetti, Violet Fane, William Morris, Walter Pater, Algy Swinburne, Johnston Forbes-Robertson, Ellen Terry, Leslie Ward. Then there were his 'many purely social lights' such as the Duchess of Beaufort, the Duchess of Westminster, Lord and Lady Dorchester and 'of course' the Rosslyns.

'One day yours too will be here,' said Wilde, 'when you find my tie-pin. How much did you adore Lillie Langtry?'

'Delightful, and of course beautiful,' I replied.

'I discovered her, you know. Frank Miles says he did, but he didn't. Jimmy Whistler says he did, but he didn't, except between the sheets. I think she's a more important discovery than America.'

'Do you see her often?' I asked.

'We are quite the gang, you see. Lillie, Frank, Jimmy and Oscar. We are her other life, her Bohemian life. When she's not ladying it with us, she's lording it with the Marlborough House set. I also invented her. Dressed her, educated her. Before *moi*, she didn't know a Ming from a Tang. But sometimes "The Lily" is so tiresome. She won't do what I tell her. I assure her that she owes it to herself and to the whole world to drive daily through the Park dressed entirely in black in a black victoria drawn by black horses and with *Venus Annodomini* emblazoned on her black bonnet in dull sapphires. But she won't. Tiresome, wouldn't you say?'

'Unreasonable,' I agreed. 'Now I would like you to lend me your other tie-pin, the ruby one you were wearing when we met.'

'Why so?' he asked. 'I'm not entirely unattached to it. It's a Burmese ruby as it happens. I wore it last night to the *Vanity Fair* reception. I'm one of their contributors, you know.'

'I didn't know. That's interesting. Regarding your tie-pin, I need it to fence it, or rather pretend to fence it. To see who might have tried to sell and buy your amethyst one.'

'And what is fencing when it's at home?' he asked.

I explained. He said 'touché' and told me I kept strange company; I could hardly demur. I left with a ruby tie-pin in its original box, but it wasn't the same as the one he was wearing in Montague Street.

CHAPTER 4
Langdale Pike

IT'S NOT JUST in the physics laboratory where opposites attract. Langdale Pike and I are surely as opposite as north and south magnetic poles, but ever since we met at college we have rubbed along well together. He studied the liberal arts; I studied science. In sport he was a team player, rugby in winter, cricket in summer; I was my own team, boxing in winter, rowing in summer. Like Victor Trevor, my other friend there, he belonged to Apollo Lodge; I doubt it ever occurred to either to invite me to join. Our common ground was the Varsity College Players, in particular the Michaelmas 1875 production of Edward Bulwer-Lytton's *Richelieu*, where he played the Cardinal (with the line 'The pen is mightier than the sword') and I played Cambronne. In London we stayed in touch with the odd lunch and theatre visits. My own deficiencies will be obvious to the reader shortly if not already, his deficiencies are best described in that he is languid, dissolute, indolent, lackadaisical, apathetic; all of these and more, and all saved by his three great attributes: curiosity, clubbability and good humour. Pike collects people and people collect Pike.

His family are comfortably off without being obviously rich, a bit like mine but maybe more so. I suppose at our age, 24, he doesn't have to work; after all he doesn't do much that needs money except loaf around his various clubs, and he has enough to pay the club fees and dues. He drifted into his line of work as a gossip-peddler to newspapers through a sense of fun as much as anything else. Ironically, his secret is discretion: nobody except a few very close friends knows how he plies his trade, so when at a party Lady A tells Pike that her cousin the Earl of B is cavorting with the actress C and they read the story a month later in one of the society columns of a newspaper or one of the scandal sheets, they never suspect it was Pike who'd picked up the guinea for the story. He was clever here, too: he would wait awhile after Lady A's indiscretion until the story had gained a little more currency before selling it on. If he felt it wasn't gathering sufficient momentum under its own steam, he wasn't averse to giving it a helpful shove along the way.

When I arrived at Arthur's at 69 St James's Street, he was perched on his usual armchair in the bow window looking out at the comings and goings in club-land. Boodle's and White's are both on the other side of the road and Brooks's is just alongside. If the pickings were too thin, he would amble over Piccadilly to the Arts Club in Dover Street. He waved and gestured to me to come in as I walked past and moments later we were each enjoying a glass of dry sherry.

I was about to ask him about the Thames House set when he gave me the latest issue of *Vanity Fair*, opened on page 3. He pointed to a boxed item halfway down:

Black-eyed Lady of Distinction

A lady well known in Society is said to have been seen with two black eyes, most certainly not the result of self-embellishment. The question asked is who, or rather which, was kind enough to give them to her? We hear that there is absolutely no truth at all in the rumour that the perpetrator is seeking a divorce, and even less truth that one of the High and Mighty, or even, 'Heaven forfend', the Highest and the Mightiest himself will have to take the witness stand.

'One of mine,' he said.

'Who is she?' I asked.

'Holmes,' he said, 'you do live in your own world. Lillie Langtry, of course. And it's true, Ned Langtry did biff her. Well, half-true, he only gave her one black eye. Mind you, I don't blame him the way she performs.'

'With the Prince?'

'Yes, with "The Bertie" and more besides. Her Jersey sweetheart Arthur Jones is never far away. Then she has been paying, let us say afternoon visits, to Rudolf, Crown Prince of Austria. Lord Londesborough is a constant rumour. They say Millais, when he painted her Royal Academy portrait, knew her remarkably well, sheets-wise.'

'And Ned Langtry?'

'Poor man. He was an older widower with a yacht when they met and married. The yacht was her way off Jersey, literally and metaphorically. He was considerably less rich than the yacht implied. What little cash he had, she spent promptly enough. The yacht soon went to pay new debts. Now neither of them is in the funds, although they say he has a place in Ireland. As a husband he has become her chaperone and is openly cuckolded. A laughing-stock. He has, hardly surprisingly, turned to drink. Port by the draught, so I hear.'

'And the divorce you wrote about?'

'When I hear a rumour, I file it away in the rumour drawer. When I hear the same rumour from a different and unconnected source, I open the drawer and give it some air. That's where we are now; the rumour is taking the air. A more assiduous correspondent would go looking for the truth, if any, behind the rumour. But I prefer to wait for the truth, if any, to come to me. It usually does.'

'And why *Vanity Fair*?' I asked.

'I like to spread my favours around evenly, even strategically. There are fifteen daily morning newspapers, nine daily evening newspapers and nearly four hundred weekly magazines. Of course, not all the weeklies are weeklies. I divide them into periodicals like *Punch*, *Illustrated Police News*, *Truth*, *Sketch* and *Sphere*, and sporadicals – *London Drum* and *High Times Here* for example. The scandal sheets or garbage press or gutter papers, people call them all sorts of things, pay the most. And they're the most fun, let's face it. Most fun to read, most fun to be around. I'm friends with George Reynolds of *Reynolds News*, friends with Fred Burnaby of *Vanity Fair*. There's a new one, *Town Talk*, started by Adolphus Rosenberg, one of the famous Solly Boys gang.'

The Solly Boys was the nickname for a violent and well-known East End criminal gang run by the Solomons family, now in its third generation.

'Odd business for a gangster to be in, isn't it?' I asked.

'Rosenberg and the press? Yes, I suppose it is. He must have married into the Solomons by his name. Anyway, why so many questions? What are you up to?'

'Do you mean, what am I up to asking so many questions or what am I up to in general?'

'Both.'

I dissembled as best I could about the former and told him all about my studies and writing in the British Museum Reading Room, my visits to the Repton Boxing Club, my rooms at Montague Street, the tranquillity of the Diogenes Club, Ellen Terry's Ophelia at the Gaiety and Kitty Clive's invitation to the Garrick, but he wasn't London's best gossip-monger for nothing.

'Come now, Holmes, you didn't ask to meet me to tell me all you already told me two months ago at the Savage. Tell me what you really want to know, I might have the answer. Wait a moment. Another sherry, a canapé?' I declined the sherry; he ordered two small glasses of India pale ale and two herrings and horseradish on toast.

'It's a trifling matter,' I said. 'So trifling that I know it's of no use to you. Oscar Wilde has lost his amethyst tie-pin and he's asked me to try to find it. What have you heard about Oscar Wilde?'

'Only that his reputation far exceeds his achievements. I haven't met him, but I hear he's charming, probably an homosexualist, takes his company with Millais, Whistler and Lillie Langtry and her friends Patsy Cornwallis-West and Gladys Lonsdale. I often see Whistler up at the Arts Club. Millais too for that matter. If you tell me what to ask either of them I certainly will. But I've got a feeling this is about much more than a tie-pin.'

'So have I,' I said. 'But he is paying me a guinea a day plus incidentals to find it. It's worth two hundred pounds on the market, and much more to him, and I have no reason to doubt him. But still, I wish I knew more about his set.'

'Then why don't you come to George Reynolds's leaving party for Jimmy Whistler at the Oriental Club on Tuesday night?' said Pike. 'They will all be there, all the people we've been talking about and more besides. There'll be an auction to raise money for Jimmy, no doubt. You might find a bargain.'

I mentioned the small matter of not being invited, but he laughed and said that I'd been invited now and was to come as his guest. I was on the point of asking him about the other little matter on my mind, and thought better of it. But then there's something about Langdale Pike.

'Blackmail,' I said in spite of myself. 'I mustn't say much more than that, but if you ever hear any rumours of blackmail in Society, I'd like to know about it.'

'Aha, you're a dark horse, Holmes. I knew there was something more than the trifling on your mind. We shall have a fair trade of information. You know what I want, to be the first to press. I know what you what, underground information. Now tell me more about the blackmail.'

'We are still at the rumour stage, so it's now in your rumour drawer, but if you hear anything else perhaps you could give the rumour some air.'

CHAPTER 5

Wiggins

DECONSTRUCTING, DECIPHERING AND decoding the
blackmail note were not as simple as I'd hoped they would
be. The study of graphology was so new that there were
few published works on the subject. The British Museum
Reading Room could only find a reference to one book,
Handwriting of Junius by Twisleton & Chabot, 1871. The
subtitle read: *On the examination of the handwriting of a
large number of letters which were critical of King George III
and his government, by an anonymous individual, otherwise
known as Junius.* They did not hold it and could only
suggest antiquarian booksellers. At the Science Museum
Reference Library I found a lengthy but inconclusive article
in *New Discovery Chronicle* by Persifor MacDonald entitled
'Studying and Establishing Handwriting Characteristics'.
This in turn referred frequently to the *Société Graphologique*
in Paris and I ordered their *Traité Pratique de Graphologie*
by Jules Crépieux-Jamin from Hatchard's.

My analysis of the ink had not moved much further
forward either. MacDonald mentions something he called
'dichroism' – an effect of the ink changing colour when
illuminated and viewed from different positions. He notes
that, 'Wherever this occurs, the facts should be carefully
noted, because it offers a means of discriminating between
the ink possessing this property and other inks with more
or less the same character and appearance.' I didn't find that

particularly helpful, in fact it was rather obvious. My own estimation is that the ink will need a reagent such as an acid or alkaline, or a bleach of varying strength, to identify certain occlusions such as ferric compound which may turn bright blue with ferricyanide.

If research into the handwriting and the ink had been slow off the mark, the analysis of the paper was even further behind. I had written to the Master of the Worshipful Company of Stationers requesting an interview and was awaiting his reply. No one else seemed to share Lewis's sense of urgency. I noticed with a raised eyebrow that the Under Warden was a member of the Diogenes Club, but for now merely filed that away for safekeeping in a back room of the brain-attic. Even less progress had been made on the fingerprinting front, the powder not even detecting a smudge, but I was never very hopeful of this anyway.

Waiting for the various strands to come together, I turned my attention again to the case of Oscar Wilde's amethyst tie-pin. So far my knowledge of criminology had come from studying it objectively, but now I needed to practise it subjectively by acting the criminal myself. I remember the feeling that day, that heady mixture of fear and excitement, of heading into terra incognita with only one's wits as a guide.

I had Wilde's ruby tie-pin in a box and my plan was to see who would buy it without asking questions, reject whatever offer was forthcoming as being too low, and then to return later, disguised, and claim to be in the market to buy an intaglio amethyst tie-pin in a gold harp setting and see if they had one as Wilde had described it. If they did, I would return with him to identify it, and if he confirmed it, confront them and if they were not obliging, call in the Constabulary. But where to go? If as I suspected it was stolen by a member or one of the staff while he was asleep at the Arts Club, I suspected they would aim higher than a pawnbroker, who famously will take any valuables without questions and part with only the minimum amount of money. Hatton Garden is the centre of the London jewel trade and so I set off from Montague Street, turned left onto Great Russell Street, right onto Southampton Row and along Theobalds Road to the north end of Hatton Garden. This time there were no unpleasant incidents en route and the one-mile walk took exactly the fifteen minutes it should take.

For no good reason my first stop was Hirschoff's, Number 19. I told them I was selling a family heirloom and asked if they would be interested in buying it. They looked at the tie-pin and asked if I had the original receipt or any supporting documentation like an insurance certificate or clause in a Will. Clearly I didn't and their interest in the transaction came to an immediate halt. At Jordan & Rappzavitch a few shops down, they were actively hostile about the lack of paperwork and presumed, reasonably enough, that I was a thief and threatened to send for the police unless I left immediately. I tried again, this time at Isadore Mitziman at Number 33. They at least showed some interest, took the jewel behind a glass screen, examined it under a spotlight and microscope and came back with the news that it wasn't a Burmese ruby but one from Siam and as such was more or less valueless. He suggested I take it to a pawnbroker, who might give me ten or fifteen shillings for it. I asked if there was a halfway house between a jeweller and a pawnbroker and he recommended a visit to Bruno Decisi's stall in Clerkenwell Road's Little Italy quarter.

The two great curses of London street life are pickpockets and street arabs, and of course the two often go together. For readers outside London, I should report that there are so many types of pickpockets that each has its own designation: dippers specialise in coat pockets; toolers prefer trouser pockets; a flimp is a snatch pickpocket; a fine wirer is the most highly skilled pickpocket and the most admired among his fellows; a maltooler works the omnibuses; a mobsman is well dressed and specialises in places where gentlefolk congregate; a snotter or wipe-hauler specialises in silk pocket kerchiefs. I am sure there are others I have yet to hear about.

The street arabs are not only London's curse, but London's shame. These urchins are often orphans, either literally or practically so on account of drunken or deranged parents, left free to roam the streets all day and having to live on their wits from the earliest age. Of course, wits means crime and crime means theft, either from shops or stalls, or people. Always dirty and dressed in rags, often barefoot, usually part of a gang and feral, their life is doomed before it has really started. It is just a matter of time before they are caught thieving, either red-handed by the victim who, being much taller and stronger, frogmarches them to the nearest Constabulary or occasionally by a bobby who just happens to be there when the crime occurs. They go to court and then inevitably to prison, are typically given a birching and a short spell of hard labour and sent back out a better informed and connected criminal than when they arrived. Along with others I help feed them in a small way, in this case by putting a sixpence in the bucket chained outside St Giles & St Geoffrey Church around the corner from Montague Street every time I walk past, the Anglican church providing them with soup or stew every evening, blankets and a pew to sleep on every night.

I mention all this because of what happened next. On the way to Little Italy, the corner of Saffron Hill and St Cross Street is abrupt and the pavement narrow, and turning it I was instantly collided into by a street arab sprinting full tilt. I was knocked back, but not down, and grabbed the urchin by his shirt, which immediately ripped, and then seized him by the neck. He was like a wild cat, arms flailing, desperately trying to wriggle free. But I had him firm in my grasp. A whistle came from behind in Saffron Hill, then another longer blast: then two bobbies came running towards us, one with handcuffs already out. They pulled up just short of us, puffing from the sprint.

'We'll take him from here, sir,' said the taller one.

'No need, Constable,' I said. 'I know it doesn't look like it, but he's with me.'

'No, it doesn't look like it, sir. Why is he squirming around like that if he's with you?'

I gave the urchin a swift clip around the ear with my free hand and said: 'Because he's a disobedient little arab who won't do what he's told. He knows when I get him home I'm going to put him over my knee and give him what's coming to him.'

'Best thing for them,' said the shorter one. 'Maybe he is known to us, what's his name?'

'Wiggins,' I said. Wiggins is a name I keep to hand and I have used it to disguise myself from time to time. When I was growing up it was the name of our gardener, now unfortunately no longer with us.

They looked at each other and shook their heads. Luckily there wasn't another Wiggins on their books.

'Very well, sir,' said the taller one, 'and give him a few extra whacks from me.'

'Wotja do that for, then?' asked the newly named Wiggins, no longer trying to escape and standing cheekily before me with his hands in his pockets.

'Because for the first time in your life you might be of some use.' I looked him over: eight to ten years old, no shoes, feet almost completely black from the soot and filth, short trousers several sizes too big for him held up by a twine belt, two layers of ragged shirt topped with an expensive-looking tweed scally cap, no doubt stolen from a resting gent. I gave him a shilling and said: 'And I might be of some use to you. How would you like to make some honest money for a change?'

'Dunno,' he replied suspiciously. 'Doin' wot?'

'First I'll feed you, then I'll explain.' We walked on to Little Italy, passers-by staring at this unlikely-looking couple. Dino's in Clerkenwell Road looked warm and welcoming. Wiggins couldn't read the menu, but didn't really seem too concerned what he ate, as long as he ate. And he ate and ate again: soup and bread, pasta and bread, stew and bread, pie and bread, all washed down with cups of hot, sweet tea. I kept him company with a glass of Sangiovese, a variety I had been wanting to try for a while; quite passable it was too.

'Feeling better?' I asked.

'Yeah, fanks,' he said between mouthfuls.

'What's your real name?'

He shrugged, and smirked. And ate.

'Not falling for that one, eh? My name is Holmes, Sherlock Holmes.'

'Sherlock's a funny name.'

I could only agree, and then explained what I had in mind, but he was really more interested in eating than listening, so when the feeding stopped, I ran through it all again.

'I have a jewel in a box,' I said opening it. 'It's actually worthless, a Siamese ruby if you must know and you'd be lucky to get ten shillings for it at a pawnbroker. I'll give you twenty shillings not to even try. What I want you to do is find out who might buy it, but whatever they say you turn down the offer and report back to me. I'm not interested in pawnbrokers; they'll take anything and pay nothing. I want you to try low-level jewellery shops, more likely stalls. Little Italy would be a start. Bruno Decisi's has been mentioned. If anything goes wrong and you get into any trouble, you'll have a signed letter from me with my address on it in an envelope in your pocket identifying you as working for me in my capacity as a consulting detective. Clear so far?'

'S'pose.'

'But first we are going to clean you up. When did you last have a wash?'

'We get jugs every Sunday mornin'. Before prayers.'

'Where?'

'Where I sleep, at St Patrick's in Blackfriars.'

'The Benevolent Society?' He nodded yes. 'I thought it was just for Irish arabs?'

'Caffolick. Any Caffolick.'

'You're Catholic?'

'Dunno. Yeh. S'pose.' He smiled for the first time and I warmed even more to the little urchin.

'First we will go to St Giles's old-clothes market and get you some better clothes. And some shoes. Then you'll come back to my rooms, so you know where I live. We've got hot water in the house now and a fixed bath. My landlady won't be too amused, but I will explain all to her later. Let's hope she sees you after and not before your bath and new clothes. I'm going to call you Wiggins – best I don't know your real name and best you don't tell me.'

And so it was done. Wiggins was fed, clothed and washed, trusted with the Siamese ruby and five shillings towards the twenty promised, given a letter from me as a firman and sent about his work. I was a little apprehensive, but I knew where he lived, or at least where he could be found, and hoped my letter would keep him out of any trouble.

CHAPTER 6

Sticky O

WHILE WAITING FOR Hatchard's to take delivery of the French graphology book and a reply from the Master of the Stationers, and having determined that there is no pre-existing forensics analysis of ink I could draw on, the only progress possible on the blackmail case was going to come at James McNeill Whistler's leaving party that evening at the Oriental Club. Reflecting on my last public outing, at the tea and-art party, I can't say I was joyful at the prospect. Given a choice of company, I tend to prefer my own, and the very thought of a party full of strangers made me appreciate even more the benefits of solitude. Also, I couldn't help but feel that my investigation into the blackmail for George Lewis would be more efficient if I were anonymous, and although the theft, or possibly loss, of Oscar Wilde's amethyst tie-pin was a good facade for investigating the blackmail case, it was a blackmail case that was increasingly preoccupying me. The air was still unpleasantly sticky, making the 1.1 miles along Oxford Street and into Stafford Place a burdensome stride that took seventeen minutes, precisely.

The truth is, at that stage I really had no more idea than Lewis who the blackmailer might be. Applying the modus operandi of ruling out the impossible and giving every consideration to the improbable didn't move the investigation very far forward. It went as much against the grain then as it does now, but in the absence of anything tangible I was relying on suspicion, instinct and feeling. I regret to say this unscientific approach even included a pecking order of likely suspects: James McNeill Whistler – with or without Rosa Corder, Ned Langtry, George Reynolds, Francis Knollys and Patsy Cornwallis-West – she somehow with Lillie Langtry. Whistler because he was broke, famously so, was international enough to have an overseas bank account, and with or without the forger Rosa Corder would know how to disguise a blackmail note. Or Whistler with Lillie Langtry; they had been lovers, and were both broke and both adventurous. Ned Langtry was also broke and could easily have stolen the notebook at any one of the Prince's functions, and had the motive of revenge for his wife cuckolding him so frequently and publicly, one might say whole-heartedly. I suspected George Reynolds really only because his name was on the blackmail note, which in a bluff move would appear to rule him out, but I reckoned ruled him in. My suspicion against Knollys was based partly on George Lewis's feeling about him, but equally because if there was a notebook, and I still wasn't sure that there was *that* notebook, he would be in a perfect position to steal it and sufficiently sophisticated to manage all aspects of the blackmail.

I had only met Patsy Cornwallis-West at the tea-and-art party, and of all the suspects mentioned she was the least likely on the basis of any sort of evidence, not that there was much of that to go round for any of them, and yet... There was something about her mischievousness and free spirit that one couldn't help but find attractive, partly out of admiration for the type of capers she might enjoy. One thing I was sure of, if it were she, she wasn't the type to act alone and her closest friend Lillie Langtry would be the ideal collaborator, one who had every opportunity and reason to prosper from her own romantic endeavours.

Thus, full of preconceived and unwarranted prejudices, I joined the party and made my first hello to my host of sorts, Langdale Pike.

'If there's anyone you want to meet, just ask me,' he said.

I noticed George Lewis in the crowd at the same time as he saw me, and we acknowledged each other with the most imperceptible of nods. I also saw for the first time his wife Elizabeth, the glamorous salon hostess, already early in the evening a queen bee to whom others were paying court.

'I'd like an introduction to George Reynolds,' I told Pike, 'but first, before he's too swamped, I'll say hello again to Jimmy Whistler.'

From Whistler I wanted some handwriting and the day before I had bought an art card from Crossman & Sons of his *Portrait of Rosa Corder*. I hoped they would both sign it. It's at exactly times like this that my fictitious sister Lottie comes in useful, as the reader will soon discover.

'Mr Whistler,' I introduced myself, 'I'm Sherlock Holmes. We met at Frank Miles's tea-and-art party at Thames House. You were kind enough to ask me about the different types of detective.'

'Yes, yes,' he replied, shaking my hand, 'you're the one looking for Os's lost jewel. No doubt he's told you it's part of the crown jewels. But did you know that one of them is fake?' I said I didn't. 'Yes,' he said, 'the Black Prince's ruby is actually a spinel. Have you found Oscar's heirloom yet?'

'Still looking, but getting closer. Actually, I'm hoping you might sign this art card for me. My sister Lottie is a great admirer of your work and when she knew I was coming to the party tonight she asked me if you could please sign this card for her, say something like "Best wishes to Lottie" with a greeting from you. Lottie with "ie" at the end.'

'With the greatest of pleasure, Holmes.' He duly wrote, left-handed: *To my rightful admirer Lottie, with very best wishes. Yours soon in exile, Whistler.* And then he drew his famous stinging butterfly signature. At last, some handwriting to analyse.

'Thank you. Will Rosa Corder be here later this evening? It would be wonderful if she could send Lottie a message on the same card too.'

'She is anybody's guess. If she does come it won't be till midnight. Midnight for her is breakfast for most of us.'

I wished him well in his Venetian exile and asked Pike to point out Ned Langtry. He scanned the room and nodded towards a tall, thin, handsome man in his mid-thirties. He was alone and looked lonely. I walked over to near where he was standing and accidentally backed into him.

'Oh sorry,' I said looking around, 'we both seem to be here on our own. I'm Holmes, Sherlock Holmes.'

He looked relieved to have somebody to talk to and owned up immediately. 'I'm Edward Langtry. What brings you here?'

'I'm here as a guest of Langdale Pike over there,' I said waving my glass of Sancerre towards my good friend.

'The newspaperman. Are you a newspaperman?' he asked worriedly.

'No, I'm a consulting detective. Let me give you my card.' Which I did. 'And you, what brings you here?'

'Oh, I'm just here escorting my wife. That's her in the yellow over there in the middle of that gaggle of young bloods.'

I couldn't think of a way of asking him to write something at that moment, so I opted for fingerprints, imprecise as the science was. I took a new glass by the stem from a passing tray of wine and asked him to hold it for me for a few seconds while I wrote something down in my card holder, took the glass back by the stem and we parted company the way one does at parties. In the cloakroom I emptied the wine glass, past my palate not down the drain, wrapped it in tissue and stored it in my pocket. Later I would send it to Henry Faulds to see if he could record the prints.

Meeting George Reynolds would be easy: he was talking to Langdale Pike as I wandered over. Pike introduced us. Curious about *Reynolds News*, I had bought a copy last Sunday. It would also have carried our blackmail reply announcement. The masthead proudly proclaimed the circulation of 400,000 and the front page was

indistinguishable from any other broadsheet, with news of
the Second Anglo-Afghan War and the proposed Anglo-
Russian Treaty of Gandamak establishing an Afghan state.
the famine in central India and a report of the British victory
at Ulindi in the Anglo-Zulu War. The back page and the
six inside were less formal. Unusually, there were images:
photographs, cartoons, etchings and point cuts. They were
evidently leading a long-standing campaign to abolish
flogging in the Army, devoting half a page of righteous
indignation to the subject. Two new football clubs had been
formed, one in Doncaster and the other in Fulham. John
Henry Newman had been elevated to Cardinal. On the other
side of the aisle, the Anglican priest was tried and convicted
of using Ritualist practices. We learned of the detailed
investigation, over two pages, of the previous summer's 640
deaths arising from the collision of the overcrowded pleasure
boats *Princess Alice* **and** *Bywell Castle* on the River Thames. In
Dumbarton, the Denny Bros yard had launched the world's
first mild steel ocean-going ship, the SS *Rotomahana*. There
was news of the ever-spreading electrification: Blackpool was
preparing for 'Illuminations'. 'Gabardine', a new waterproof
clothing material, was introduced by Thomas Burberry
of Basingstoke. There was a review of Anthony Trollope's
final Palliser novel *The Duke's Children*. And there was the
obituary of the poet Charles Tennyson Turner.

But the curious part of it was that among all this variety
of foreign and home news, gossip and scandal, sports,
entertainment, fashion and other stories there was no
mention at all of the royal family or any of its numerous

offshoots. Royal news is the bread-and-butter of every other publication. I had asked Pike, who knew Reynolds well and was after all a contributor, about the omission. The monarchy was, generally, equally popular and unpopular: popular among the upper and lower classes and unpopular among the middle classes, but to ignore the subject altogether was singular. Pike reported that Reynolds was a fervent republican, and his undeclared way of making his point was to imagine a world in which royalty didn't exist. This of course raised interesting questions about the blackmail: either the blackmailer didn't know the newspaper's policy or considered it such an explosive story, a story that might tip the equilibrium in the abolitionists' favour, that even it would print it, giving greater credence to the scandal. And of course, who better to decide that course of action than George Reynolds himself?

Trying to gauge him for myself, after Pike introduced us, I proposed to offer him a story about illegal international banking to see if there was any uneasiness in his reaction. I said that as part of my detective work, I had come across a story where gold was smuggled into the UK and placed illegally in a Swiss bank here, mentioning that of course for professional reasons I would have to change the names, but that even without any names it was a scandalous story in itself. His eyes looked directly into mine all the time and he showed no sign of unease or recognition of the blackmail proposal. I concluded the interview and was none the wiser: either he really knew nothing about the blackmail or equally he was a first-class card-player.

For readers outside London, in fact outside central London, I should explain there was a strange phenomenon then known as the 'Professional Beauty' or 'PB'. The origins of this recent development are unclear. The word 'professional' would seem to indicate the women concerned do some kind of work, but nothing could be further from the truth. The word 'beauty' however does indeed apply, so these PBs are beautiful young 'ladies of quality' who have largely invented and promoted themselves as such for purposes of their advancement in Society. The next stage was for them to be drawn, painted or usually photographed and the resulting postcards to be displayed in shop windows along Fleet Street and sold for a penny each. These soon became collectors' items. From Fleet Street the craze spread throughout newsagents of London, so for reasons no one could quite explain PBs had become the talk of the town. Lady Dudley, Lady Dalhousie, the Duchess of Leinster, Lady de Grey and Lady Londonderry were all popular, but the two most popular, Patsy Cornwallis-West and Lillie Langtry, were in front of me now. In my front pocket was a PB card of each one of them and my sister Lottie was about to be pressed into service again when Jimmy Whistler appeared from nowhere and, clasping my shoulders with his hands, steered me away from my quarry.

'Social gatherings are such a bore, don't you think? After entertaining everyone for five minutes, there is nothing more to be said. Rosa Corder – you asked to be introduced to her. That's her with the bright red scarf and green jacket just leaving the room. Quick, you'll catch her.'

By the time I'd squeezed and sidestepped through the throng she was at the far end of the hall, heading for a door in the passage-way. She opened the door and disappeared down the stairs into the basement. I followed her down.

The light was flickering dimly from candles, and the air was thick with a sweet, sickly but not wholly unpleasant odour. On makeshift layers of rugs on the floor lay three gentlemen and a lady, well dressed if partially *en déshabillé*, all with their heads on low stools acting as pillows. In the centre of them all a Chinaman in flowing clothes was squatting near a candlelit stool. On it he seemed to be preparing some kind of decoction. He looked up at Rosa and she joined the circle.

'Ah, Rosa-koh,' he said.

'Hello, Johnny,' she replied, settling on the floor. 'Room for one more?'

'Sure, sure,' said Johnny, as she made her own space on the rugs. Johnny? This must be John Johnston, as the famous Ah Sing is known to all the habitués of London's better opium dens. I had heard of him of course, and not just through Charles Dickens's John Chinaman in *The Mystery of Edwin Drood*. He inhabited a semi-illegal underworld, mysterious in itself and, due to the oriental component, exotic. By some strange quirk of the law, owning opium was not illegal, in fact it was widely available in pharmacies, but enjoying it in public was illegal. Like everyone else, I had taken opium powder as a constituent part of laudanum when in pain. He gestured for me to lie down and smoke with the others.

'Thank you, but no,' I said. 'Maybe at a later date. Can I

sit here quietly and see?' I tossed half a crown into a silk sack by an oil lamp next to him. He smiled his agreement.

The four incumbents seemed to be in a deep sleep, a smiling sleep, as Rosa lay down on her side with her head resting on the wooden ledge-pillow and Ah Sing gave her a black pipe to hold, about two feet in length with a mouthpiece at one end and an open bowl sticking up at the other. She was left-handed. Still squatting, he moved closer to her with four black balls on a saucer, gesturing to her to choose one, which she did. They all looked identical to me, so I gestured him to show them to me. He picked one up, held it between his thumb and forefinger and said, 'Sticky O.' He gave it me to touch as well and it was indeed sticky and was indeed opium.

Next, he pierced the ball with a long thin needle and held it over an oil lamp until it started to smoke, and then moved the open bowl to the smoke and she breathed it in; one, two, three times. She fell into the kind of waking sleep propounded by opium enthusiasts, to enjoy what dreams only she will ever know. Clearly, my planned interview with Rosa Corder would not make sense tonight, but at least we had met after a fashion, and in a fashion that might prove fruitful later on. The immediate lack of fruitfulness continued: by the time I had resurfaced to the party, the Professional Beauties had left, along with many other guests, and so I walked home alone to Montague Street, only slightly the wiser. But at least I now knew she was left-handed, as well as being a forger.

CHAPTER 7

A New Blackmail Note

As I was soon to discover, when not face-to-face George Lewis communicated mostly by telegram. On the morning of 8 July a messenger knocked on the Montague Street door and handed me this telegram:

NEW NOTE COLLECT FROM HARRIS IN OFFICE STOP IN COURT ALL DAY STOP GL

I set off immediately for the Lewis & Lewis & Co office at 10 Ely Place, just off Holborn. Lewis's secretary Harris handed me the latest blackmail note in its envelope.

'You've come quickly, Mr Holmes, and you're lucky. Mr Lewis is within minutes of leaving,' he said.

'Ah, Holmes,' said Lewis emerging through his office door. 'I was just off to the Central for the day. Have a quick look at this before I go.'

The envelope itself and the handwriting looked identical to the first blackmail note. Inside, the note had the same handwriting too:

The Prince of Wales's notebook. The first of many mistress names is ALW. Her code entry is 1x1 2x1. I have the codes too. India is also slandered. My price is 2 gold bars, deposited with Rahn+Bodmer Co. Zurich, London account 8006. Now 3 weeks to pay. Once paid,

the notebook is burned. Or Reynolds News prints.
The Times seen. Why don't you trust me? The Jew can
organize pay.

I spent a short while examining it over by the window
with my lens. I felt Lewis impatient to leave. In all aspects
except the contents, it was identical to the first blackmail
note.

'The message is certainly more succinct than the
first one,' I said. 'Less obviously archaic usage, though
"mistress names" is irregular. As is "code entry". It sounds
again like it is written by someone deliberately trying to
be somebody else. "ALW" initials or acronym or another
code? But why bother? It was sent to you, and you of all
people know all the mistresses. So, although the code
isn't important as such, it seems the blackmailer thinks
we don't know who these mistresses were or are. This
may well be the most revealing part of the note. Equally,
it could be another blind, and a clever one at that.'

'Take a seat for a minute, Holmes. You're missing half
the point. Or more precisely half the blackmail. India
being slandered, and in writing, and by the heir to the
Empire. And previously Ireland of course. We will solve
this by concentrating on the mistress clues, probably.
But what will bring the pack of cards down, the scandal
that will erupt, will be diplomatic and not moral. It's not
just me who knows who the mistresses are, everybody in
the *tout le monde* sense of the word does. By my counting
there have been fourteen of them and that doesn't

include his, shall we say, short-lived indiscretions. I think the definition of a mistress is a lady who has coupled with a gentleman on multiple occasions, at least half a dozen. That's not a legal definition as such, but from my experience of divorce cases that is an eighteenth-century precedent that stands firm.'

'All noted about the broader inference. But as you say, the clues are in the codes. ALW and 1x1 2x1. Sexual positions and frequency as we thought before. I can't think what else it would be.'

'Nor I,' said Lewis. 'So, the price has doubled to two gold bars. Far from going away, it looks like our blackmailer is upping the ante. But they've clearly seen your announcement in *The Times*. Why don't you put in another? At least it's a form of communication.'

'Yes, but they haven't replied in kind. I look every day, as I'm sure you do. And the question of why we don't trust them. Which in turn begs the question, why would we? That part makes no sense at all. And as you say the ante has indeed been upped – doubled. The "burnt" has now become "burned", which I take to confirm my theory that the former was another blind. Another change is we now have "prints" not "will print". The significance of that isn't clear. And we still have the personal Jewish reference. Could be another bluff, like "burnt" and "burned".'

'I must go or I'll be late. Harris, copy that note, would you, and give the original to Holmes? I don't like the way this is doubling up: we need to double up too. Get to the bottom of it smartly. And well before the three-week deadline. Right, I must go.'

Later that day I placed this announcement in *The Times*:

Edward's lost notebook: there is trust and a reward. For proof, send a page.

CHAPTER 8

The Leander Club Regatta Day

To SAY THAT Brother Mycroft is a creature of habit is to understate his preference for his regime of rigid regularity. His routine is simple and never-changing, a constant clockwise triangle between his office in Whitehall from exactly 9.15am until 4.30pm, his afternoon and early evening refreshments at the Diogenes Club from 4.45pm, and the return to his rooms in Pall Mall East at 7.40pm. There were only two exceptions to his daily round, and the exceptions were so routine that they hardly counted as exceptions: the yearly Christmas visit to our parents in Yorkshire, from where I'm now writing this account, and the annual visit to the Leander Club Regatta Day in Putney to watch the River Thames rowing races.

At school, for reasons that are hard to imagine now, Mycroft was actually quite good at the sport of rowing. Back then he was solidly rather than superfluously built and powered his scull along with considerable alacrity; if he tried to embark on one now, I fear for the poor scull's ability to remain afloat. Rowing was the only school activity for which he showed any enthusiasm. At studies, a form of logical brilliance came to him so naturally that he deemed it unnecessary to make the slightest effort to improve on the intellectual powers that nature undoubtedly bestowed on him. After university, where he rowed even more and studied even less, he was recruited into a branch of government that necessarily has to remain obscure, at which point all sporting activities stopped and the routine described above took over. Later it became clear that he would remain a bachelor; or rather become a husband to his own regime. It was not as if he were otherwise inclined, but the whole enterprise of courting and suiting, of sweet nothings and love-making, was so disruptive to his habits, so exhausting to his frame and so demanding of his reasoning that he preferred the company of Mycroft alone.

I could I suppose sympathise with him in that regard. I was also conscious of trying not to become like Mycroft as the years passed. Mycroft could never live here in Yorkshire and could only live in London because the potential for random events in the country was too great, the mealtimes too imprecise and then the meal never quite enough, whereas my reason for becoming a Londoner was precisely to seek out the unknown, to develop my powers of logic and deduction, to discover the great city's back alleys and Royal Parks and to pursue a career that I wanted to present me with a different challenge every day. I was even content with my slim pickings, a guinea a day when a day was employed, for the living was as simple as it needed to be and as long as the intellect was challenged and the storeroom of knowledge added to, my lot was not unhappy. No, my enemy was not living modestly; it was being bored to any degree.

I must admit to enjoying our yearly excursions to Putney, for Mycroft always invited me as his guest. Most years we boarded a steamboat at Westminster Pier and took the floodtide up to Putney, eight miles and an hour along the River Thames. This year the unending hot spell had made the river stench so foully that only commercial traffic could bear to use it, so we took the Fulham and Hammersmith omnibuses instead as the excursion. Very jolly it was too, with all the passengers on the top deck using umbrellas as parasols and hawkers at the stops enjoying a brisk turnover in lemonade and pale ale.

The Leander Club lays on a splendid lunch for its members, served in a marquee decked out to match the members' black and pink blazers, and normally eaten and drunk on the lawn sloping down the river so they could cheer on other members rowing by. This year, however, the weather won, the air on the river being so putrid that the lawn was uninhabitable, and the lunch moved to inside the clubhouse. Later the main event, the Gentlemen v. Players Cox'd Eights, was scrubbed when the Gentlemen refused to take part due to the overpowering stink down on the water.

After lunch Mycroft and I wandered over Putney Bridge to Hurlingham Park. Sitting on an old oak bench and looking back over the river to the Leander, we lit our *Reina Cubanas* and I had a strong premonition of what would be coming next.

'So, I hear you're on the Bertie blackmail case,' said Mycroft.

'How did you know about that?' I asked, playing the game, and also protecting Lewis's discretion.

'My dear chap,' he replied.

'Yes?'

'It's an affair of State. Nowadays I hear about these things. A minor affair of State I grant you, but with potential for expansion.'

'Hmmm.'

'Do you feel like talking about it?'

'No.'

'You're not being very helpful, Sherlock.'

'Well...'

'Have you investigated Francis Knollys or Lord Gifford yet?'

'No.'

'Why not? Knollys in particular is an interesting cove.'

'Blast and damnation!' I said, 'I forgot to bring my violin.'

'What's that got to do with Francis Knollys?'

'Nothing at all, but I like to play my violin in a park after lunch. Maybe I could borrow one from the Hurlingham Club now we are here.'

'Don't be so silly. I was saying that Knollys is an interesting cove.'

'I'm sure he is one such, an interesting cove, so you keep saying.'

'Try to be more receptive, Sherlock, I'm only trying to help. Francis Knollys is not only Bertie's Private Secretary, but also Gentleman Usher to the Queen. And a

Companion to the Most Honourable Order of the Bath. He is also a Chevalier of Ordo Supremus Militaris Templi Hierosolymitani.'

'Let me guess,' I said, now paying more attention. 'The Sovereign Military Order of the Temple of Jerusalem. One of yours?'

'No,' he said with false patience, 'mine is Pauperes Commilitones Christi Templique Salomonici, the Poor Fellow-Soldiers of Christ and of the Temple of Solomon. As you very well know.'

'In other words, he is a Knight Templar,' I said.

'Do you see the connections?'

'He is caught in a secrecy bind,' I offered. 'As Private Secretary to the Prince, or Bertie as everyone seems to call him, he must be totally discreet. As Gentleman Usher he is bound to relieve that discretion to Her Majesty. As a Companion his duty is to his Queen first and to his Prince second. As a chevalier he would be obliged to share his discretion if requested, but only if requested. Then the discretion is only as safe as the most closed mouth.'

'Very good. But there is something else, something harder to define. He's too smooth, at least too smooth for my liking.'

'An annoying character trait doesn't make him any more or less of a suspect,' I said. 'What about the other one, Lord Gifford?'

'Even smoother. He is Master of the Royal Household at Marlborough House. If Bertie has Knollys to run his state life, Alix has Gifford to run her domestic life. And unlike Knollys he is loyal. He knows what's happening in every nook and cranny at Marlborough House. If the blackmail is home-grown, he either knows about it or soon will.'

'How do you know about it?'

'Sherlock, you know better than that.'

I must say I could have done without the complicating factor of Mycroft being involved. But involved he was. He hadn't mentioned George Lewis, and I wasn't going to do so either.

'I presume you've seen the blackmail note?' I asked, referring only to the first one.

'Which one, I hear there are two? But I know you have. I hear Ireland and India and codes are mentioned. What do you make of the codes?'

'At the moment, I can only presume the numbers refer to the type and frequency of activity and the letters to the ladies concerned. There also seems to be a separate record of the codes, without which the book on its own would be worthless.'

'You mean Greek, French or German style, two, three or four times with Daisy Greville, that sort of thing?'

'Thanks for putting it so delicately, Mycroft, but yes, that's about the long and the short of it. But I'm not even sure if the blackmailer has the lost notebook or is bluffing.'

'What do you mean?' he asked.

'We can't be sure either way. Bertie has lost a notebook; that much we know. In that notebook there may well be embarrassing entries; that much we presume. It would be quite feasible for the blackmailer to have heard about the lost notebook without actually possessing it. It could be an invention.'

'True. That would be just the type of manoeuvre I'd expect from Knollys.'

The heat of the day was easing enough to remind Mycroft of tea-time. On our way back to Earl Grey and scones and jam and cream at the Leander he asked me to keep him abreast of events. I suspected I was wading into waters too deep for my current ability to allow me to swim, so I gave him a polite assurance that it would be so; Regatta Day is after all a time for brotherly love. But from tomorrow onwards, brotherly vying reasserts itself and if I could defuse the blackmail without Mycroft's assistance, I would. And no doubt he knew that.

Chapter 9
A Cuckold's Tale

THERE WAS A partial spring in my step as I opened the front door of Montague Street. After the excursion to genteel Putney, it was good to be back in central London, back among the crime, back among the denizens of crime. Delivered that day were three envelopes waiting on Cousin Sara's mat: a note from Hatchard's saying the graphology book had arrived from France, a letter from the Master of the Worshipful Company of Stationers, and this note from Edward Langtry Esq:

17 Norfolk Street   *Tuesday*
Park Lane,
London W.

Dear Mr Holmes,
You were kind enough to give me your card when we met at the Oriental Club.
   After much determination, I now find I need the services of a 'consulting detective' as mentioned on your card and I would be grateful if you could attend the above address at 11.00am on the 11th inst.
Yours in faithful anticipation,
Edward Langtry

To: Mr S. Holmes, 24 Montague Street, London, WC

Well, at least I now had his handwriting as well as his fingerprints, with which so far I'd not had a chance to do anything. What arose most strongly from his card was the expensive address; all I had heard was that the Langtrys were without funds, and yet here, quite to the contrary, they were in Norfolk Street, just off Park Lane, and in a whole house too.

The 1.5 miles from Montague Street along the length of Oxford Street took 22 minutes as expected. I arrived early to see what could be observed from a discreet distance. Norfolk Street is a row of recently built red-brick 10-room houses with stabling in its own Norfolk Mews behind it. Number 17 was still in the process of being occupied, with frequent deliveries of furniture, rugs and other household items. At the appointed time I was shown into the drawing-room by a pageboy, and there standing by the mantelpiece was Langtry and another person, a man of similar age – and I could tell immediately by the familiar clues, a solicitor. Langtry looked no happier now in his own den than he did behind enemy lines at the Oriental Club. The lawyer looked eager and bright and was keen to introduce himself before Langtry did so, as would be expected.

'I'm Lee Shipley of Shipley & Grout. I'm very pleased to meet you, Mr Holmes.' His accent was from northwest London, first generation with a formal education, but his tone was confident, more so than his handshake. I returned the compliment, while Langtry looked more careworn than even a few minutes ago, sitting on a side chair, gesturing to us to make ourselves comfortable.

'Have you managed to take yourself away from London in this terrible hot weather, Mr Holmes?' Langtry asked.

'I'm afraid not to any great extent. The day before yesterday I found myself in Putney, but the stench on the river there was as bad as in Westminster. And you?'

'I went for a short spell with my wife to Jersey. We both come from there. But it was not a pleasant sojourn. In fact I was humiliated, and the humiliation is the reason I've invited you here today.'

There was no need to ask him to expand, as by now he was off his chair and pacing across the room, talking as if relieving himself of a burden too closely held for too long a time.

'I have no doubt you've heard of my wife's amorous entanglements; you saw for yourself at the Oriental Club how she attracts those who should know better than to play along with her games. You have also no doubt heard that one of her admirers is the Prince of Wales. It is one thing for her to have discreet affairs with the more tactful members of the aristocracy, but quite another for her to be flaunting her faithlessness with the most indiscreet Prince in all of Christendom.

'You've heard about the villa he had built for her in Bournemouth?' I hadn't at the time, but Lewis later told me that he had indeed done so, built by him for her so they could continue their tryst away from London eyes and ears.

It occurred to me that Langtry was in his own way almost as indiscreet as the Prince, but before I had a chance to reply he continued.

'Mrs Langtry and I had determined to attend a relative of hers wedding in Jersey. She told the Prince and he immediately laid on the royal yacht *Hildegarde* to take us there, wait for us in pride of place in St Helier harbour attracting the widest possible attention, and take us back again. Of course, while we were there, my wife was quite the attraction. Her so-called success was all everybody talked about. Her photographs were for sale in all the shops, and every time she went out people stopped and waved approvingly. Of course, many of them we knew from our childhoods. Because of her we were not only invited to lunch at Government House, but she sat at the Governor's right hand while I was on a far table over by the door. It was worse than being in London, at least here one can get lost in the size of the place.'

'And where is she now?' I asked.

'The Prince and his family are in Norfolk, so she is taking advantage of his absence and cavorting with Moreton Frewin. They are over in Hyde Park right now.' Here was a suitor that, possibly, Lewis didn't yet know about. I had heard of Moreton Frewen, in the sense that everybody had. In the scandal sheets he even had a nickname, Mortal Ruin. He was one of the most famous horsemen in England, Master of Hounds at Cambridge, and in the news recently as the winner of a midnight steeplechase run against one of Patsy Cornwallis-West's lovers, Lord Rossmore. A recent magazine cover had him leading the hunt through a railway cut in Leicestershire, with – incidentally – Gladys Lonsdale's husband Lord

Lonsdale close behind him. I need hardly have asked Langtry what they were doing in the park. 'He is teaching her how to ride, dammit. She knows how to ride perfectly well, she just likes being manhandled on and off his horses.'

'You had better tell Mr Holmes about this house,' said Shipley.

'Yes,' said Langtry pacing anew. 'This house, how could we possibly afford it? We could not is the answer; it's another gift from the Prince. He pays the first month's rent and then expects us to take it on from there. It's the only possible reason for us to be living off Park Lane. Now the delivery men are coming all the time and asking me where to put the effects. As if I should know. My wife should be telling them, not riding in the Park with a beau. Half of the goods I don't even recognise. They are more gifts from the Prince. And come five o'clock, do you know what happens at five o'clock?'

'Yes, I have heard,' I replied, to save him the embarrassment of having to explain it. At five o'clock, between tea and dressing for dinner, the gentlemen visit their lady friends. The lady rings for tea and it is acknowledged that she's not to be disturbed until she rings again to have the tea taken away at seven o'clock. The wags suggest that there's little chance of her being disturbed by her husband, who himself would be away on his own dalliance. All the husbands that is, I thought, except poor Ned Langtry who was quite incapable of mixing in such louche society, let alone enjoying amorous adventures therein. According to Lewis, he didn't even belong to a club, so couldn't seek refuge where other gentlemen would.

'Next week,' Langtry continued, 'Baron Ferdinand de Rothschild will give a dinner for Crown Prince Rudolph of Austria, followed by a ball for four hundred. And the Crown Prince has asked particularly that my wife sits next to him. Again. Do you know what that means? That after the Rothschilds have had the first dance, my wife and the Prince will be next, and in front of four hundred guests. I will be seated heaven knows where, and only invited at all to give her some semblance of respectability. And the dress, have you any idea of the cost of the dress, Mr Holmes?' I said I regretted to say that I didn't, and I didn't need to ask who was going to be sent the bill: poor Ned Langtry.

'And now we must talk some business, Mr Holmes', said Shipley, who had clearly heard Langtry's laments several times before. 'Mr Langtry has instructed my firm to file for divorce. I need hardly tell you of the repercussions.'

'No, indeed,' I said.

'But we need more evidence. So far we only have these,' he said handing me four envelopes tied by a ribbon. He asked me to look at them. They were all notes from the Prince to Mrs Langley, which I presumed Mr Langtry had either intercepted on arrival or removed from her quarters later. They were more like silly billets-doux than passionate love letters, but still embarrassing and best kept away from public gaze. I gave them back to Shipley who returned them to his attaché case.

I could see Shipley's point: they were insufficient proof of adultery for the purpose of divorce.

'If I could ask the obvious question,' I asked, 'if the

objective is simply to obtain a divorce, why aim so high and at so hard a target? If as you say her lovers are legion, you only need to find her compromised adulterously with any one of them. That, combined with the inevitable speculation of further misdeeds in the press and public discourse, will be sufficient for the court.'

'Sufficient for the court, Mr Holmes, but not sufficient for me,' said Langtry agitated again.

I understood at once. He wanted to ruin him *and* her, and asked, 'What do you need me for?'

'To seek out evidence,' said Shipley. 'Our firm uses a private detective, but he is not in your league.'

I asked: 'If you would forgive me for being so frank, Mr Langtry, in view of what you said regarding your finances, how are either of us to be paid? I may be only a guinea a day, but I imagine Shipley & Grout will be on a firm's pay scale.'

'My firm is to be paid on settlement, Mr Holmes, but we cannot ask you to accept the same terms. We have within our means enough to afford a guinea a day, plus incidentals no doubt.'

I thought of Lillie Langtry's half-hearted attempt at the tea–and–art party to engage me to spy on her husband, for the same reason he was now trying to employ me to do the same to her. This time I gave the proposition more consideration; but not for long. I had after all resolved at the beginning of my career never to be involved with anything as sordid as the reasons behind a divorce, but on the other hand in this instance the players involved might help forward the blackmail case. If I took this on at all, I would only do it with Lewis's knowledge, and only for the furtherance of Lewis's goals. There were indeed attractions in taking on Langtry's case: there was a better than evens chance I would uncover some evidence pertaining to the blackmail; an even chance that Langtry would somehow be intertwined with the blackmail case; and an outside chance that it would lead me to the blackmailer. I wanted to keep a foot in the game without committing to join the team.

'You are an insider with that set, Mr Holmes,' said Langtry. This was a worrying statement, as if he knew I was involved with the blackmail case. But then he added to my relief, 'I hear you are looking for Oscar Wilde's amethyst tie-pin. My wife thinks that is highly amusing. Mr Wilde is my wife's best friend. At least he is not a lover. I suspect his interests lie elsewhere. And I met you at Mr Pike's party for Mr Whistler. You clearly move in the appropriate circles to help me find evidence, evidence for which I'm willing to pay beyond your fee once there is a settlement.'

'I don't think I can take on the case,' I said, 'it's really not my line of country. I'm not a hawkshaw. But I will keep my eyes and ears open and if anything lands in my path, I will inform Mr Shipley.'

There was then a commotion at the door. The lady of the house had returned from her riding lesson in the park. Langtry quietly locked the drawing-room door and we heard her skip up the stairs and the closing of a first-floor door. Langtry let us out, and with a handshake and exchange of cards Shipley turned left and I turned right.

CHAPTER 10

Complicating Factors

BEFORE THE APPOINTMENT with Ned Langtry, I collected the *Traité Pratique de Graphologie* book from Hatchard's and followed up the suggestion from the Master of the Worshipful Company of Stationers to take my enquiry to a Mr Frank Smythson who had just established the Stationers' Company's Foundation School at Bolt Court near Fleet Street and knew as much about household stationery as anybody in the city. We made an appointment for the following day.

But first, an exercise in graphology. I have mentioned briefly that my landlady at 24 Montague Street was my cousin Sara Holmes, but to be more accurate she is my cousin-in-law, having married my father's brother's eldest son Herbert in 1855. They were barely married at all: after a few months he was sent on his first commission to India to serve in the British Indian Army and was part of the Thirty-Second Regiment of Foot at the Siege of Lucknow where he died with honour, being awarded the Indian Order of Merit (First Class) posthumously. When newly married they were living with Sara's parents at 24 Montague Street, having carved out an apartment for themselves from the rooms upstairs; these are the rooms I am renting from her now. When one after the other of her parents died, she inherited the house together with the Maltese housemaid Ruby and enough funds to live comfortably, if not lavishly;

comfortably enough to be able to afford to rent me the rooms at a family rate. By now forty-one years old, she has never shown any interest in marrying again. Rather more than that, she seems to go out of her way to avoid appealing to potential suitors, dressing dowdily and seeding her conversation with little gaiety. It's not so much that she is ill-humoured, rather that she has no humour at all; but what she lacks in humour she makes up in kindliness. Although only seventeen years older than I, she looks after me like a son and I warm to her as a mother-figure.

'Ready for an outing, Sherlock?' she shouts up the stairs three times a week.

She has three outings a week, twice to nearby Covent Garden for victuals and once, on Sundays, to St George's Bloomsbury.

'I'll be right down,' I reply on the Sunday, for I could hardly refuse.

Inevitably during the service my thoughts turn to the reasoning and deductions of Charles Darwin. After the service we have Sunday lunch and for this, thankfully, we are always joined by two neighbours, both spinsters in their forties and both of interest. Miss Owens is a librarian at the Reading Room at the British Museum and if conversation were allowed, we would greet each other there beyond the permitted nod, and Miss Cranshaw is a nurse at St Bartholomew's. Much later in the year, when they allowed me to use their laboratories for some experiments, we would see each other more often.

It was into this company that over lunch I introduced

the subject of graphology and afterwards we amused ourselves by turning the subject into a parlour game. I brought down Jules Crépieux-Jamin's treatise from upstairs and gave the others a summary of his theories: that our handwriting reveals a lot about our character; that the size of the loops above and below the letters in cursive script indicate our level of faithfulness, trustworthiness and honesty, the larger the better, the smaller the worse; that where we cross the letter 't' indicates our level of confidence, the higher the better; that where we dot the letter 'i' is a guide to our level of self-sufficiency, the closer the better; that how we complete the loop on lower case letters such as 'a', 'e' and 'o' shows how well organised we are, the more complete the better; that how we complete our hanging letters such as 'g', 'j', 'p' and 'q' reveals how decisive we are, the less elaborate the better; that how our cursive letters lean indicates how confident and optimistic we are, the more forward-facing the better; and so on.

For the parlour game I passed the book around, covering up Crépieux-Jamin's conclusions and we all had to guess what they would be. Time after time we came up with disagreeing conclusions, often with four different variations on his surmises. We rapidly began to lose heart in the whole exercise and tried a different approach. Miss Owen suggested this pangram, a sentence containing all the letters in the alphabet: 'the quick brown fox jumps over the lazy dog'. Sara produced pens and paper and we all set to work. Sara and I knew each other's handwriting, but not that of the other two, and the other two didn't know anyone else's script but their own. In spite of knowing each other reasonably well, we passed the papers around and we comprehensively failed to recognise each other's characters from the handwriting. We seemed to have so completely disproved Crépieux-Jamin's theories that we could only laugh at them: even Sara managed a passing smile.

With the blackmail note in mind, the reason why we were investigating graphology at all, I asked each of them to write the pangram again underneath their existing ones, but this time with their other hand. There was absolutely no similarity between the writing of the two hands, and so even if we had been able to detect the character of the blackmailer by their usual handwriting, if they wrote in the other hand the exercise became futile.

Thus, with one avenue of detection closed, the next morning I made my way to meet George Lewis in his offices at 10 Ely Place, Holborn, nine-tenths of a mile away and a horrible nineteen-minute walk through the sticky heat. These nineteen minutes included a small diversion to Carper & Sons news stall by the Museum Tavern to buy my two dailies, *The Times* and the *Record*, note-takers of the highs and lows of society's misdemeanours, when I noticed headlines in 16-point bold on a new scandal sheet, *Town Talk*:

COMING SOON:
The Scandal to End all Scandals?

Is it true that London is shortly to be regaled with a highly sensational divorce case, in which a well-known beauty, rumoured to be "professionally" such, will play

> *a prominent part? And is it also true that someone*
> *occupying a very high position in society will be called*
> *upon as a witness? And could it be that this "Scandal to*
> *End All Scandals" will be the one that crowns them all?*

So this was the *Town Talk* that Pike had mentioned, connected somehow to the Solly Boys gangsters, and the new scandal sheet addition to London's scurrilousness. I bought two copies, one to keep and one to take to Lewis.

It is easy to be impressed by the size of George Lewis's operation, using all five floors of a substantial Georgian townhouse. I was expecting to be shown up to the top floor, but instead his own office is on the ground floor behind a lace-curtained bay window, 'so I can see who's coming and going', as he explained.

After the usual pleasantries, I reported on the graphology dead-end and the forthcoming meeting with Smythson and, partly in case he already knew, of the meeting with Ned Langtry but without going into details.

'There's a problem,' he said, 'although it was only a matter of time. Francis Knollys knows about the blackmail and wants to know what we know.'

'You know about his conflicts of interest?' I asked. 'He's the Prince's Private Secretary, but also a Gentleman Usher to the Queen and a Knight Templar.'

'I didn't know about the last one, not really on the Jewish horizon,' he laughed, 'but on anyone's horizon he is trouble. A complicating factor we could do without.'

'There is another complicating factor,' I said. 'The

press has opened up a new front, a divorce rumour not too far removed from the blackmail by the look of it.' I gave him his copy of *Town Talk* and explained its antecedents.

'We could convince ourselves the story is unrelated,' I said, 'but the reference to "professional beauties" rather narrows it down. There are, let's say, a dozen of them in total, and maybe only half a dozen of them are being flagrantly unfaithful at any one time, and only one with the so-called "highest levels of society". And then there's the "crowns it all", if anyone was still in doubt.'

'The Prince and Mrs Langtry.'

'Exactly.'

'And I have news on that as well,' I said, and proceeded to tell him about Lee Shipley from Shipley & Grout, about how Shipley was talking about Ned Langtry filing for divorce and how Ned Langtry had showed me four letters from the Prince to his wife.

'There's no smoke without fire,' he said. '*Town Talk* is the smoke and this news is the fire. I'll find out about Shipley and Grout. They're not a top firm, and certainly not divorce lawyers like we are, or I'd have heard of them. What was in the letters?'

'Nothing really incriminating, certainly not evidence for divorce. Flirtatious more than adulterous. But embarrassing all the same.'

'Hmmm. They need more evidence. Did they ask you to find it?'

'Yes, but I refused.'

'Two things, young Holmes. First you must be

completely open with me. We must trust each other, and you should have told me this at once, not when I asked. You are new and learning and we won't talk of it again. But it also means they don't know that you are engaged either on the blackmail case or have any connection to me, or they wouldn't have asked you, so that's good news.'

'It looks like Shipley knows he doesn't have enough evidence and so has spilt a rumour to *Town Talk* knowing they won't be too careful about checking it. Nevertheless, it will now be talked about, making a divorce seem inevitable.'

'Maybe,' he replied, 'or he has actually filed for divorce and a clerk in the court has sold *Town Talk* the information. It wouldn't be the first time that's happened. I'll look into Shipley and you will look into *Town Talk*.'

'I've heard Lord Gifford's name mentioned. Is there any suspicion there?'

'You mean the Earl of Gifford as the blackmailer? I wouldn't have thought he had the imagination. Runs Marlborough House efficiently enough, devoted to the Princess, her children love him. Totally loyal to Alix, unlike Knollys to Bertie. They are close, though, Gifford and Knollys.'

'And what about meeting Knollys?' I asked.

'It's a good idea with a schemer like him to hold the initiative. So, we will go there and find out what he knows. And more importantly what he doesn't know. We'd better hurry that up.'

'We?'

'We. You must come too. To take the blame when we make mistakes later. It's the fate of the young.'

CHAPTER II
'You're a Diamond'

'THE POLICE ARE here to see you, Sherlock,' Cousin Sara shouted up the stairs. I put my head round the door and invited the young policeman up to my rooms.

Before me stood a pasty-looking man of about my age, with weasel eyes and greasy hair; short, shabby and shifty. He introduced himself as Police Sub-inspector Lestrade of the Metropolitan Police. I couldn't immediately think of any felony I had committed; I was certain he could not know anything about the blackmail case and saw no obvious connection to Oscar Wilde's amethyst tie-pin.

'Are you Mr Sherlock Holmes of 24 Montague Street?' Lestrade asked. His voice and manner were more impressive than his appearance.

'I am he, and you are here.'

'Do you know a hooligan called Wiggins?'

'I do.'

'And have you written a letter taking responsibility for his behaviour?'

'Not exactly, but go on.'

'I have been asked by the Bow Street Magistrates that you report to the Surrey House of Correction in Wandsworth, where the governor would like to interview you concerning said Wiggins.'

'Do you know any other details? Has he been convicted, or is he on remand?'

'I fear I have no inkling, Mr Holmes.'

'And how is he? Is he hurt in any way?'

'If he wasn't before he was admitted, he will be by now. And now if you will excuse me, I have carried out my instructions and have other duties to attend to.'

'Of course. I'll go to Wandsworth at once. Before you go, you introduced yourself as Police Sub-inspector. A new role at Scotland Yard, I believe?'

'Yes, sir, it's part of the new Criminal Investigation Department.'

'I know. I take a keen interest in these matters. I'm a consulting detective myself. Is the new department proving successful?'

'I believe it will be so, given time. I haven't come across a consulting detective before: what does that mean, exactly?'

I gave him my card. 'If ever you need a fresh pair of eyes or an unofficial approach, please call me.'

'I'll bear it in mind, sir,' he said, giving me his card in turn. 'Now if you'll excuse me.' With that he was gone as briskly as he'd arrived. I didn't know then that we would meet again later in the year to our mutual benefit.

Every morning the newspapers were headlining that the Royal Observatory at Greenwich was reporting the driest and warmest early summer since records were started there two decades ago, and this morning was no exception. The six miles from my rooms to Wandsworth took only an hour and a half, but by the time I arrived I was so covered in dust that I needed a good wash and brush-up before presenting myself to the Governor to see what could be done about young Wiggins, and indeed about what young Wiggins had done.

Governor George Cresley, CB, of Surrey House of Correction in Wandsworth was quite the contrary of what would be anticipated of a gaol governor. From his countenance and fingers I could tell he was equally jovial, in terms of alcohol and tobacco consumption, at home as well as at work. His clothes were about as imperfectly pressed as his rank would allow and this with his missing wedding ring hinted that he was a widower. His right ear lobe, voice inflection and nodding manner told me he had seen service in India. His office was light, with windows wide open on three sides, posies in vases and all the furniture polished to perfection. A greater contrast to the putrid squalor I'd seen on the short walk from the main gate up to his office would be hard to imagine.

'Wiggins,' he said, standing up to look into the filing cabinet. 'Just arrived. Yes, here we are, a most unusual case. For a start, there is just his name – Wiggins. That's all he said, no Christian name, no surname – just Wiggins. I presume that's the surname, that's what we've entered and put three XXXs against the Christian name. He doesn't know his birthday, but that's not unusual with street arabs, he thinks he's ten, which looks about right. It's not that important. I presume you must be the same Mr Holmes that is mentioned in the letter,' which Cresley first read aloud then gave back to me:

TO WHOM IT MAY CONCERN

The bearer of this letter, if a 4' 6" 10-year-old (est.) urchin called Wiggins, is working for me in my capacity as a consulting detective. I would be grateful if you would render him any assistance, and if his behaviour is in anyway unconventional please bear in mind that he is acting under his own initiative on an important case. If complications arise, please refer to me in the first instance.

Yours faithfully,

Sherlock Holmes, Esq.
24 Montague Street,
London, WC

'Tell me how all this came about?' he asked.

I explained how, as per the letter, I was a consulting detective and Wiggins was a street arab whom I was paying to help me on a case of lost jewellery. He resided, if that's the right word, at St Patrick's Benevolent Society in Blackfriars. This morning a young policeman knocked on the door of my lodgings and told me to report here. I was about to ask the governor to tell me the circumstances of his retention, and why I hadn't been contacted earlier as requested, when the shock of a sudden scream came from the floor below, then seconds later another.

'Sorry about that,' said the governor, 'must be a whipping. We normally do them all together on Sunday after the service, but this one must be more urgent. It won't last long; we're only allowed a dozen lashes each time these days.' We waited for the swishing and screaming to stop and a long minute later he carried on the conversation.

'Why is he here? Larceny in a word. Caught red-handed. Bow Street Magistrates gave him the child convict's standard sentence, four strokes of the birch and three weeks of hard labour.'

'Does it do any good?' I asked.

'None at all,' he said jovially, 'except the gratification of the great British public. The boys used to spend their three weeks here mixing with other delinquents, which only made them worse, so now we keep them in solitary confinement.'

'And the hard labour?'

'For the likes of Wiggins we just use the crank, mainly because we can put one in their cell. There is a box with a crank and two handles and a counter. They have to crank it five thousand times for each meal. Ten thousand cranks a day. Of course if they don't crank enough, they don't eat and so we save money. It's all completely pointless, but that's the idea. If they act up, the wardens make the cranking harder by tensioning it with a screw.'

'Which is why they call them "screws"?'

'Exactly. But forgive me, the mystery for me is why Wiggins didn't produce the letter when he was first arrested. That's another reason I said it was a strange case. He could have showed the letter to the sergeant or the magistrate. The magistrate would have asked for your confirmation, might even have dismissed the case or at least given him a much lighter sentence. But all the time he kept that letter in his pocket, even when sentenced, brought here and given his birching on arrival. It was only when we were changing him into prison clothes that a warden saw the letter. And even then, he was reluctant to ask us to contact you. Can you explain it?'

'No, I really can't,' I said. 'May I see him?'

'Yes, of course. I'll have him sent up.'

'If you don't mind, I would prefer to go to the cell. I am a criminologist and keen to see it for myself, if that is permitted.'

'Normally not, but in the circumstances I don't see why you shouldn't. I never go anywhere near the cells myself, they're too disgusting. You'll need a mask at the very least.' Then he went over to the door, opened it and shouted, 'Warden!'

Warden Courtlea was about as misnamed as a warden could be: short and stocky, a brute of a man, heavily tattooed, with all the bearing of the ex-prisoner. He growled, 'Wiggins, D43. Child lags' wing. Thievin' little bastards. Follow me. I was the one what birched him, squealed like a pig, but they all do. Four I gave 'im, can't do more than that these days. Not like when I was in 'ere. Fair bleedin' they are by the time I've finished with them.'

The governor was right about the mask: the stench of human waste was overwhelming, the air dank and damp, lessened only by the relative cool in the corridor; I thought of how the damp conditions in the winter without heating must be almost unbearable. The only sounds were the whirrings of cranking machines from inside the cells. The only light in the corridor was Courtlea's oil lamp, and it was a light as ineffective against the damp as the dark. He opened Number 43; inside Wiggins was working his crank; he carried on as if in a daze while I looked around at the hard wooden bed, with one blanket, a wash jug and waste bucket. The smell was the air. The only light was through a small high window.

Wiggins was by now a very different creature from the jaunty little urchin I apprehended near Hatton Garden, or the cocky little urchin I had said good-bye to in Montague Street. Physically depleted and exhausted, and he'd only been here two or three days.

'Mr 'Olmes, sir,' he half whispered.

There was no point in explaining to him my feelings of regret, for I guessed I was at least partly responsible for his current predicament. But I was regretful.

'They sent for me,' I said, 'and somehow I'll arrange to have you released. You may stop that now,' I said, pointing to the crank.

'Ahem,' Courtlea coughed.

I reached in my pocket and gave him a shilling. 'There'll be no more hard labour for the boy, and I want him to have a good meal tonight.'

'Ahem.'

I gave him another shilling, then another. 'That's for an extra blanket.'

I nodded good-bye to Wiggins and repaired as swiftly as possible back to the Governor's office and the fresh air of normality.

Yes, the governor could arrange his release, but it would take some paperwork, a visit by me to the Bow Street magistrates and back, maybe twice, probably a surety or some kind of bail, but in the meantime he would ensure Wiggins was at least spared the worst of what his prison had to offer. And so it was done; I went to the magistrates, explained all the circumstances, and Wiggins and I left the gaol the following day.

We repeated the bathing, clothing and feeding exercise, and I made sure he was welcomed back to St Patrick's and soon heard what Wiggins had to tell me.

'I took the ring to a dozen or so places like wot you told me. 'Ventually I found one geezer to buy it in Li'l Italy, an Eytalian, Forna-Chary he's called.'

'Forna-Chary?'

'Sounds like that, yeah. All the ovvers were tryin' me on for five or ten bob, but this Eyetalian, Forna You-know, tried me at a quid. Then I did like you said, turned 'im down and came to find you in your home, but the ol' girl there said you'd knocked off to Putney for the day.'

'Yes, I had. So what did you do then?'

'I went back to the Eyetalian and said, like I remembered wot you told me, I really wanted an amyfist tie-pin in a gold 'arp thing. Told him there was another word I couldn't quite remember, sounded like inter-galo. Forna-Chary knew right away, said he'd just sold it to some blouse from up norf. Give 'im the ruby, he said, and he'd tell me wot's-wot about the amyfist. You told me the ruby was chaff, like, and the amyfist was bona, so I made the swap. I done right?'

'You done very right, my little friend, and I'm sorry for the spot of bother along the way.'

I looked on young Wiggins with a sense of admiration. Not only had he tried to keep me out of whatever sordid little piece of larceny that got him into trouble, but with the stolen jewellery he had made exactly the kind of trade I would have made. Explaining it all to Oscar Wilde was going to be a different matter, especially as I remember he quietly exchanged the ruby tie-pin I'd seen when we first met for this other one. Whether or not he had any idea of the financial, rather than the sentimental, value of either would have to wait for another day.

'Tell me,' I asked Wiggins, 'why didn't you show my letter to the Bow Street Magistrates? It would have saved you a lot of trouble.'

"Cos I didn't wanna get you into no trouble. I like wot we done, hope we can do some more. Jobs, like. We can, can't we?'

'We can and we will. Let's start right away. Could you take me back to this Forna-Chary?'

'Yeh,' he replied, 'but I can remember wot 'e said. 'E said the buyer was a young bride wot wanted to buy it for 'er 'usband wot was about to go to war in Afganittan, or sommit. That's all he knew. Honest.'

'You did well, Wiggins, very well. You are what's known in the vernacular as a diamond. And I'm sorry for your inconvenience at Her Majesty's pleasure. Here's twenty shillings for your trouble. And stay out of trouble.'

'Yes, Mr 'Olmes,' he smirked.

'I mean it, Mr Wiggins.'

'No one's ever called me that before.'

'What, Mister or Wiggins?'

'Neever. 'Cept you.'

Wiggins was coming back to life, and very useful to each other we would prove to be too.

CHAPTER 12

Dead-ends

Now I MUST backtrack two days: the letter from the Master of The Worshipful Company of Stationers waiting for me after the Leander lunch had read as follows:

Dear Mr Holmes,

Further to your enquiry about determining different types of writing paper, I would suggest you contact Mr Frank Smythson, who is at present Acting Headmaster at the Stationers' Company's Foundation School at Bolt Court near Fleet Street. I should mention that the school is co-educational and exists for the benefit of the children of the Liverymen and Freeman of the Company and is of the Quaker persuasion. The school also has a small laboratory and I am sure that if you bring along the writing paper in question Mr Smythson will attempt to analyse it. He has been informed about this communication.

Yours respectfully,

Basil P. J. Cardew, CMG
Master

By a further exchange of messages, Smythson and I arranged to meet at the school the next day.

Before the unpleasant interlude that follows, the walk had started as a particularly agreeable one mile, fifteen-minute stroll from Montague Street to Bolt Court, meandering through Lincoln's Inn Field and round the back alleys of the building site that will soon be the new Royal Courts of Justice. There was an element of topicality about this part of the walk, too: the newspapers had been full of stories of how the original workforce were on strike and barricading the building, while the imported German workers had to eat, sleep and work inside the site fearing the ruffian treatment that would be dealt them if they ventured outside. I walked past the protesting Londoners, but in my pressed cotton I did not appear to be a German worker and so passed without being set upon.

I confirmed I was being dogged when I looked back at the protesters as I was leaving Carey Street. The pursuer was good enough at his task: everything about his appearance was average, everything about his clothing non-descript, everything about his crowd-mingling was invisible. I had first noticed him crossing Holborn to join Kingsway; not that I picked him out in particular, he was part of a throng and I observed them all equally.

At times like these it's helpful to know London as well as I. Just off Carey Street is the small cul-de-sac alley of Bell Yard, which is also the back entrance to the White Hart pub on the Strand. I darted into the pub yard with my back pressed against the wall. I soon heard the shuffle of confused footsteps in Bell Yard as my pursuer realised he had lost me. As he walked past the alley,

I said:

'You are looking for me, I presume?' I stepped into the centre of the alley to block his escape.

'Who says I am?' He was shorter than me, but more powerfully built. By his bearing and haircut I'd warrant a soldier, by his manner a private.

'Holmes, Sherlock Holmes, as you very well know. Now who sent you?'

'I ain't telling you nuffink. Get outa my way or I'll smash yer 'ead in.'

'I don't suppose the Princess of Wales would be too pleased to hear about one of her trooper's off-duty activities, do you?'

'What's she got to do wiv it?'

'She is your Colonel-in-Chief. Second Dragoon Guards by the tattoo on your wrist. And that cross scar on your neck. Should be easy enough for your lieutenant-colonel Lord Gifford to track you down.'

'You don't know them, you wouldn't dare talk to them.'

'*You* may not dare talk to them, but I'd have no compunction. Now what you don't know is if I really know them or not. But seeing as harassing civilians off-duty is a flogging offence, you have got to ask yourself one question: "Does he know them, or does he not?" Well, do I or don't I, trooper?'

'All right, it was Lord Gifford wot sent me. Now what you goin' to do about it? I ain't done nothing illegal.' He had a point.

'And what did he tell you to do?'

'To dog you wherever you went and tell 'im.'

'You won't say anything about this and neither will I. Tell him I just went for a walk. Do we agree?'

'Yer, all right,' he mumbled.

'Now be gone with you.' I stepped aside to let him pass back into Carey Street.

'Wait,' he said, looking back. 'I've got to know. Do you know them or not, the Princess and the Colonel?'

'Not in the slightest,' I said.

I didn't believe Gifford would have done this on his own; in fact there's absolutely no reason for him to know I even exist. It had to be Knollys who instructed him. The more I knew about Francis Knollys the less savoury he became.

Inside the school, Smythson welcomed me warmly. He was certainly among the neatest people I had ever met. In the same way that Darwin's new evolution and Fauld's new fingerprint theories work by exploring variations on theoretical perfection, Smythson could be that very model of perfection. Each hair was tailored precisely, his eyebrows perfectly trimmed, the shaving sharp and recent, and his nails ordered Bristol-fashion. Likewise, his clothes: the wing collar and tails freshly starched, the shirt just laundered, the frock jacket and trousers neatly pressed and the boots gleaming. I realised then that like Darwin and Faulds my powers of deduction were based on observing abnormalities and that a perfect specimen has few secrets to reveal, not even whether or not the person concerned is a deliberate perfectionist.

It was not until he spoke that I was able to find out more. An Englishman is incapable of uttering the simplest sentence without revealing to those with ears to hear almost all there is to know about him. Thus, when Smythson said: 'Welcome to our school, Mr Holmes. The Master told me about your visit and request. I'm Acting Headmaster because Mr Dunnwitty is ill, terminally so, I'm sorry to say', I knew that he was from Dulwich, almost certainly educated at the excellent Dulwich College, that his father was in trade, probably a prosperous shopkeeper or warehouse-wallah, that the family had newly arrived from the lower-middle into the middle-middle classes and that he himself was aware of this ascendancy and determined to continue it. By his tone and manners as much as his accent it was clear he was outgoing and generous, as he was presently to prove.

Of course I could not give him the blackmail note in its entirety, but I had made a sketch of the central watermark and cut off the one-and-three-quarter inches above and two-and-a-quarter inches below the handwriting, and I was hoping this would be enough for him to tell me the manufacturer and supplier of the paper, and from that the likely retailer or distributor, and from one of these perhaps the customer and eventually, perchance, the blackmailer. I had also brought along the envelope to see if he could shed any light on the ink; just Lewis's name and address revealed nothing of the blackmail itself.

The Stationers' School laboratory was really no more than a large workbench with some sophisticated scales, a collection of magnifying glasses and a microscope, and a series of mirrors to direct light.

'It's certainly hand- and not machine-made,' he said, looking up from one of the glasses. 'They have used esparto grass mixed with wood fibres, that's what gives it the slight cream colour and the even texture. Laid not woven. I see there is a small watermark on the bottom left-hand corner.'

'The main watermark under the writing had two capital letters MM, with each M made to look like a mountain peak.' I gave him my sketch of the motif. 'The small one you're talking about I couldn't see clearly enough with any of my lenses.'

'The MM will be Mayr-Melnhof, a large mill in Austria. They also have mills in Hungary and Bohemia. If I can find a good angle on this small watermark, we might be able to find out the mill.' For a minute he adjusted the different lights and glasses and then said 'ULM77. I'd say 77 was the year, so it was pressed two years ago. Let me have a look in the mills gazetteer.' He took a hefty book down from the shelf and said, 'We know it's Mayr-Melnhof, so we only need look through the mill list. Nothing obvious. Ah, this could be something. ULM, there is a mill at Usti nad Labem in Bohemia, that could be the UL. There is nothing else that comes close, so I'd say that was certainly the mill. Let me look under that; yes, still hand-made there. Now what the M is, well it could be anything.'

'Could it be the customer or importer?' I asked.

'Yes, it could be, but first let's see what grade it is, that might give us a clue.' He weighed and re-weighed the two scraps I had given him. 'It's hard to be accurate with so little raw material, but it will be close to two hundred pounds per ream. The paper size is almost certainly Large Post 10 Quarto, halved to give eight-by-five inches if that central strip you've kept is what it should be. Here we would call this size and weight 32 Bond.'

'That's helpful, thank you,' I said, storing the data away in the brain-attic.

'Only up to a point, I fear. I presume what you really want to know is who wrote on the writing paper, and discover that you need to know where they bought it from.'

'Correct. Do you have an opinion on that?'

'The M letter, probably, I have, but it's not very useful.'

'Please continue,' I urged.

'It wasn't bought from anyone, at least not anyone in London. My guess is that it was bought directly from the factory in Bohemia, or through the factory's agent somewhere on the Continent. I'm sorry, that's not really very helpful.'

'On the contrary, you've been most helpful by eliminating very many possibilities. Is the envelope of the same paper?'

'Yes, identical. The gum has dried but it's weighted at the peak in the Continental fashion. The Whatman seals are more evenly spread.'

'Whatman?'

'Whatman of Kent, the leading British supplier. If this 32 Bond had been British that's where it would have come from. It's what the customers expect, and all other mills follow what they do. So, a blank there too, I'm afraid.'

'How about the ink?' I asked. 'The ink impression on the envelope is duller than on the letter. I presume that's because the writer used blotting-paper on the envelope and not on the letter.'

He looked again at the envelope. 'That would be so. The type of ink is much harder to determine as it's so easy to manufacture it. There are dozens of makes. I sell and import several myself on my stall. Why don't you bring the envelope along and you could try different inks and compare them directly on to the envelope?'

'You have a stall?' I asked.

'Yes,' he said, 'I live in Richmond and trade at the Kew Gardens market every Saturday. Come along tomorrow and we'll see which ink matches. I have dozens to choose from.'

So that's exactly what I did. Montague Street to Kew Gardens and back is too far to walk pleasurably in one day in the heat spell, seventeen-and–a-half miles, so I decided to rent and try out one of the high-wheeler bicycles that had nearly run me over so many times. Somewhere in the back of my mind too was the thought that if any footpads from Knollys or Gifford were trying to dog me, they'd have a far harder job if I were on a high-wheeler then on foot. A short walk down to Holborn and the garage of Gossinge & Co, a quick lesson in their yard and off

I set. Embarking is easy: left foot on the peg at knee height, right foot 'scooting' a few times to gain gyroscopic momentum, then leap on and pedal accordingly. The reverse pendulum and torque steering effects were of much interest to me, as were the other vehicles that I was consistently overtaking. As all pedestrians know by now, stopping promptly is easier said than done, but the rider can alight, and therefore stop, as easily as embark if the requirement is not too urgent. Gossinge explained the main danger was hitting a pothole or any immovable object and being thrown over the handle-bars, this occurrence being known among aficionados as 'doing a header'. A further peril in my case was my extreme height, so that my knees touched the handle-bars unless I bent the legs slightly; in the event of doing a header there was also a chance of breaking a femur. By the time I reached Kew Gardens unscathed one hour later, I had become an enthusiast for this new form of transport with its commanding views; an enthusiasm that was not to survive the return journey, as the reader will soon discover.

Smythson's stall was as spick and span as Smythson himself and displayed a splendid collection of writing and blotting-paper and envelopes, all expensive and weighty; Waterman, Cross and Faber Castell fountain pens; bottles from a dozen ink-makers in a variety of colours; diaries, note-books and journals; recipe- and address-books; and leather-desk items for storage. There was one particularly attractive leather-bound drawer-case for filing, and I determined to buy it, partly to assuage Cousin

Sara who was always criticising my untidiness with files, papers and cuttings, especially now with these two new commissions with their attendant notes. She was right, of course: although I keep the rooms in my brain such that every piece of data is exactly where it should be, the pieces of data in my room are scattered around in rather a ramshackle fashion. After buying the case, I asked him to bring it to the school from where I could collect it.

'That won't be necessary, Mr Holmes, I'll have it delivered directly to your rooms,' he said.

We set to work with the ink varieties using blotting-paper and to reduce half an hour's experiments to a summary: the ink on the envelope and therefore the blackmail note was Pelikan Ultramarine Finest.

Again, Smythson apologised that he wasn't being very helpful as this particular type of ink was widely available and could have been bought from almost anywhere.

'Royal Warrants for suppliers,' I asked, 'who holds the one for stationery supplies?'

'Whatman again.'

'All the royal palaces?'

'Yes, all of them. You may laugh, Mr Holmes, but one day it is my intention to have a Royal Warrant to supply all the palaces.'

'I'm not laughing in the least, Mr Smythson; if the way you have treated me is any indication I'm sure you will fulfil your ambition.'

I admit I wasn't giving all my attention to navigating the high-wheeler back home successfully when I had my accident; I was more concerned with what the sessions with Smythson had revealed: that the blackmail note had almost certainly come from Marlborough House, written on privately imported paper from a source known as M. That lessened the likelihood that any of the suspects who I'd loosely classified under Bohemia could be the blackmailer, so removing from my list all the residents and artist visitors, though not the Society visitors, to Thames House, together with everybody at Langdale Pike's Oriental Club party for Jimmy Whistler. That still left a handsome list of suspects: either or both of the Langtrys; Lord and/or Lady Lonsdale; Lord Londesborough and/or his daughter Lady Edith Denison; the Cornwallis-Wests, although likely to be Patsy on her own; Christopher Sykes and Francis Knollys. I was just thinking that of course the stationery could have been stolen by any of the numerous other visitors to Marlborough House beyond the inner circle, so my list of suspects had now grown back to what it was, when a landau with its roof let down turned sharp right directly in front of me and with no time for anything other than a direct hit, I 'did a header' over the handle-bars and landed most ungallantly on an elderly lady and a Pekinese dog in the back of the contraption. Before I could apologise the wretched little dog bit me on the left hand. Fortunately, not the passenger, nor my own contraption, nor the Pekinese, a breed with which under normal circumstances I share an excellent relationship, were damaged, but my left hand needed bandaging and the upper-right body parts were bruised and uncomfortable for the next few days. I fear my high-wheeler days are short-lived; the experience is novel, exciting mostly but ultimately too exciting, and so not to be repeated.

While recovering I designed a simple frame-to-rear-tyre lever brake and wondered why no one had thought of it before. It also occurred to me that, in spite of my best endeavours with graphology and my analysis of the actual raw materials of the blackmail, I had come to as much of a dead-end in the investigation as I had on the high-wheeler.

CHAPTER 13

Wringing Wilde's Neck

I HAD SENT a card to Oscar Wilde at Thames House suggesting we meet there again soon so that I could report on the missing amethyst tie-pin. He replied suggesting a meeting at the Lyceum Theatre instead, 'soon after lunch' the following day. I was pleased to comply, excited to do so too as I was well aware of the excitement still surrounding Henry Irving's new theatre company with the re-opened Lyceum as its base, and having a few months earlier much enjoyed the opening production of *Hamlet*, with Irving in the lead role and Ellen Terry as Ophelia. Taking 'soon after lunch' to mean 3.00pm, I arrived to find Wilde and a few others in the stalls while on stage Ellen Terry was in technical rehearsal for her Portia in *The Merchant of Venice*, with Irving directing her from the front stalls nearby.

During a 'fresh-air break' I asked Wilde about his involvement with the Lyceum. His old Dublin and Oxford friend Bram Stoker had not only married Wilde's first inamorata Florence Balcombe but had recently become the Lyceum's business manager and Henry Irving's personal manager, although Wilde couldn't help adding, 'as far as I know Florence's white knight couldn't run a bath, let alone a theatre'. One of Irving's ideas was to start a new periodical called *The Theatre* that would appear to be independent but be heavily weighted towards the Lyceum's activities. They needed contributors, and Stoker suggested Wilde, and Wilde revelled in his new critic-and-gossip role with the magazine and his association with a great thespian of the day and his theatre company. Towards the end of the break I met Stoker too, and he didn't seem particularly business-like to me either, but it transpired that we were neighbours in London WC and may meet up some time at the Museum Tavern.

After rehearsals I asked, 'Shall we go to Monico's next door to talk about your amethyst tie-pin?' On the way he made the startling revelation that he was considering using me for one of the characters in the new play he was writing.

'I didn't know you wrote plays,' I said.

'You didn't because I don't. Yet. But I think I will. Poetry is so convoluted; the stage so unswerving, so forthright. So much more democratic. In fact, theatre is the only democratic art of the day.' There was clearly no stopping his new enthusiasm. 'Drama, you see, Holmes, is the meeting place of art and life. Drama deals not merely with man, but with social man, with man in relation to God and to humanity. What are we if we are not *humane*? You have to say the word as an actor would so as to clearly hear its distinct sounds.'

'About your amethyst tie-pin,' I tried.

'To you it's an amethyst tie-pin, to me it's Lady Wilde riding bareback wrathful and vengeful, her younger offspring soon to die heroically at the end of her lance. Yes, now; what news?'

'In theatrical terms, if we are to head straight to the climax, I can tell you that unfortunately the tie-pin has been sold. Worse, it is by now on its way to Afghanistan.'

'Does the climax have a crisis?' he asked.

'It was sold by a stall holder in Little Italy to an army bride as a keepsake for her recent husband who is on his way to serve with the Royal Berkshire Regiment in that mountainous outpost. I wrote to her, explaining that the familial value is far greater than the economic one, and offering to make amends should it not be too late. She replied that unfortunately it was too late, her beloved was *en passage*. I am afraid therefore that enquiries are exhausted and that we should give up the investigation and the jewel as lost, at least until the husband returns.'

What I didn't tell him was how all this came about. With Wiggins I went to see 'Forna-Chary', actually Fornaciari, and laid out the facts before him in the most reasonable way possible. At first, he was reluctant to give me any useful leads to pursue, but when I pointed out that the ruby tie-pin currently on display in his vitrine was in fact stolen, and that the Constabulary would view this as an unfortunate occurrence, he relented. His receipt book revealed the details: sold to Mrs Rachel Barraclough, 14 Bedford Road, Harpenden, Hertfordshire for nine pounds, seventeen shillings and sixpence. Furthermore, when Wiggins tapped on the vitrine, he was reminded to return the ruby tie-pin too.

'Nine pounds, seventeen shillings and sixpence.' Wilde shook his head sadly. 'A pretty price for a new army bride no doubt, but I'd give ninety pounds seventeen shillings and sixpence for that now. Not that I have the sum, you understand, but I never let minor inconveniences discourage me. You have done your best and I thank you. Strangely, my mind is more at rest knowing that it has been stolen than if I had lost it. The horseback woman would never forgive me for that.'

'All is not totally lost. Let's wait for her husband – and the tie-pin – to return from Afghanistan.'

'If he ever does return from Afghanistan. I hear the natives are decidedly fearsome.'

'A fair point,' I said, 'but if he himself doesn't return there's a good chance that his personal effects will. It's an outside chance, and not one easy to submit to Lady Wilde, I grant you. Here is the ruby tie-pin you lent me at Thames House. Not the Burma one you were wearing when we first met, but the Siamese one you gave me instead.'

'You are most observant,' he smiled.

'Most people see, but I observe. For instance, it is obvious you have been up all night, and were writing this morning before attending the theatre. You had porridge for—'

'Not all that again, Holmes, for the love of God. Actually, I have a more pressing problem.' He spoke softly.

'I'll help if I can.'

'Yes, I'm sure you can. It's right up your street. But do detectives have a Hippocratic Oath? – at least the secrecy part. You seekers after justice must all be disciples of Astraea, and so you must have an Astraean Code. You know Gladys Lonsdale, I believe?'

'Only in the sense that I saw her at the tea-and-art party you invited me to, and at Langdale Pike's party at the Oriental Club. But we have never spoken.'

'Your impression of her?'

'Strikingly tall and flamboyant was the impression from your party. Romanesquely beautiful. She was sitting for Frank Miles, so she was still as an idol, and as silent. At the Oriental Club my impression was of her popularity, surrounded by admirers and general jollity. As I said we have only been in the same room together, and separated by crowds, and so never sufficiently close for me to properly observe her. And your impressions?'

'I know her well, very well. We share best friends; Lillie Langtry again. Striking, yes, yes. And trouble. Tons of trouble. That's why we love her; Lillie Langtry, Patsy and I. And *tutto il mondo* too.'

'And she being trouble; is that the problem you mention?'

'Yes and no. It's her husband, really. I don't suppose you've met him? George, the fourth Earl.'

'No, but I understand he spends most of his time out of London hunting, shooting and fishing.' This much I remembered from George Lewis.

'And drinking. I hear he's in the New Forest now shooting with Bertie. I fear he'll shoot me too when he's back in London and finds out what has happened.'

'And what has happened?' I asked.

'She has married a complete brute is what happened, a foul-mouthed, short-tempered heathen of the worst possible kind. And God knows I like heathens. And only God knows why she married him. Well, He does know why. Money and rank, the usual waylayers. More, she knows she is twice the man he is. But I don't suppose that is what you meant. Do you know Vamberry the wine merchant?'

'Slightly. I met him briefly at my club.' I had met him once at the Diogenes Club with Mycroft. We are both on the wine committee and Vamberry was touting for our trade.

'What club is that?'

'The Diogenes Club. You wouldn't like it. The strangest club in London, and Brother Mycroft one of the strangest men. He was one of the founders and I have myself discovered it to have a very soothing atmosphere.'

'Yes, well, he's the wine merchant to the Arts Club and that's where the problem starts. The problem will end with a resolutely angry Lord Lonsdale blowing my head off with a 20-bore shotgun because his dear wife has fallen for a Vamberry swindle with his money and he thinks I put her up to it. Which I did, but that's not the point.'

By now Wilde had gone from subdued and cowed to agitated and anxious. I asked him to tell me the story from the beginning. To wit: Vamberry has a scheme whereby members of the Arts Club join him in a wine investment. Wilde said he couldn't afford to join in himself or he probably would have done so, and I would need to ascertain the details later from Gladys, but from the few details he could impart it sounded to me like a variation on the old three-card trick. Vamberry invites a member to buy two cases of wine, one for their own investment and one for him to sell by the bottle, with the profit from the bottle sales paying for the investment, so granting the member a free case of wine and Vamberry free wine to sell. Quite probably, replacing labels would feature somewhere along the way in this tidy game as well.

However, the immediate problem, as Wilde and now I saw it, was that Gladys had used money from her husband's account to finance her share in this little scheme, the fourth Earl had found out due to reasons with which she would no doubt furnish me later, she had accidentally let it be known that all the members of the Arts Club were in on it and that it was Oscar's great idea – and that the said Earl, notoriously ill-tempered and violent, would prefer to wring Wilde's neck rather than blame his poor, sweet, innocent wife.

'And another point,' Wilde said. 'The good lord strongly disapproves of the company she keeps; Thames House, Lillie, Jimmy Whistler, anybody vaguely interesting and above all me. She tells it aloud to everyone's great amusement that he absolutely hates poems and poetry, and that according to him nothing will ever come of poets and that we all need a damn good shooting. Preferably up against the wall that he has built specially for the purpose, with him pulling the trigger. Are you with me?'

I said I was and that a meeting with Gladys Lonsdale would appear to be a priority. He would arrange it post-haste. What I didn't mention was that a meeting with Gladys and her handwriting was also a priority for the blackmail case, and indeed a meeting with her husband, if it could be arranged, equally so.

CHAPTER 14

The Queen

I HAD KEPT in constant touch with George Lewis about the blackmail case all the while, telling him about the graphology and raw materials dead-ends and my widening social interchange with the cast of suspects. In fact, our work together deepened beyond this immediate conundrum and he invited me when the blackmail case had been resolved to help him on a case involving Bertie's younger brother Alfred, the Duke of Saxe-Coburg and Gotha, and his racing stable where some malfeasance had been afoot. Another of his clients, a Mrs Farintosh, had fallen adrift of her opal tiara, and I was quickly able to solve the mystery behind that strange case too. Although I prefer to live and work alone, I must admit that having an older colleague with whom to confer on cases and to wonder at life's anomalies and inclinations I found most rewarding; Lewis was after all old enough to be my father, apart from being the most influential lawyer in London. His wife Elizabeth had invited me to one of her famous salons, and it wasn't quite as tiresome and insincere as I thought it might be. In fact, she was to take me under her wing socially just as much as Lewis would do professionally.

With the Oscar Wilde amethyst tie-pin case now over, or at least suspended, and the Vamberry route into the Lonsdales not yet alive, I was planning a visit to the

Repton Boxing Club gymnasium in Bethnal Green for a practice bout or two. I was on the point of leaving when a telegram arrived from Lewis & Lewis with just six words:

NEW NOTE STOP HITHER FORTHWITH GL

On arrival I found that Lewis was out with a client, and so his secretary Harris found me a desk in a quiet corner and I examined the latest note.

> The next mistress name is TID. Her codes are 1x3 1x1; 1x3, 1x2, 13 more codes. I have the code keys. Now he insults Emperor Alexander II over Afghanistan. My price is now 3 gold bars, deposited with Rahn+Bodmer. Once paid, the notebook is returned to Lewis & Co. Not paid next 4 gold bars or Reynolds News prints it. Now 2 weeks. I'm losing patience. News for us in The Times. The jew can find the gold.

TID, following ALW in the second blackmail note, was evidently a code for a particular mistress. In one column of foolscap I wrote down in capitals the full names of the eight recent significant, or Society, mistresses that Lewis had mentioned and in the other column the initials TID and ALW. I wondered if the blackmailer had deciphered the codes in a similar way.

In any event, it didn't take long to distil the very simple code: the blackmailer took the fourth letter of the Christian name of each of the mistresses and carried on spelling it backwards from there. So TID was Edith. ALW fell into place when I recalled Gladys Lonsdale had spelled her Christian name Gwladys until her husband asked her to change it on marriage to Gladys on account of his aversion to the letter double-u. All that really signified was that the blackmailer knew Lady Lonsdale before she was married, which was only a year ago, so new intelligence of limited significance at this stage.

The initials TID threw out the challenge of determining to which Edith they referred, as from Lewis's list there are two Ediths. Lady Edith Henrietta Sybil Denison, Lord Londesborough's daughter was the more recent inamorata, whereas previously that honour had belonged to Edith, Countess of Aylesford, wife of the seventh Earl of Aylesford. As Lewis recalled, apart from Bertie she was also in a liaison with the Marquess of Blandford, Randolph Churchill's brother and therefore brother-in-law to Jennie Spencer-Churchill, Lady Randolph Churchill, herself another of Bertie's conquests. The Countess wished to divorce the Earl and elope with the Marquess, leaving a breathless Bertie to call Blandford 'the greatest blackguard alive'. Identifying the right Edith could be significant, because this earlier affair was now five years old and would indicate whether or not the blackmailer knew of Bertie's liaisons at that time – if indeed the notebook went back that far.

The next clue, if such obtuse signifiers could be called clues, was: 'Her codes are 1x3 1x1; 1x3, 1x2, 13 more codes.' The irregular punctuation could be significant. If these were indeed quotes from Bertie's notebook – and the word 'if' is significant because I still wasn't convinced that the blackmailer in fact possessed the lost notebook or was bluffing – but if it did exist I would have to agree with Lewis and Mycroft that these were cyphers for the different activities during the match. Taking into account the thirteen more codes, that would appear to indicate that they had coupled in some way or other on multiple different occasions.

About Emperor Alexander II of Russia I knew little in depth, beyond the fact that he was father-in-law to the Princess of Wales's sister, so perhaps the insult was familial and not relating to the Second Anglo-Afghan War, where Britain and Russia were engaged in the Great Game. But in either event the insult would be unlikely to prove helpful to the Prince or the monarchy and could well cross over into the scandalous.

The ransom now stood at three gold bars; an increase so far of one gold bar per blackmail note, with at the end the threat of a further increase of another gold bar with the next blackmail note, should there need to be one. I worried that at four gold bars the ransom would become unaffordable, or at least not worth paying; the case would then collapse and I would have failed.

When Lewis returned I told him what I had learned and asked, 'It's reassuring we can contact them through *The Times*, but have you any idea why someone sufficiently sophisticated to hold a Swiss bank account doesn't know how to spell the proper noun Jew?'

'It's either a deliberate insult or plain ignorance. I can't think of an alternative.'

'But I'm sure it's the alternative we are looking for. In the meantime, does Francis Knollys know about this new blackmail note?'

'Not unless he wrote it as it has only just arrived. He's been wanting to see us about the first one and I've been putting it off, but we should delay no longer. I'll arrange it right now.' He scribbled out a note to a clerk, presumably the message to Francis Knollys.

'Have you read this morning's *Times*?' he asked.

'Not yet, I came straight here.'

'Have a look at the Court Circular,' he said, then read it out for me: "The brother of Alexandra, Princess of Wales King George I of Greece, King of the Hellenes and his wife Olga, Queen of the Hellenes are visiting Marlborough House". So Knollys will have his mind on keeping Alix and her clan amused at the moment. As will Gifford. Good time for us to visit, in other words.'

'So King George of Greece is Alix's brother. Who is Olga, Queen of the Hellenes?'

'She was the Grand Duchess Olga Constantinovna of Russia. A Romanov. And a real tough old broadsword. No *Venus in the Lilies* either, if I may be so ungallant. Apparently he married her for the money, then found out she doesn't have any, just a few enormous old palaces that are crumbling around her. There's an old Russian woman in Alix's household: childhood nurse to Alix, her sister Dagmar and her brother George and now the royal nanny,

Valentina Kasperskaya. She must be as old as Rome by now. We'll find out more from Francis Knollys.'

'Going back to the blackmail, Alix must know about her husband's peccadilloes. That's a motive.'

'Yes, she must. He makes absolutely no attempt to hide them, which is what makes my job so difficult.'

'And do we know if she objects or not?' I asked.

'Well, we don't know. No one ever knows what goes on behind bedroom doors. She may be relieved that he is expending his energies elsewhere. She may be having revenge affairs, although if that's the case, she is remarkably good at keeping a secret in the most indiscreet court in the world. In fact, I'm certain she isn't.'

'She is very popular with the public, far more popular than he is.'

'You're right,' he said. 'Let's face it, she could hardly be less so. He could be seriously harmed by what's in that notebook. Funds cut off at the least. Questions of accession at the worst. Alix loves being loved; if not by him, then by the people. They lead their own lives and leave each other in peace. That too I suppose is a form of love. At least that's what my wife says, so it must be right. But you are not married.'

'No, the opportunity hasn't arisen,' I replied.

'Is there a yet at the end of that sentence?'

'No. I have observed in others that emotions interfere with reason, and that most crimes are caused by motives of emotion and solved by the clarity of reason. Maybe one day when my intellect is honed enough to admit emotion,

I may relent. But for now, I must pursue the perfection of reason.'

'You may be right, but your view is singular, as you will admit. It's like a wind, marriage. You never know from whence it blows, and even if you knew there isn't much you could do about it. My business is divorce, so I have seen marriage from every direction in which the wind blows. I don't know more about it now after these dozens of cases than I did when I started. So, I know how to dissolve them, but I offer no advice on stopping it reaching that stage.'

'Is Knollys married?' I asked.

'Yes, certainly. Why do you ask?'

'Just wondering.'

'You are wondering about everything. That's good in one so young. And in your line of work.' A clerk knocked, entered and handed him a note. 'Aha, Knollys is free now. Let's go and see him. I don't trust him an inch, but I'm curious to discover what you make of him.'

Twenty minutes and a mile later, (we were travelling at Lewis's pace), we were walking through the Grand Hall at Marlborough House. Lewis contrasted the well-ordered calm that normally prevailed to the hubbub that we saw that morning as a scurry of red-uniformed men and women prepared for the foreign royal visit. One of Knollys's pageboys had come to meet us at the front entrance and was taking us through the passage-ways that snaked around the back of the house until we are in Knollys's his office on the third floor with views over the bare trees of Marlborough House Gardens, The Mall and St James's Park.

Knollys was forty-two years old, already balding with thinning white hair and a robust and equally white moustache. He was dressed formally, and yet there was a surprising touch of the unkempt about him, from his uneven shoelaces to his no-quite-right collar and tie. He welcomed us cordially, told me he knew about Musgrave and the crown and that he knew Mycroft. When I asked how, he simply said, 'From the Ministry.'

Lewis enquired about the royal visit, and Knollys leaned back in his chair, folded his arms and gave us the following briefing:

'I am personally organising the visit of Her Royal Highness Alexandra, the Princess of Wales's brother King George I of Greece, King of the Hellenes and her sister-in-law Olga, Queen of the Hellenes. As you surely must know, Princess Alexandra and King George's family are at the centre of European royalty. Their father was Prince Christian of Schleswig-Holstein-Sonderburg-Glücksburg and is now King Christian IX of Denmark. Their mother was Louise Wilhelmine Friederike Caroline Auguste Julie von Hesse-Kassel and is now the Queen of Denmark. All this and more I must, and do, have at my fingertips.'

'Quite a scattered brood,' said Lewis.

'They are, but they're a surprisingly close family in the circumstances. Every Christmas they gather in Copenhagen and throughout the year one branch is always visiting another, albeit usually far less formally than this. Queen Olga and her children were here two months ago.' Then, turning to the matter in hand, 'So, Lewis, what news on the blackmail front?'

Lewis gave him a progress report to date: regarding the second (but I noticed not the third) blackmail note; my efforts on the subjects of graphology and writing paper; and the circle of possibilities. I noticed Lewis didn't tell him specifically about the royal palaces' connection with the writing paper.

'Does all the writing paper and ink at Marlborough House come from the same place?' I asked.

'The Repository Office in Buckingham Palace Mews requisitions everything from there.'

'Could you find out from where?'

'Could I find out from where? Well, I suppose I could, yes. Why do you ask?'

'It's just a factor. Is that the palaces' writing paper on your desk? And the ink?'

'Yes.'

'Could you please write something, anything, on a piece of paper for me?' I asked.

'No,' he said, 'and I must assure you that the blackmail notes did not come from Marlborough House.' He immediately realised the trap he had fallen into and quickly added, 'At least I imagine it's very doubtful. We don't employ those sorts of people here.'

'On which subject,' asked Lewis, 'just so we haven't missed anyone significant, the Prince's staff consist of you as his Private Secretary, and who else? And if you don't mind, the same question for Princess Alexandra's staff.'

'As well as me, there is a Deputy Private Secretary, William McLeod, and an Equerry, Major John Lavery. The Princess has just her Private Secretary, Commander Stephen Sandeman, and her lady-in-waiting, Alice, the Countess of Derby. Then Marlborough House has a Master of the Royal Household, the Earl of Gifford, and a Treasurer, Captain Peter Stacey. Those are the immediate senior staff, but of course there are many more. I can find you a complete list if I must. Then there are the children of course, they have their own royal nanny, currently Valentina Kasperskaya. The Princess has just made her Mistress of the Bedchamber, a new role and one that makes her formally part of the Household.'

'I thought a Mistress of the Bedchamber was a lady-in-waiting. Surely a royal nanny cannot be one such?' asked Lewis.

'You are referring to a Lady of the Bedchamber and a Mistress of the Robes; these are the ladies-in-waiting. The Mistress is the Princess's invention. I must say it's a break with tradition, something which I normally don't approve, but really it's the Earl of Gifford's purview rather than mine.'

'If I may,' I said, taking a sheet from the pile of blank writing paper. He was unamused, and bristled. I asked: 'Do people work normal daytime hours here or are they also expected to work overnight sometimes?'

'That's a strange question. They work the usual working hours only. We go home every night.'

'Yourself included?'

'I haven't missed a night at home for years. Why do you ask?'

'Because I'm interested,' I said.

'Your interest is bordering on impertinence, young man. Most unlike your brother, I might add. I suggest you take stock of whom you are addressing.' Then he turned to Lewis. 'There is something else, something of far more significance than your young assistant here looking for tittle-tattle. The Queen has asked for this matter to be settled.'

'Settled in what way?' asked Lewis.

'Settled by paying the blackmailer what he wants, bringing the whole sorry episode to a quick conclusion.' His tone had changed to combative.

'But why this one?' I asked. 'It can't be the first blackmail attempt against the monarchy, and I presume they are not all paid off. We don't even know for sure if this is significant or not at this stage. We only know the Prince has lost a notebook. What makes this one so special?'

'Because,' he said with a tone of false patience, 'I need hardly say there is a growing sense of popular discontent with the monarchy. The evidence is all around us. I can't take the chance that the blackmailer is bluffing, as you suggest.'

'I see the intention,' said Lewis. 'But has Her Majesty considered who is going to pay the gold bars?'

'I don't suppose Her Majesty has given much thought to such grubby considerations. Her Majesty has instructed me, and I am instructing you. It couldn't be more simple.'

'Excuse me,' I said, 'I thought the Prince of Wales instructed you, not her Majesty.'

Knollys stood up angrily and snarled at me, 'Do you know of my importance around here?' And to Lewis: 'Better get him out of here before I do something he regrets. The interview is over. Good day to you both.' He rang his desk bell and shouted, 'Hopkins!'

The same pageboy showed us out and in St James's Park George Lewis and I compared notes.

I said: 'I hope I haven't overstepped the mark, but I needed him to stand up and step back so I could see his waistcoat.'

'For what reason?'

'Because I wanted to confirm my suspicion that the bottom button on his waistcoat was not done up, as a gentleman dressing himself would surely not do. I missed it on our arrival, foolishly.'

'So, what's he been up to? Although I suspect I know the answer.'

'When I leaned forward to take the sheet of paper, I inclined further than was necessary and could smell scent on his sleeve. Putting these together I knew he had come straight from a mistress or a bordello that morning. Hence my question about their working hours.'

'I told you he wasn't my favourite.'

'Mine neither now. He lied about the writing paper. When I asked about the repository, his eyes looked left for a few seconds before replying and then he repeated my question. He writes with his left hand, yet chews his right-hand fingernails. I'll have to investigate that.'

'Did you see how he changed when he mentioned the Queen?'

'He shifted his body shape to the left and looked over our heads when he was talking. I think he made up that part in an effort to persuade us to pay the money, in other words to pay it to him. Only he knows if the Queen really does know or not, and if she does, if she is concerned about it. From what I've heard a further embarrassment to her son would only give her some satisfaction.'

'Well partly, yes. But she will also be seriously worried about a scandal, if this becomes one, and the effect that will have on her and the House of Hanover. And he's anti-Semite I can tell. Something you can't.'

'Well, I noticed that when he was talking to you, he was cleaning his glasses unnecessarily vigorously. Something about you agitated him.'

'You have made an enemy, Holmes, and a powerful one, but my experience of divorce cases suggests that having a catalyst in the camp can work to our advantage; and anyway, I will shield you. You were right about the Queen and whether or not she really knows. I think you're also right that he is the most likely suspect.'

'The most likely of many suspects, though,' I said.

'Unfortunately, yes. The fact is we are no further forward at the end of today's work then we were at the beginning of it, in fact with some new names coming to light we are even further away from solving our little problem than we have ever been. We are moving backwards. If the Queen is involved, we have a whole new layer of complications too.' He took a gulp of air before continuing rapidly: 'We need to stop going backwards and start going forwards, and fast. I'd say that Bertie doesn't know about the blackmail yet or he would have told me. If the Queen really is demanding payment, she would have confirmed the story with him first, or why press to settle? Which either means she doesn't know and hasn't asked him, in which case Knollys is the blackmailer, or that Bertie has denied it and she doesn't believe him. The payment will have to come from him in some form and I know him well enough to know that he will fight that to the end. That's why we must find the blackmailer before he has to find the money. Quickly too, if it keeps going up every week.'

I had an additional little problem, which I decided to keep to myself: Mycroft and his obvious closeness to Knollys, even if Mycroft clearly didn't trust him. But on the other hand, I thought, Mycroft might also be able to shed some light on how powerfully the Queen was really pulling the strings, if at all.

'I'd like to put another announcement in *The Times*. Keep our discussion such as it is alive.'

'All right,' he said. 'Play for time. Not that we've got much to play with.'

Later that evening I placed the announcement:

Edward's lost notebook reward. We are raising the bars. Not as easy as it sounds. Need time.

CHAPTER 15

Vamberry the Wine Merchant

ONCE AGAIN THE blackmail trail found me walking along Oxford Street, in this case the whole length of it up to Marble Arch, and then a right turn into Great Cumberland Place and a left turn into Bryanston Street. Very pleasant it was too, 1.5 miles in 22.5 minutes, and with evidence that the City of London Corporation's recent purge on predatory beggar gangs, at least along Oxford Street, has been successful. The Lonsdales lived at Number 14 Bryanston Street, opposite the Central North Synagogue and almost next door to one of my favourite coffee shops, La Madeleine.

I was shown into the drawing-room by a pageboy and within moments Gladys, Lady Lonsdale wafted in, dressed in a simple Moroccan kaftan, without make-up, jewellery or having had her hair coiffured. Twenty years old, six feet tall in flat moccasins, with a slight scent of masseur's cologne, she cut a striking and singular figure, moving like a tigress; she was also the first woman I have ever met who was within striking distance of my own height. Informality, at least at home alone, was her trademark and no sooner had I started the conversation with 'Lady Lonsdale—,' than she broke in with, 'No, no, you must call me Gladys, I absolutely insist. For a friend of Oscar's to use anything else would sound too far too solemn. He has given you the greatest acclamation, you know.'

'That's very kind of him and thank you, Gladys,' I said a little awkwardly, 'and on the subject of Gladys, I notice that you have changed the spelling of your name from Gwladys with a double-u to Gladys as you use it now. Was there any particular reason to do so?'

'None whatsoever, except my husband insisted on it. I was, as I'm sure you know, the Honourable Gwladys Herbert with a double-u, but for some reason I can't explain on marriage my husband insisted that I change the spelling of my Christian name. He has a thing against double-ues, you see.'

'Quite. So, Wilde told me briefly about your dealings with Vamberry the wine merchant. Could you please start from the beginning, including every detail, no matter how small?'

While the coffee and *biscuits rose de Reims* were being served she told her story. Although women are not allowed into the Arts Club, she was friends with many of the members, not only Oscar Wilde, Jimmy Whistler and John Everett Millais, with whom I'd seen her before, but also Thomas Hughes, Paolo Tosti, Franz Liszt, Frederic Leighton, Walter Sickert and many others. But she digressed, she said; the Arts Club's wine merchant was Vamberry and Wilde had told her that a few of the members had come up with this devilish cunning wheeze whereby they all got free investment wine through

Vamberry. Knowing her boys there, she suspected that not many of them waited for their investment to mature, but rather drank their investment dry before it had a chance to do so. Wilde wrote her an introduction card and she turned up at Vamberry's cellar in Bury Street, off St James's. She explained that she wanted to invest in wine along with her boys at the Arts Club as it was shortly to be her husband's birthday and she wanted to give him a case as a gift. Very well, you are in the right place, madam, said Vamberry, and explained the arrangement.

This time the wine wasn't wine as such but port, specifically the 1871 Serafim Cabral from Oporto. He buys directly from the family *armazenamento* there at *vinhedo* prices. His London partners buy twelve cases at a time; six they keep for investment and six they give to Vamberry to sell. He pays back his partners from some of the profits on the 72 bottles he sells, so the partners have a free case of investment wine and Vamberry a profit from his case too.

'And may I ask how much money is involved?' I asked.

'Certainly,' she said, 'I've written it down here. Each case is fifteen pounds, so twelve cases cost me one hundred and eighty pounds.'

'Can I please keep that note?' I asked, although it was really for my handwriting collection. 'And do you know how much Vamberry was selling his bottles for?'

'He said for four pounds each,' she said, handing me her note.

'So he has seventy-two bottles to sell at four pounds

each. That's two hundred and eighty-eight pounds, from which he pays you back one hundred and eighty. So he makes one hundred and eight pounds profit and you have a case of free port. Wilde, that is Oscar, said it sounded too good to be true, and so no doubt it is. The question is, where lies the problem?'

'The problem is currently killing everything that flies in the New Forest with his friend Bertie, the Prince of Wales.'

'And how is Lord Lonsdale involved with this Vamberry business?'

'Well, he gives me a monthly allowance, but there have been so many parties recently for which I needed new dresses. So, I had overspent before the next month's payment. His birthday falls just after that date and so I thought I could borrow some money from his account and pay it back without his noticing and he would be none the wiser. So I went to see his bank, spoke to some director or other, took out the cash as Vamberry asked, and thought all was well and good. Next thing I know I receive a stinking letter from George, that's my husband, from Northumberland where he's fishing something or other out of a stream, saying his banker has told him of my little loan and to make sure I'm here when he spends the night on his way down to Hampshire. Which I was. That's when I promised to pay it back by the time he returns.'

On one level I found her candour useful, even if I was rather shocked by it. 'I take it he wasn't sympathetic?'

'That's one way of putting it, Sherlock. I thought I'd make a clean breast of it and tell him everything. I've got nothing of which to be ashamed. And anyway it was all for his benefit. Unfortunately he can't understand why I don't want to go round the country by his side while he kills everything in sight like the other wives and why I'd rather stay here in London in Society. And even when he's in London all he does is organise cricket; he is a founder of the Marylebone Cricket Club, whatever that is. Apparently it's frightfully important to what I call the bat-swingers. He can just about tolerate my enjoying the company of what he calls "people of rank", but he has no comprehension at all about my Arts Club friends. He has formed a particular dislike for Oscar. They've only met once, at a salon I gave here. I must admit Oscar was laying it on a bit thick and poor George was, well, dumbfounded in his company. Not his game of soldiers at all, you see. I fear for Oscar when my husband comes back from Hampshire, for he will blame it all on him.'

'The bank you borrowed the money from, which one was it?'

'It's a Zurich bank with a branch here in London. Rain and Bognor is it?'

'It could be Rahn and Bodmer.'

'Yes, that's it, Rahn and Bodmer.'

'Do you know why he banks there and not with a British bank?'

'I'm not sure, it's his family's bank. Something about death duties. I don't know.'

'And Vamberry has not paid you back yet?'

'Exactly! I need the hundred and eighty back in George's Rain and Thingy account before he gets back.'

'Then I have no time to lose,' I said.

An equally pleasant 1.3 mile, nineteen-minute stroll back halfway down Oxford Street and along the length of Bond Street found me in Bury Street. I analysed that these two criminal cases were taking me into new territory, dealing with what I could only refer to as the Thames House set. The artists among them, Frank Miles and James McNeill Whistler, and Oscar Wilde, thought of their lives as works of art, and art that broke convention. The women around them, Lady Lonsdale, Lillie Langtry and Patsy Cornwallis-West broke convention too, in their cases with informality in manners and candour in conversation, as I'd just seen and heard.

By now I thought this would be a relatively easy case to solve. I presumed Vamberry was simply switching bottles and labels and all I would have to do is buy one from him, then buy another from Berry Bros & Rudd around the corner, compare them, return to Vamberry with the exposition and demand Lady Lonsdale's money back. Later when occasion demanded I was resigned to having two bottles of port to drink; presumably one of them a fair deal better than the other.

Vamberry's cellar was laid out much as one would expect. On the ground floor was a small room off the street entrance that counted as a shop, at the back of which was what is called a dumbwaiter which transported the stock up and down from the cellar below. There was a desk with a clerk and piles of paper and a counter across the width of the space with Vamberry behind it. Vamberry himself made an expensive impression: by the signatured buttons I could tell he was wearing a Henry Poole & Company ensemble from Savile Row, Church's shoes and a monogrammed Hudson & Greaves shirt. He had enjoyed a good night's sleep in a well-ordered household and gave every impression of prosperous solidity, but to my eye, suspiciously so. He certainly appeared too prosperous for one whose income derived only from the cellar we were in.

I asked for a bottle of 1871 Scrafim Cabral. He repeated the order through a voice-tube to the cellar and moments later a bottle came up. Four pounds changed hands, we bade each other good-bye and I left. During my time in the cellar a phaeton had drawn up outside and a footman was rubbing down the horse. The contraption was immaculate and on the side a coat of arms had been conjured up, built around a rather too ostentatious V. I soon fell into conversation with the footman, initially about the characteristics of the phaeton, and soon learned that it spent every night in a mews behind one of the Nash terraced houses off the Regent's Park. Whatever else could be learned about Vamberry, he was clearly living beyond the means of a minor cellar-keeper off St James's.

Any investigation could benefit from a slice of luck and just as I was repairing to Berry Bros to buy a similar bottle of port, a goods growler drew up. It was from the Piccadilly Circus department store Swan & Edgar. The driver and loader jumped down and took off two large cardboard boxes with Swan & Edgar Ladieswear printed on the side with the delivery note made out to Vamberry's. I told the loader I thought the boxes were for me and could I have a quick look at the chit to make sure. The quick look suggested there were four complete outfits; frocks and skirts and blouses, bonnets and scarves and shoes, all the same size and colour. I told the loader that I was mistaken and it was for Vamberry and they took the boxes inside. I waited for two minutes, went back into the cellar on the pretext of having left my best pen behind, found out the closing time in case I wanted a second bottle and saw one of the boxes being loaded onto the dumbwaiter ready to go down to the cellar.

A few moments later I was in Berry Bros & Rudd where I again bought a bottle of 1871 Serafim Cabral. This one cost £5/10s, or £55 if I wanted a case. Five minutes after that I was in the peace and quiet of the Diogenes Club ready to examine the difference between the two bottles of port wine. A minute after that, I discovered that in fact there was no difference between the bottles of port. Whatever mischief Vamberry was about, it wasn't hoodwinking his wine investors; quite the opposite, he was giving them the fairest of bargains. Logical conclusion: he made his money not by swindling his customers at this end, but at the other end of the transaction, buying wine that had been stolen. In all probability this had happened in Portugal and there was little point in pursuing that avenue further.

It was time to employ young Wiggins again. He had helped me on the Mrs Farintosh case for Lewis and now I needed him to spy on Vamberry. He couldn't read or write so we had developed a simple communication system: if I sent him a card with an X he was to report to Montague Street or with an O to the Diogenes Club, in both cases at nine o'clock the next morning. I wrote an X on a card, and marked it Wiggins, c/o St Patrick's Benevolent Society, Blackfriars, and gave it a runner to deliver. Meanwhile, I wanted to find out exactly where Vamberry lived. Just before the closing time I hailed a hansom, tarried further down Bury Street, waited for the cellar to close and with a cry of 'follow that phaeton' pursued him to his destination: 55 Cumberland Terrace, one of the Nash terraces on the Regent's Park.

Wiggins not only couldn't read or write, he couldn't tell the time, so I had to treat the nine o'clock instruction with a degree of laxity. We both took it to mean sometime in the morning, although I'm sure he wouldn't have expressed it quite so precisely. Nevertheless, just before eleven o'clock he did arrive and I gave him the following instructions:

'Here is half a crown now and there's another half a crown when you've completed what I'm telling you to do. I'll take you to Bury Street and show you a wine merchant there, Vamberry. The man himself is smartly dressed and has a crested yellow phaeton parked outside—'

'Wotsat?'

'An open carriage, four wheels. Throughout the day

customers will come and go and if anyone looks like an ordinary customer they are of no interest to me. If any young ladies should leave, they are of the utmost interest and you must dog them to their destination.'

'Any young lady?'

'Yes, and similarly, overly well-dressed gentleman. If any of them look what I'm sure you would call poncy, dog them and report back. But be careful, if there's any trouble, run for it. I'll be here this evening. Call back then with whatever news you have and your second half a crown will be here waiting for you. Off you go. Now, what are you going to be?'

'Spy.'

'No, you're going to be careful.'

'Careful spy, then.'

There was little for me to do all day except shuffle through some files and papers and organise them in Smythson's excellent smart filing drawers. Bored with that, I walked round to the British Museum Reading Room and made some notes there, the ones I am copying from now as it happens, then repaired home to wait for Wiggins. Wiggins. Fate's a funny fellow. I hoped I was helping the young rascal. Maybe I should be sending him off to Sunday school rather than asking him to be a scallywag in the streets. Maybe I will one day too.

It was worth the wait. He came back with startling news. A man matching Vamberry's description had left with a girl and walked her round to Shepherd Market. He dropped her at Number 3 Marston Street, stayed a few minutes and left. And there was more: there was a poncy-looking man who left Vamberry's and Wiggins dogged him all the way to his destination: Marlborough House.

After Soho, Shepherd Market is London's most notorious red-light district and I presumed that 3 Marston Street was a bordello. I was heading into terra incognita, and more than a little apprehensive as I had never attended a house of ill repute before. I waited until dark, and at about 8.30pm saw a red light shining on the first-floor window of the house in question. I pushed open the door and climbed the grubby stairs to the first floor. Sitting on a chair by a table was a rough-looking chap of my height; thickly built, with a small scar on his left cheek and his neck and hands liberally adorned with naval tattoos.

'Yes, mate, what can we do for you?' The menace with which the words were spoken belied their politeness.

'My friend Mr Vamberry told me of a new girl who started here earlier today whose company I might enjoy.'

'There's only one started today, Rosa I call 'er. Don't know 'er real name. Don't speak no English, not broken in yet.' Giving me a riding crop he added, 'Give 'er a bit of this if you get any lip from 'er. Two pound.'

Inside, 'Rosa' was sitting nervously on the edge of the bed. She was slight, clearly still a teenager, with a skin hue from southern Europe. Her eyes were red from crying and she had bruised wrists and another bruise on her neck. I sat away from her and tried to explain that I wanted nothing untoward from her, but she clearly didn't understand. She started talking softly and the only word I could understand was 'Portugal'. Not knowing how long I was supposed to be there, I drew a chair up to the window, opened it and smoked a pipe. Ten minutes later I gave her a five-pound note for her troubles and left.

In the hall the ex-sailor was standing menacingly in front of the stairs. 'Oy, what's your game then?' he asked. 'You a rozzer or summit?' Before I could answer he said, 'I was watchin' you through the peep-hole and you didn't do nuffink, just sat there smokin' a pipe. And I'll have that fiver off her. So what's your game?'

'We each take our pleasure in different ways, do we not?' I replied.

'So you're a bloody prancer. Get out of 'ere and don't come back.' He escorted me down the stairs, opened the door, shoved me out and shouted down the street, 'Dirty prancer, don't come back!'

Somewhat chastened, yet somewhat exhilarated, I repaired immediately by hansom to 55 Cumberland Terrace. I gave the pageboy my card; he told me that Mr Vamberry and his family were just sitting down for dinner. I asked the pageboy to mention the words Shepherd Market when he gave the master of the house my card.

Moments later the immaculately smart Vamberry came skipping down the stairs to meet me in the entrance hall. To my left and his right was a large mirror, and the lit candles on the hall table between us gave the scene a ghostly impression.

'I don't know who you are, but I'm about to eat dinner with my family and I don't appreciate the interruption. What's all this about Shepherd Market?'

'My name is Holmes, Sherlock Holmes. I was at Shepherd Market this evening, as were you this afternoon.'

'Wait, I know you; you were in my cellar earlier today. You bought a bottle of Portuguese port. Is that what this is about?'

'No, it's about your other Portuguese business, the one in Shepherd Market.'

'And if I had another business in Shepherd Market, what business is it of yours?'

'I am a consulting detective. It is a crime to live off immoral earnings, and you seem to be living very well off them.'

'What is this consulting detective? Some sort of secret policeman, a morals vigilante? Are you blackmailing me?'

From the top of the stairs a woman's voice shouted: 'Desmond! Where are you? We're ready for grace.'

I said: 'The white slave trade will be of interest to Scotland Yard, but not to me. I have a client who invested one hundred and eighty pounds in the Portuguese wine scheme. The client wants the money back sooner than anticipated; in fact right now.'

'Desmond!' again from above.

'Coming! Jesus Christ, bloody women. You will take a cheque I presume?'

'Yes, if it's made out to me and crossed. Sherlock Holmes.'

He darted into a side room and came back with a cheque book. 'So, tomorrow's date, then S-h-e-r-l-o-c-k

H-o-l-m-e-s. I haven't written the amount yet. How much more would it take to persuade you to forget about the other business?'

'One hundred and eighty pounds will be grand, thank you,' I replied.

'You know you're not entirely innocent in this whole affair. It seems to me that if as you say you went to Shepherd Market and found out the strumpet was Portuguese, you must've enjoyed yourself with her.'

'You are mistaken. I also met her pimp who, unreliable witness though he is, will confirm what I have said.'

'Carl is not her pimp. She doesn't have a pimp. I own the slut and Carl protects her.'

'Desmond! What *are* you doing?'

'Coming, for God's sake! You say grace. I'll be up in a moment. Look, Holmes, here is the cheque. I still haven't filled in the amount, in case you see sense later. If you are greedy with my money, I'm sure I'll find you with a funny name like yours. Now you'd better go. And I'd better eat.'

The following morning I paid the cheque into my bank and repaired to Bryanston Street and another interview with a very grateful, and equally informal, Lady Lonsdale.

'I have your hundred and eighty pounds in my account, Lady Lonsdale – I mean Gladys, apologies. In return I'd like to ask a favour.'

'Of course, what would you like?'

'I'd like to pay the amount into your husband's Rahn and Bodmer myself.'

She looked slightly quizzical, but said, 'All right, if it's not too inconvenient. But it has to be done today. The great white hunter is back tomorrow.'

'I will go there directly,' I said. 'I just need the account number.'

'Of course,' she said, 'let me find it. Here it is: 8009. And send me your own account soon. I'll settle it immediately. I can't tell you how grateful I am to you.'

I can recall now my mounting excitement as she read out those numbers, a perfect match with the blackmail note bank account until she reached the last digit. Of course, if as Lady Lonsdale said it was a family bank, the likelihood was that they had more than one account. But there was another form of satisfaction soon to hand: in Smythson's filing drawers I found Police Sub-inspector Lestrade's card with his Scotland Yard address and I wrote him a full of account of Vamberry the wine merchant's white-slaving activities with a strong recommendation for an immediate investigation.

CHAPTER 16

Pike's Fair Trade

COUSIN SARA IS more than a little fond of her set routine and while we are both quite happy that I fend for myself during the week, she likes to give me a robust traditional breakfast on a Saturday, as well as the Sunday lunch that I have already mentioned. The weekly breakfast was not only on the same day, but at the same time, 8.30am, and consisted of the same components: into very hot goose grease she would float two eggs, two slices of bread, four tomato halves, four sausages, four rashers of bacon and two kidneys, followed directly by a bowl of porridge, 'to soak it all up and set you up for the day'. Reading back this paragraph now, I hope I don't sound ungrateful. I am not; and I'm also well aware that I only eat properly twice a week, on both occasions thanks to my considerate cousin and landlady Sara Holmes, helped by the faithful housemaid Ruby.

But on that baking July Saturday our routine was disturbed by a knock on the front door and the delivery of a telegram addressed to me. It read: COME URGENTEST SAVAGE STOP PIKE. The instruction was clear enough: my friend Langdale Pike had some urgent news to impart and was waiting for me at one of his clubs, the Savage Club in Adelphi Terrace, as it happens the street adjoining Salisbury Street and Thames House.

In under an hour later I was enjoying a second, more

modest breakfast of toast, butter and marmalade with Langdale Pike. As usual, Pike took up station by the front window so he could see the comings and goings outside. It was good to be back in the Savage, the Bohemian den of the fourth estate, and with the incessant chatter and jinks a stark change from the Trappist tranquillity of the Diogenes Club. We reminisced for a while about the Oriental Club party, and I thanked him again in person as I had already done in writing for inviting me.

'Now, Holmes,' he said, 'before you bring me up-to-date on your blackmail and Oscar Wilde's amethyst tie-pin cases, I have something for you. Tomorrow morning at first light this is going to be delivered to news stands all over London.' He reached down into his attaché case and put a Berliner size news-sheet on the table. It was the next edition of *Town Talk*. 'Page two, columns three and four are what you need to see,' he said. I read:

A Poor Husband Laments

About the warmest divorce case which ever came before a judge may shortly be expected to come off. The respondent was a reigning beauty not many centuries ago, and the co-respondents – and they are numerous – are big 'pots'. Some say one is the biggest 'pot' of all. Even the smallest 'pot' is a big 'pot'. The poor husband is almost frantic. 'Darn this country,' he says, 'nothing belongs to a fellow here. Even his wife is everybody's property.' No wonder he seeks satisfaction from m'learned friends. The shame of it – to him, to her, to all the 'pots', to the country and

---

> *our reputation in the Empire for fidelity and rectitude!*
> *Oh that woman, that woman! Woe betide any man*
> *whose eyes fall upon her, for he is smitten unmercifully.*
> *I myself loved her. I bought her portrait in thirty-*
> *five different shop windows and all positions therein,*
> *alongside, underneath and on top of the greatest sports*
> *in the land. How I wept over it in the silent hours of*
> *the night.*

'The Prince of Wales and Mrs Langtry, obviously,' I said. 'How do you receive it before publication?'

'I know the printer, Frank Paisley in Walthamstow, we are in brother Lodges. He gives me printer's advances of all the scandal sheets. Many of the stories are mine anyway. I can tell you who didn't give *Town Talk* that story: me. What do you make of it?'

'I would say it's almost certainly tied in with a blackmail case, as indeed I suspected the first one was too,' I said. 'It's the perfect way for the blackmailer to catch our attention. Public exposure, first like this in the press, with the threat of a court case to follow. How about you?'

'I don't know enough about the blackmail case because so far you've only hinted at it. But my inner Sherlock Holmes tells me that it has to be something to do with Bertie's extra-curricular activities, as we put it at *Reynolds News*. Just now the outer Holmes, the real Holmes tells me that the blackmail is somehow tied in with putting Bertie in the witness box, or if ransomed, avoiding same. He is so unpopular, that could be the end of him. And he would pay a pretty price to avoid it. I wonder if his mother knows? That would certainly change things.'

'I really don't know about that. But yes, that would certainly stir the pot, somewhat.'

'I'll tell you some things you don't know. Lillie Langtry is what at university we used to call a naughty girl. Apart from bedding Bertie, if I could put it so journalistically, she's been having an affair with Jimmy Whistler, that's well known, and also with her Channel Islands sweetheart Arthur Jones and Bertie's first cousin Prince Louis of Battenberg.'

'Does Bertie know about these?' I asked.

'My dear chap, Bertie has the morals of an alley cat. I'd be surprised if he doesn't know about Whistler. He may not know about Jones, but he actively encouraged his cousin Louis, in fact they were on the same yacht together when Lillie and Louis first joined forces, as it were. Ha, I'm starting to sound like *Town Talk*.'

'So if the blackmail and the press stories are linked, I need to find out how *Town Talk* got hold of the stories,' I said.

'If you remember the first mention of the divorce in *Town Talk* – it was just a stage-one rumour, but on the basis that there's no smoke without fire, Ned Langtry was obviously thinking about it and thinking about it aloud. He told someone, or did something. That's when it first went into my famous rumour drawer.'

'Did you know he's found a lawyer, Lee Shipley of Shipley & Grout?'

'Never heard of them, but no I didn't.'

'We know Langtry can't pay him, so they must have come to some post-event arrangement.'

As there were no probabilities, over the next pot of coffee we explored the possibilities. The most obvious source for the *Town Talk* stories was one of the court clerks; they are notoriously bribe-able, especially if there's anything related to the Prince of Wales in a love scandal. But for this to happen there would need to be a case filed in the court. As far as we could tell, this hadn't happened by the time of the first *Town Talk* story, but may well have happened with this one. Pike could and would find out from a tame clerk. But there was something else against this scenario: especially with a story like this, the clerks would tout it around likely bidders and Pike was certainly on their bidding list, yet he had not been approached.

If the story had not originated from the court, it had to come from one of the players. Ned Langtry was an obvious candidate, but I didn't think he had the guile to tie this in with the blackmail, and his lawyer Shipley, who did have the guile, didn't come on board until after the first *Town Talk* story, and for that matter until after the first blackmail note. At least, not that we knew of. On the basis of not ruling out the impossible, it was not impossible that the Langtrys had somehow combined to conjure up the whole plot, although Pike had heard that they lived totally separate lives, albeit under one roof, and were barely speaking to each other, let alone colluding on something as sophisticated as this. Less impossible was Lillie Langtry acting with someone else, maybe this new lover Arthur Jones. Lillie and Whistler acting together, one of my previous possible scenarios, now seemed a deal less likely since Whistler had fled to Venice and their affair had ended.

'My money is on someone else,' said Pike and before I could ask who he continued, 'Patsy Cornwallis-West. You know the Decorum Vanitas column in *Vanity Fair*? That's her. She knows her way around the press. She knows her way around the world.'

'But she doesn't have a motive. From what I've heard she is extremely rich. The Langtrys are the only ones who are broke, well, cash-broke, I've heard he has something in Ireland.'

'You don't understand people like Patsy Cornwallis-West and Gladys Lonsdale. Of course they are rich. But they are also adventuresses. Free spirits. Easily bored. They live to break rules and because they're so rich they can get away with almost anything. That's why they've adopted Lillie Langtry into their set. No one breaks more rules than Lillie, but she really does put herself on the wire because she has no money to fall back on. But of the three, if you're looking for one who could orchestrate a blackmail and be published, even in *Town Talk*, it has to be Patsy. Anyway, I'm sure they'll all be at the ball on Saturday night.'

'What ball?' I asked.

'The Marlborough House ball for King George and Queen Olga of Greece. Three hundred and fifty guests from what I hear. He is Alix's brother. He's so poor Bertie had to buy him a new crown for his coronation. She's as rough as

Old Harry and tough as old boots. They're staying for a few weeks. Anything to get out of Greece is the word around town. Why they are the King and Queen of Greece is all part of the Great Game. He is Danish and she is Russian. He is as licentious as Bertie from what I've heard, and she's no stranger to the vodka bottle and with a foul temper too, so my eyes and ears will be peeled for good stories.'

'You're going to the ball?' I asked.

'Of course. You're not, I presume. Strictly invitation only, so I can't do an Oriental Club wheeze for you. But the point you probably missed is that Lillie Langtry will be there too, and what that means.' Before I could agree, he continued, 'Alix will be there too, and Lillie will be presented to her. Without anyone saying so in as many words, it signifies the end of the affair between Bertie and Lillie. She couldn't be presented to the Princess of Wales if she were still the Prince's mistress.'

But I needed to be there for the blackmail case and so we hatched a plot: I would go incognito. Marlborough House would certainly need extra staff for the night and Pike suggested I write to their staff provider Baxter Bros offering my services. I would certainly need a letter of recommendation, a referral, and he would provide that too on some metaphorical Pike Towers writing paper. I would make myself as unrecognisable as possible and go disguised as a young retainer able to perform any task that was required.

'One last point,' I asked, 'you said Adolphus Rosenberg of *Town Talk* was also connected to the Solly Boys. Can you tell me more about that?'

'He married one of the Solomons daughters. I presume the Solomons family are financing him. A number of them are trying to live more honestly. I've met him a few times, selling him stories. Nasty piece of work. Always has a bodyguard, Negev, with him. He's young and ambitious; tough too, used to be a boxer. A slogger, as the Solly Boys would say. He's without scruples like all good journalists, and he knows there's good money to be made from high-circulation scandal sheets. I'd say he's at the racier end of the band of respectability. If he's on it at all. I'd file him under A for Avoid, if I were you. So after all that, what do you have for me?'

I certainly didn't want to tell him about any further blackmail notes or the Knollys Marlborough House visit, so I gave him the whole Vamberry story, wine flanker and slave trader. His main interest was which members of the Arts Club had invested and I repeated all that I knew except my client's identity. He told me to look out for the next issue of *Illustrated Police News* as it would likely be their main story.

'One important point,' I said, 'is that the story cannot be traced back to me. Do you know Police Sub-inspector Lestrade at Scotland Yard?' He didn't. 'Make sure he gets all the credit for solving it.'

'Very well, Holmes, this is what I call a fair trade. I solve your blackmail case and you provide me with publishable stories. I'll find out about the court filing even if it does costs me two shillings.'

CHAPTER 17

Break-in

ONE BOWL OF shag didn't help, and the second bowl didn't help much either. Nor did I have much confidence that this would be a three-piper. Every turn I took in the blackmail case only seemed to widen the scope of likely suspects. Instead of narrowing the possibilities down as would be expected, every new player, every new scenario only increased them. There was an abundance of motives from the financial to the mischievous. The weapon, pen and paper, were as widely available as any weapon can be. The opportunities too were endless: all that any one of the suspects had to do was push an envelope through the Lewis & Lewis letterbox after hours; worse, the suspect didn't even have to do that, just summon a messenger to deliver it on their behalf. It was not as though I was up against a worthy opponent, a criminal mastermind, but rather against a myriad of circumstances over which I had no control at all. To add to these woes, none of these circumstances had left any meaningful clues behind them. The one certainty I had, that whoever wrote the blackmail note was also giving *Town Talk* their stories, on closer examination couldn't really be called a certainty at all; it did however score high in the probability stakes and was all I had to build my case around.

All this was only making me more determined to succeed, to crack this nut with a dozen kernels. That third pipe was lit and, as absentmindedly I watched the smoke swirl its way upwards in spirals of satisfaction, it seemed to signal back to me that a slight infringement of the law might be excusable: I could only further my cause by breaking into the *Town Talk* office, an imperceptible intruder who would take or disturb nothing but simply observe what clues might lie there and leave as discreetly as he had arrived. I'd known the day would come in my chosen career when I would have to infringe on the letter of the law in order to prevent a greater infringement against it, and not without a sense of foreboding did I undertake tonight to put this idea into practice.

From the recent *Town Talk* masthead I learned the address: 4 Ludgate Circus Buildings. These were on the corner of Fleet Street and Farringdon Road. That bode well: the Fleet Street area was busy all night and through the early hours as newspapermen put their first editions to bed. Ludgate Circus Buildings had dozens of small press offices like *Town Talk*'s, again with many open until just before dawn. If the usual pattern was followed, Number 4 was likely to be on the ground floor, so the only door I would need to trespass would be Rosenberg's own; the greatest danger of discovery would be from other pressmen coming and going near the main entrance.

Unfortunately to reach Ludgate Circus from Montague Street meant crossing a part of London where only the foolish or country-folk might venture at night: Gray's Inn. It is one of those London areas that changes its character with nightfall, from the hubbub of legal offices and artisan shops in daylight to a perilous warren infested by ne'er-do-wells and malcontents when darkness calls. Although I'm taller than most, young and fit, can box well enough and carry a swordstick, even I would be hard-pressed to escape the gangs of mug-hands and feral street arabs unscathed. Instead, with my pockets full of a burglar's trade tools, a jemmy, a six-inch flat blade, some eighth-inch wire cutters, a muffling rag, a half-shade lamp and matches and my ever-present lens, at midnight I took a hansom from outside the Museum Tavern with instructions for Ludgate Circus Buildings. Unsurprisingly the cab-man chose the well-attended and well-lit High Holborn and Chancery Lane approach to Fleet Street.

Ludgate Circus Buildings offices had no front door, but a wide open main entrance arch leading on to six floors of mostly single occupancy offices. As expected, Number 4 was just inside the main entrance. On the left side of the corridor, it had a simple three-lever mortice deadlock on a softwood door on a similar frame. It would jemmy open easily enough, but I preferred to pick my way in so that Rosenberg would never know of the break-in.

But no! Someone else had done the dirty work before me, and none too subtly: the front door had been smashed open with a hammer and claw. I didn't need the lens to see the splinters were fresh; I could smell fresh wood. Stepping inside with the half-lamp lit I saw the office had been well searched, every drawer and file had been opened, emptied and left ajar. What was taken from them I could never know. But something had been left behind. In the centre of his desk was a cream-coloured, unsealed envelope on which was written 'Adolphus Rosenberg, c/o *Town Talk*. Private.' Even in the dim light the envelope looked familiar, as did the blue ink. In a hurry I opened the envelope and written on equally familiar writing paper were the words:

DESIST WITH THE LANGTRY / PRINCE DIVORCE REPORTS. MORE IMPORTANT PEOPLE THAN YOU WILL TAKE VENGEANCE. YOU HAVE BEEN WARNED.

This time no attempt had been made to disguise the handwriting. At last: a clue! Finding a blank side of foolscap in a drawer I copied out the message exactly and left it in precisely the same place. The original message and envelope I pocketed as my prize. I hurried to leave as the broken door and light lamp would raise suspicions from passers-by, but on the way out I noticed something the earlier intruders had missed and I too had missed on my way in: an envelope lying under the letter flap on the floor. The envelope was embossed with the words Shipley & Grout. I closed the *Town Talk* door and took it to read in the brighter light near the entrance.

It read as follows:

Adolphus Rosenberg, Esq.
c/o Town Talk
4 Ludgate Circus Buildings
London EC

Wednesday
Dear Mr Rosenberg,

Shipley & Grout represent Mr Edward Langtry in the matter addressed herewithin.

As you are aware, two recent editions of 'Town Talk' have alluded to an impending divorce and subsequent scandal involving the highest levels of society. Although you have not specifically mentioned our client or his wife Mrs Langtry by name, readers could only gain the strongest possible impression from what you have published that it is to them you are referring.

We need hardly remind you that the laws of libel are in force to protect innocent parties from scurrilous attacks in the public realm. We therefore hereby inform you that we are undertaking libel proceedings against you.

We remain, sir, in anticipation of acknowledgement of receipt of this notice.

Lee Shipley
Shipley & Grout
14F, Charterhouse Street
London, EC

Returning to Number 4, I posted the letter through Rosenberg's door. There was nothing I could do about the opened envelope except remove it from the scene and hope Rosenberg would not be too suspicious of a bare letter.

If a Londoner survives the surrounding night-time gangs to reach it, there are few places in England, and I would venture in the world, more enthralling in the early hours of a day than Fleet Street. On either side the printing presses whir and thump, printing-men rush from presses to public house and back again, journalists on the morning editions scurry in and out of *The Times*, the *Daily Telegraph*, *the News*, Reuters, the *Gazette*, and many dozens more national and regional newspapers that line each side of the 'street of ink' from Ludgate Circus to The Strand. In any of the coffee shops and pubs the gossip and intrigue flow as readily as the fare, and it was into one of these, the newly opened El Vino's, that I called in for a glass of club claret and a Partagas No 3 cigar and sat still to take stock of the new evidence gained from the *Town Talk* break-in.

There was good news; a proper clue for the first time. A quick examination of the letter and envelope with the lens in the better light confirmed that the writing was indeed made on royal palaces paper, as determined by Smythson. But also new doubts: if the blackmailer and the *Town Talk* contributor were the same person, on which supposition in the absence of real clues I had been hanging my hat, why would this person want the news-sheet to stop printing the rumours of the forthcoming divorce? Surely, if my supposition was correct, the opposite would be the case?

And what to make of the Shipley & Grout letter? If any element of the Langtry camp were behind the blackmail, why would they take away from themselves the important advantage of scurrilous, anonymous publicity? Unfortunately, there was no logical conclusion other than that I was dealing with two, not one, separate sources of villainy: one a blackmailer and the other a paid gossip-monger. Admittedly the levels of villainy were far apart, one heinous and the other trivial, even if they shared the same motive: reward. By the time the second draught of claret was consumed and the Partagas had fulfilled its destiny, I knew the conclusions from the Ludgate Circus Buildings adventure had turned my investigation on its head; and more importantly, stopped it heading in the wrong direction.

Maybe now I should take Langtry's motive at face value: he was tired of being humiliated socially and cuckolded publicly, and a simple yet honourable man was genuinely hurt to see *Town Talk* spread accounts of his misfortune around to a wider audience than those who already knew of it. How he was going to pay Shipley & Grout was still a mystery, as was their role in all this. Langtry did after all have letters from Bertie to Lillie, and they were embarrassing enough to be used to some advantage. Shipley must be advising Langtry to save them for later use. Although Shipley could take them to Lewis and exchange them for Lewis paying Rosenberg to desist, Shipley must know that the moment *Town Talk* desisted, *Vanity Fair*, *Sphere*, *Truth*, *London Gazetteer* and a dozen others, even *Reynolds News*, would quickly take up the story.

So if logic declared that it would not be in the blackmailer's interest to have *Town Talk* stop reporting the divorce case rumours, in whose interest was it to silence the organ? Bertie's certainly, but according to Lewis he didn't yet know about the blackmail. According to Knollys the Queen did know about it and would not want a royal scandal even if it had the advantage of embarrassing her wayward son. Against that, Lewis and I had concluded that Knollys could have invented her involvement to hasten a settlement in his favour. If Knollys were the blackmailer, and I believed he would attract the best odds, that would put him in an interesting dilemma: to obey the Queen and frighten off Rosenberg, or somehow to pretend to have done so and retain his blackmail advantage by encouraging more *Town Talk* rumours. All this supposed that the Queen really knew, which Lewis had called a 'known unknown'.

By the time the hansom cab had dropped me back at Montague Street my conclusions were as follows: Ned Langtry was not the blackmailer and Francis Knollys, in one of his many machinations, probably was. Furthermore, if he were the blackmailer, he had just made his first mistake, hand-writing the note to Rosenberg on palace stationery. This was significant: when Lewis had looked for Knollys's handwriting on official papers he had only found ticks and squiggles in margins or initials at page ends, and his scribbled signature on official documents. My next tasks were clear: I had to find some of Francis Knollys's handwriting for comparison and I needed to make a more serious, even if only autodidactic, study of graphology.

CHAPTER 18

The Marlborough House Ball

IT NEVER SITS easily to cut a comical figure, but at least with two levels of disguise the embarrassment can be mitigated. Baxter Bros gave their hired waiters a chit to let them into Marlborough House, and then they went into a withdrawing room to change into their uniforms. My first level of disguise was applied before arrival: with a moustache and goatee, spectacles and fair hair I was sure I would be unrecognisable, if only to Knollys and to the pageboy Hopkins who had shown Lewis and I in and out on my previous visit. The uniform would complete the job: all sixty-five of us looked suitably servile in black pin-striped gas-pipe trousers, red 'bum-freezer' jackets, white semi-dress shirts and black bow-ties. Not unexpectedly, even the largest size was too short for me, so that the cuffs rode a good two inches above my wrists and my turn-ups an equally good three inches above my ankles; hence cutting the comical, albeit satisfactorily unrecognisable, figure.

Moments later we were standing in a loose line of attention in front of the Earl of Gifford for our instructions, but in truth we were all just as interested to see the electric lights as we were to hear of the night's events; Marlborough House was the first grand house in

London to be equipped with the new phenomenon of electric lighting, about which the newspapers had been trumpeting so fulsomely.

With a clap of the hands the Earl drew our attention. 'Important occasion tonight, men. The Princess of Wales is giving this ball for her brother, the King of Greece. Also in attendance will be the Prince of Wales and the Queen of the Hellenes. The full guest list of three hundred and ninety is posted there.' He pointed to two large cards of paper on a green baize board by a door. 'I need hardly tell you that the very many relations of European royalty will be in attendance and the Prince and Princess wish to give the best possible impression. I too will be one of the guests, as will many of the other grandees of London.

'I must also remind you that strict confidentiality and anonymity is required in all circumstances. And now a new instruction. If you find yourself in a dark pantry or storeroom, you will notice that the electric light will come on if you pull the lever down, and it will go off when you push the lever up. Under no circumstances are you to pull or push the levers up and down within five seconds of each movement.

'Don't forget that as ever you will be pocket-patted on your exit. We don't want any pilfering, do we? Now my two subalterns here, Cartwright and Williams, will give you further instructions.'

These further instructions were issued with military precision. Each one of us waiters was allocated six guests and we were each shown our charges on a chart with the guest names and placements. The tables were laid out in an E-shape and my six guests were on an outer table and unknown to me, but a quick perusal of the full guest list contained many names by now familiar, including Langdale Pike, George and Elizabeth Lewis, and to my great surprise Brother Mycroft. It must have taken an almighty departmental instruction, a three-line office ministerial whip to persuade Mycroft to attend such a function.

I noticed a waiter named Parkes was serving Francis Knollys and the five guests around him, and half a crown soon persuaded him to exchange duties with me. I was confident enough that my double disguise combined with Knollys's arrogance towards anyone who served him meant he would not recognise me. I also saw that the Cornwallis-Wests and the Lonsdales were sitting close by. The royal parties were sitting at the head of the central E. Off the centre but still at the top table, Lillie Langtry was placed with Prince Rudolph of Austria on her one side and Prince Louis of Battenberg on her other. If Pike's reading of her status was correct, she was no longer officially the royal mistress, but was now being passed down the princely line, from Prince Bertie to Prince Louis to Prince Rudolph. I would also be able to see Christopher Sykes for the first time as well as Princess Alexandra and her lady-in-waiting, the Countess of Derby. Beyond them were Lord and Lady Lonsdale, and next to them two other new players for me to see: Lord Londesborough and his daughter Lady Edith Henrietta Sybil Denison, this latter according to Lewis another of Bertie's mistresses.

My espionage mission was initially disappointing. Eavesdropping was impossible with any two hundred of the four hundred guests talking at the same time and the fact that a waiter couldn't tarry more than the few necessary seconds needed to carry out his duties. On the other hand, I was able to observe Knollys close up. Significantly, he was ambidextrous, although he wrote left-handedly. He was inattentive towards his wife, who was sitting opposite him. Lewis had said that he was poorly paid but lived well with the perquisites of the job, but still I was surprised to see him attired in a Monroe & Canning dinner suit; I doubted that Savile Row tailoring would be included in his list of allowances. He had cut himself shaving, which suggested that he shaved himself; a sign that he was not quite from the top drawer, despite superficial appearances.

And so unproductive course followed unproductive course. The Baxter Bros regulars reckoned this was a light supper compared to some royal banquets, nevertheless guests were served turtle or vegetable soup, boiled salmon or fried sole, chicken breast with truffles, spiced fillets of beef with madeira sauce, all with a constant supply of complementary vegetables, and all helped along by bottles of 1870 Château Beychevelle red and 1877 Larue Puligny white wines. An 1875 Château Dudon Sauternes accompanied the cake rings with kirsch and apricot sauce or orange jelly and meringues with sweetened whipped cream. When all this had been cleared away, there would be decanted port and brandy, followed by the royal toast, Punch Coronation cigars for those so inclined and a fifteen-minute commingle for the guests to circulate, followed by speeches – and finally my chance to realise my intention: a search of Francis Knollys's office upstairs.

At last the clearing away was finished and as I passed Mycroft I slipped him this note: 'After the toast and before commingle, summon me and ask for pen and paper. Sherlock'. I then took my place with other waiters lining the wall and waiting for their orders, all the while watching for Mycroft's signal. In the meantime, he acknowledged me with the slightest lift of an eyebrow.

The toastmaster toasted, cigars and cigarettes lit, the chairs scraped backwards for the commingle and soon Mycroft was sending me on the mission to find him some writing paper. The permanent staff were keen to help us 'one-timers', and a chambermaid led me directly to the stationery storeroom on the mezzanine floor. There was a satisfactory novelty in pulling down a lever on the wall and seeing the room instantly lit; this was clearly an invention with a future.

I gathered up a few sheets of writing paper and envelopes, a couple of fountain pens and an ink bottle and told the chambermaid that I had been asked to deliver these to the Private Secretary's office, and could she please send me off in the right direction. She did, and I was soon on the stairwell that I'd used before with Lewis during our previous audience with Knollys.

His office door was unlocked and I was presently inside it and pulling on the lever for light. His office and desk were as well ordered as I remembered them: he had made no special effort to impress us when we visited. On his desk was an abundance of his handwriting and I slipped a full sheet with random writing into my inside pocket. In his tray I noticed an opened envelope with the Rahn & Bodmer emboss; that too found a new home inside my jacket. I was putting his fountain pen in there too when I heard urgent, approaching footsteps from down the hall. I rushed over to switch off the light and dived under the centre of the desk between the twin pedestals of drawers.

Close to the five-second limit, the light went back on again and the footsteps marched up to the desk. I recognised Knollys's shoes and trousers from waiting for him to take his seat at the table earlier. If he sat at his desk now with his legs beneath it, I would surely be discovered as my tall frame used up all the space and I could not shuffle back unnoticed, even less as I was squeezed tight all round by the uniform. From the noise at the desk I could tell he was searching for something and hoped it wasn't now residing in my pocket. I heard an anxious 'Blast and dammit!', and as urgently as they had arrived, the footsteps retired. I waited a minute until the hall was quiet again, and then slipped out with the stationery for Mycroft and my pockets lined with evidence for Lewis.

On the landing between the third and second floor I came across an elderly, stoutly built woman in a full-length apron who put her hand up to halt me where I stood.

'Who are you?' she asked in a thick Eastern European accent.

'My name is Sherrinford,' I replied.

'And vot are you doink?'

'I am delivering a message for a guest.'

'I don't believe you. I call a soldier.'

'By all means, madam. I'll wait here for you.'

She looked me and down. 'Vere you come from?'

'Here, I live here in London.'

'No, idiot, come from just now.'

'From Mr Benson's office.'

'Who is this Benson?'

'I don't know, he works here. I'm just here for the night. For the ball.'

'I check for this Benson. I find not, I see you, you in trouble. Now go.'

'And might I ask who you are?'

'I am Valentina Kasperskaya. Go on.' So I had just met Alix's childhood Russian nurse who was now the royal nanny and Mistress of the Royal Bedchamber. She was over eighty, but not by much, and devoid of any charm at all. I also noticed that she was right-handed; it seems to be the first thing I look for in everyone I meet these days. 'Go on, go!' she snapped again just as I was doing so.

In the ballroom the commingle was ending and during the speeches we waiters had to line the wall and could only be summoned for the minute or so between speeches. From a distance I saw that Patsy Cornwallis-West was in her element; Christopher Sykes was left out, and left-handed; the Countess of Derby distracted; Lord and Lady Lonsdale equally bored; Lord Londesborough restless;

Lady Edith slightly drunken; Francis Knollys constantly surveying everything around him; and the Earl of Gifford mostly conducting the arrangements on his feet, albeit as discreetly as the occasion allowed.

Half a restless hour later the speeches were over, the orchestra struck up, King George of Greece and the Princess of Wales, followed by the Prince of Wales and the Queen of the Hellenes, led the dancers onto the floor. It was 10.00pm precisely. Carriages had been announced as 'Midnight, sharp'. Once the dancing started the hired waiters had to go downstairs to help with scullery duties. I needed to move quickly to bring Mycroft into my employ and hand George Lewis over the trophies from Knollys's desk before I attracted attention to myself, let alone being pocket-patted on the way out.

Mycroft was easy to find, sitting exactly where he had been sitting all evening and exactly where he would certainly remain until Carriages. He was expecting me. I gave him fresh sheets of paper from the stationery storeroom and a fountain pen and asked him to write down what he observed on the dance floor, and then put it in my pigeonhole at the Diogenes Club. He nodded absently.

George Lewis was harder to find; in fact he was dancing with Elizabeth when I arrived at their places. The neighbour asked if he could help. I declined, saying I had a personal message to deliver from another guest to Mr Lewis. An awkward half a minute later the Lewises returned to their seats. I intercepted George Lewis before he had a chance to sit down within earshot of his neighbour.

'Lewis,' I said, 'this is Sherlock Holmes.' For several seconds he could barely contain his surprise. Pointing to an imaginary guest on the other side of the ballroom I said: 'The guest over there would like me to hand you these documents and artefacts.' I suited action to words. 'Shall I see you in your office on Monday morning?'

'No,' he replied, 'I'm in court all day Monday. The house is full of guests, so come to one of my clubs for a change, the Oxford and Cambridge. Mid-morning tomorrow, say eleven o'clock?'

I shall not overburden the reader with an account of the rest of the evening. Before Carriages at midnight we were down in the kitchens, scullery and storerooms cleaning and putting away, and after Carriages back upstairs in the ballroom, clearing and cleaning up until there was no evidence that the ball had taken place at all. We finished shortly before 2.00am, when Baxters gave everybody the customary shilling to find their own way home. I spent my shilling on a hansom; and slept soundly.

The next morning I called in at the Diogenes Club and in my pigeonhole was the following note from Mycroft:

My dear Sherlock,
Your ingenuity impresses me, but I fear my efforts as a correspondent may be less than satisfactory due to my immobility in general and the fact that among my near neighbours, who all hailed from government departments, there were very few ladies on whom to inflict my two left dancing feet. However, observed

from a sedentary position, and not close to hand, I can report on events on the dancing floor as follows.

Lillie Langtry was in the greatest demand, partly from being effectively single, her husband leaving, noticeably drunken, even before the speeches. Particularly persistent was Prince Rudolph, whose wandering hand she had to readjust on several occasions. She also danced twice with Lords Lonsdale and Londesborough. Francis Knollys and Patsy Cornwallis-West danced together several times and never stopping talking; I could almost say scheming. Christopher Sykes was very attentive towards Lady Edith. Two dull people are William Cornwallis-West and the Countess of Derby.

The royal party were wholly consumed with themselves, dancing with each other and only conversing with each other. Of them, Princess Alexandra is by far the most elegant on the floor, but I doubt if that is the type of intelligence you were hoping I could gather. My observations were hindered by my position, so I'm reporting what I saw from a distance.

Yours aye for now,
Mycroft

It is only a minute's walk along Pall Mall to the Oxford and Cambridge Club. George Lewis was waiting for me in the magnificent first-floor library, with its back-of-house views over the courtyards of Marlborough House. Coffee and ginger biscuits were already to hand.

'You are a master of disguise, Holmes,' he said. 'Even

when I knew it was you, I didn't know it was you.'

'It is a useful skill. At university I was in the theatre company. I hope my trophies were worthwhile.'

We compared the written sheet and bank statement from Knollys's desk with the note left in Rosenberg's office. It only took a matter of moments for us to agree that the handwriting was the same: Knollys's.

'Very worthwhile. Well done. What do you make of it?' he asked.

'On the face of it, if Knollys is the blackmailer, it would seem he is going against his own interests in trying to silence *Town Talk*, as surely having an apparently unconnected second flank in the public realm is in the blackmailer's interest. The Queen is the key to understanding this. If she ordered him to silence *Town Talk* to save the royal family embarrassment, he would surely have carried out her wishes, or at least been seen trying to do so. Yet the only reason we think she is involved is because he told us so, and he also told us that it was her wish that the ransom be paid, and the matter put to rest. And now we see he too has an account at Rahn & Bodmer. It is, at the very least, suspicious.'

'So, whether or not the Queen really does know about it is a known unknown. That is probably the key.'

'Precisely. Is there any way you could find out?' I asked.

'You mean make it a known known? Her regime is more or less impenetrable.'

'And I don't suppose he's found his lost notebook? Put all our minds at rest.'

'No,' Lewis said. 'I asked the other day. I even asked him what was in it.'

'And?'

'He just said, "Oh this and that, you know, musings about love and war. Private stuff. Best left unfound or your Prince is in a spot of palaver." Then he asked if he could offer a reward or would that make it worse. Worse, I said. I should've told him about all this Knollys-and-the-Queen business; maybe I will next time. I'm just worried he'd make everything worse, as he usually does.'

'Yes,' I said, 'difficult for you, I see. Also there's Knollys's bank statement. There are only sixty-five pounds and fifteen shillings in there, but also monthly payments of the equivalent of three guineas, anonymously of course. Which brings me on to my next line of investigation, Rahn & Bodmer. Do my incidentals run to the cost of hiring an expensive suit? I want to investigate the bank by seeing what it takes to open an account. There is something too coincidental about the blackmailer, Lord Lonsdale and now Francis Knollys all banking there.'

'How will you do it?' Lewis asked.

'I'll disguise myself as a rich Australian who wants a safe deposit as well as a transaction account.'

'I think the incidentals could run to that. Now, if you'll excuse me Elizabeth has a house full of guests.' With that we both left, me with the prospects of a hearty Sunday lunch back in Montague Street and time to plan the next moves over a pipe or two afterwards.

CHAPTER 19
The Divine Sarah

WHEN I WRITE that all of London was agog at the prospect of the *Comédie-Française* and its leading lady Sarah Bernhardt performing Racine's *Phèdre* on the Gaiety Theatre stage, I realise I sound as though I am part of that cream of London's social and artistic elite with whom I was spending most of my waking hours. 'All' of London is clearly imprecise usage, but it would be fair to say that among the habitué of that elite, 'all' is a fair summation of how those insiders viewed themselves; and they *were* all agog at the prospect outlined above.

My own attendance as one of the 'all' at the Divine Sarah's Chester Square house one late June evening needs some explanation. I have already mentioned that Lady Lonsdale was grateful I had managed to recover the money that Vamberry the wine merchant had temporarily borrowed from her. She had thus managed to ward off a disgruntled Lord Lonsdale who had been threatening to vent his displeasure on her Arts Club friends, all of whom he disapproved, especially Oscar Wilde who had led her into the minor misadventure with Vamberry.

A few days ago Wilde, who was Sarah Bernhardt's leading London admirer and who had even gone to Folkestone to welcome her to these shores, at her request arranged an artistic soirée at her rented house in Belgravia. Of course Wilde invited Gladys Lonsdale and therefore, for the sake of good form, had also to include her husband, but fortunately in his lordship's view he was hunting wild boar in Upper Saxony with Christopher Sykes that week and couldn't attend. He insisted however in making sure she was accompanied by someone of whom he approved, someone who wasn't part of the Thames House or Art Club sets and someone who wasn't part of their social scene and therefore wouldn't set tongues wagging. I'm not exactly sure how during their conversation my name came into the frame as a chaperone, but it did, and soon enough the two tallest guests to the party arrived together in the two-horse brougham with impeccable attendants; she in a multi-coloured Watteau kaftan and I in a new J.W. Dore's dark blue woollen suit in which Cousin Sara had insisted I invest for what she hoped would be the first of many such glamorous outings. My own feelings about my new attire were more ambivalent, but nevertheless accommodating.

I realise I was fortunate to be there, and so I hope readers will excuse the small digression as I describe Sarah Bernhardt and the scene around her. She herself is of the most striking aspect: thirty-four years old, five feet tall, very thin around the waist but broader than expected of shoulder and hip, of extremely pale complexion topped by ostensibly disorganised but clearly carefully coiffured and hennaed hair. She was wearing white silk overalls, with no jewellery or make-up, and with a chisel in one hand and a paintbrush in the other she moved from one work of art to another as she circulated. Soon we learned they were all for sale for her animal charity. We also learned that in the garden were the creatures she had brought with her from Paris: a cheetah, a Russian wolfhound, a monkey, a parrot and six chameleons. Quite what the neighbours thought of this menagerie, one can only imagine. Sarah Bernhardt may well have been the slightest person in the room, but her personality dominated it with an enormous confidence and joy in her surroundings.

While on the subject of digressions, pray permit one more: my first impression on entering the drawing-room was the pleasure at hearing a string quartet, as that very week I had purchased a Stradivarius, worth at least five hundred guineas, for 45 shillings at a pawnbroker's shop in Tottenham Court Road. I was there looking for a particular type of Faber Castell fountain pen that Smythson could not find when I stumbled across the violin. Of course I had to buy it immediately. They were even playing my kind of introspective music; German. I was equally pleased that I would have somebody like-minded to talk to in case I found myself alone, for the quartet had a young assistant or manager on hand.

There were perhaps two dozen guests spread evenly between the company of *Comédie-Française* and Wilde's inner circle. I was pleased to see Langdale Pike because as soon as Gladys Lonsdale noticed Lillie Langtry and Patsy Cornwallis-West, she left me to fend for myself. I also recognised Wilde's housemate Frank Miles and Sir John Everett Millais from Thames House. With Pike were George Reynolds, and Thomas Gibson Bowles of *Vanity Fair*. There were two waiters busy circulating, both dwarfs, both French, each holding a tray on their heads with three glasses. '*Absinthe, champagne ou Cabot cheval pas d'origine, monsieur?*' one of them asked upwards. '*Qu'est-ce que c'est Cabot cheval pas d'origine?*' I asked. '*Un cocktail à base d'absinthe et de champagne,*' he replied. I took a glass of absinthe, one of Wilde's favourite spirits, tried one sip of the liquid explosive and reverted to champagne.

'I say, Holmes, you do get around,' said Pike as we met. 'You remember George Reynolds?' We both did and greeted each other. 'And here is Thomas Gibson Bowles of *Vanity Fair*. This is Sherlock Holmes, an old friend and the keenest detective in London.' Before I could protest, Pike continued, 'Holmes, as you might guess when three pressmen gather together they talk of current affairs, and the pun is intended. There are rich pickings for us here tonight, which no doubt is why Wilde invited us.'

'And you, sir, how do you come to be here?' Bowles asked me. 'A detective in our midst is bound to arouse a good journalist's interests.'

I explained as briefly and discreetly as I could about helping Lady Lonsdale with an investigation and why I was chaperoning her at Lord Lonsdale's suggestion, he currently at large inconveniencing wild boar on the continent.

'Crime sells, we all know that,' said Reynolds. 'Next Sunday we are giving up six columns to a new crime science, graphology. From what I can gather it's a bit like astrology, except it uses handwriting.'

'Written in the stars,' joked Pike.

'Droll as always, Pike. No, but seriously,' said Reynolds, 'I think there's something in it. I've met the man and he tells a good story. Asked me to write a couple of sentences and he summed me up quite well, I thought. Flatteringly of course, but after all I was buying and he was selling.'

I said: 'I'm interested in any new crime science. May I ask his name?'

'Persifor MacDonald.'

'Ah yes, he wrote an article on graphology I read in the *New Discovery Chronicle*. Would it be possible for me to meet him?'

'Of course. Come to the paper on Friday afternoon and he'll be there filing his copy. We're at 147 Fleet Street, second and third floors.'

Our conversation stopped when our hostess, followed by several fawning Frenchmen, appeared in front of us. During the introductions, it became clear that probably due to my ancestry I spoke the best French of the four of us and so I found myself leading the conversation on our behalf, although I am certain the others could follow it. I'm translating it into English as follows:

SB: I love newspapermen. You have a very lively press here in London, much livelier than ours in Paris. I hear there is a great scandal involving the Prince of Wales and one of my guests. (She pointed her paintbrush towards Lillie Langtry). Oscar tells me there will be a divorce case and you gentlemen of the press will be reporting every crumb. In Paris, that would be impossible. Not the divorce, you understand, that happens all the time, but not a word will you read of it in the newspapers.

SH: Yes, we are lucky, there are two dozen daily papers and almost four hundred weekly papers and magazines. My friends here own two of them, Reynolds News and Vanity Fair.

SB: And I hope you will be reporting on tonight's event. I am sure that is why Oscar invited you. I hope to read wonderful accounts. Ah, and here he is.'

At that moment Oscar Wilde strode into the drawing-room. Sarah Bernhardt rushed over to greet him: she, all in white, tiny in comparison to him, all in black; yet there embraced the two most charismatic personalities in London that July evening.

Wilde cried out: 'A chair, a stool, a ladder, a stage, for I have fresh rhymings to impart.'

Someone found him a chair, on which he stood and read directly to Sarah Bernhardt as the room fell silent around them:

> *How vain and dull this common world must seem*
> *To such a One as thou, who should'st have talked*
> *At Florence with Mirandola, or walked*
> *Through the cool olives of the Academe:*
> *Thou should'st have gathered reeds from a green*
>   *stream*

For Goat-foot Pan's shrill piping, and have played
With the white girls in that Phaeacian glade
Where grave Odysseus wakened from his dream.
Ah! surely once some urn of Attic clay
Held thy wan dust, and thou hast come again
Back to this common world so dull and vain,
For thou wert weary of the sunless day,
The heavy fields of scentless asphodel,
The loveless lips with which men kiss in Hell.

I must admit to thinking it was rather overblown at the time, and reading it again now (it was published along with Wilde's full account of the evening in *Vanity Fair*) I haven't changed my opinion. But a poet, I am not. Nevertheless, the room burst into enthusiastic applause and Wilde, it would be safe to say, was in his element. But he hadn't finished yet. Still standing on his chair, he produced from his inside pocket the latest issue of *Town Talk* and with a broad smile and a blown kiss to Lillie Langtry read as follows:

'Adolphus Rosenberg from *Town Talk* writes, starting here:

Langtry in a Pickle

I am informed that Mr Langtry, famous only for being married to the beautiful, iridescent, loose-limbed Mrs Langtry, has announced his intention suing me to libel and if that does not work, then of breaking my neck. For reporting the truth about the divorce, can you imagine such effrontery? And how does clever Mr Langtry imagine Town Talk finds out about his machinations? He that consumes the gateau cannot admire it too. Now, if the brave gentleman wants to go in for neck-breaking, surely he can find plenty of his friends (?) who have injured him more than I have. His wife I might include, to boot or to put in the boot – oh what a fool he has been. Desist, man, desist before it is too late.

I thought the use of the word 'desist' was informative, an uncommon word and one taken directly from Knollys's warning-off note at the *Town Talk* office. It was as though Rosenberg was not only ignoring the threat, he was cocking a snook at it.

'Oscar Wilde, you are a very naughty young man, spreading stories around like this,' joked Gladys Lonsdale to the quietened room.

Patsy Cornwallis-West stood up. 'I think for the first, last and probably only time in his life Oscar is innocent, if only because he'd have sold to a higher circulation than *Town Talk. Vanity Fair* and *Reynolds News* are here tonight, far likelier customers I would venture. Let's play a game. Can anyone guess who is giving *Town Talk* these titbits?'

'I think I know,' said Lillie Langtry looking directly at me. 'I think it is Mr Sherlock Holmes, who seems to be everywhere all at once these days, even when he is invisible. Including, so I hear, with my husband's lawyer. Am I right, Mr Holmes?'

I can still remember that moment of acute embarrassment five months ago as if it were earlier today. Two dozen guests looked at me, waiting for an answer. The room was totally silent. On my left I heard Pike say softly, and unhelpfully: 'This will be interesting.'

I raised my voice. 'Unfortunately for this game, it is not I. Nor am I able to tell you the name of the person responsible. Like Mr Wilde I am an innocent party. Like everyone else I would like to find the guilty party.'

'Very well, Mr Holmes,' said Lillie Langtry. 'We believe you. But say no to my husband's offer of employ. He hasn't got a penny!' Thankfully, the room laughed and the pressure was relieved and then she said: 'He hasn't got a clue either!' to even louder laughter and more applause and the unfortunate episode was over as quickly as it had begun.

But my singling-out wasn't over yet: before the conversations resumed Sarah Bernhardt took over the floor and pointing at me announced in French to one of her camp followers to make sure that I had an invitation to the opening night of *Phèdre* and the celebrations thereafter.

I rejoined the three pressmen and the conversation unsurprisingly turned to *Town Talk*. Not, I was relieved to hear, about the libel threat, which could only mean that they hadn't heard of it, but about Adolphus Rosenberg's Solly Boys connection, how the Solomons family could use him and he them, what his circulation was, if he were making a profit, if he even needed to, or if he were cleaning money for the family business.

An hour and a half after we arrived, Lady Lonsdale

found me and announced that it was time for her carriage. As she waited for her coat a smoothly dressed, well-presented man of about forty approached me and said: 'Before you go, Mr Holmes, I'd like to introduce myself. I hear that you are a detective, but not a policeman. That is perfect for my purpose. I am Edward Jarrett, theatre impresario. I am arranging the *Comédie-Française* season at the Gaiety Theatre. Unfortunately, the contract insisted that they bring the theatre company's charity with them, *Waifs et Errants*, which in English translates as Waifs and Strays. I am certain that it is a form of protection racket. Or embezzlement. Or plain theft. They take six per cent of the box, every night on closing. I have been told they have now registered Waifs and Strays as a charity in London and six per cent of the takings here has to go to them. Would you help me expose them? Looks like you will be at the opening night. I could show you him then.'

'Him?'

'The man behind the so-called charity. He is called Ricoletti. Once introduced, you won't miss him. He has a club-foot. He is bad enough, but his wife is quite abominable.'

CHAPTER 20

Ambushed

I HAVE MENTIONED before how Cousin Sara likes a set routine and every Wednesday when the hall clock chimes ten she sends Ruby up to my rooms to give them a thorough clean. The ten chimes are also the signal for me to leave the house for the hour or so that Ruby needs, a little more in the winter due to the soot and ash from the fire. That particular Wednesday morning my leaving coincided with a messenger from Lewis & Lewis arriving on the doorstep and handing me a company embossed envelope within which was the following handwritten message:

SH, I'M IN COURT ALL DAY SO PLS COME TO PP AT 6.00PM TO DISCUSS ENC, THIS SENT TO E! AT HOME GL

"PP" was Lewis's house in Portland Place to which this new note had been sent, addressed to "E!" for Elizabeth and the "enc" was the following enclosure:

Page after page, the codes. Next is STA. 8 codes. 1 know them all. Also Disraeli is now ridiculed. My price, it is now 4 gold bars, deposited with Rahn+Bodmer Co. 1 have many names, each one has a gold bar. Your time is running out. 1 week now to pay. 1 repeat 1 week. Paid, and the notebook goes to Lewis, if not send to scandal

press. 7 have it ready to send, losing patience. You must
act now. Typical the jew not to pay!

What was new, and most unpleasant, even sinister, was
it was addressed and delivered to his home and that his
wife Elizabeth had obviously seen it.

The ransom now stood at four gold bars; an increase so
far of one gold bar per blackmail note, with at the end the
threat of a further increase of another gold bar with the
next blackmail note should there need to be one.

Before I set off to Rahn & Bodmer to investigate
opening an account, I was hoping that to do so would
prove rather difficult, and so help me find the blackmailer
by narrowing down the account holders to those who in
some way qualified. But, on the contrary, it could hardly
have been easier. I arrived at the impressive, double-
column-fronted four-storey building at 106 Old Jewry
and was met by an immaculately dressed chief clerk who
ushered me into an enclosed room, sat opposite me across
an enormous desk and gave me his card. I was about to
introduce myself as J. Sherrinford when he held his hand
up and said, 'No, sir, we never deal in names here, only
numbers.' I asked about opening an account and if it were
possible to deposit objects, for example bullion, as well
as money. 'This is the largest branch outside Zurich and
you may deposit anything you like with us with complete
confidence. But do you know if you have an account here
in London you can use that in any city where we have a
bank? We are in all the major capitals of Europe as well as

Moscow and New York. It's really very convenient.'

On my way out I observed a person in front of me about to leave. What made him especially noticeable was that he had a club-foot. This is rare indeed, and I wondered if it might be the gentleman involved with the Gaiety Theatre, Ricoletti. I went back to the desk he was using, looked at the blotting-paper and saw the impress of a capital R, followed by less distinguishable letters except for a line as if it were the cross of a double T at the end. I followed Mr Ricoletti, for I was convinced it was him, to his destination a mile away and shall report on that later.

I spent the rest of the day at the Repton Boxing Club in Bethnal Green and set off back to my newly cleaned rooms to change into more presentable attire for Portland Place; no visit there could avoid a meeting with the fashionable Elizabeth Lewis who had been so kind to me, albeit her idea of heaven – a salon full of chattering socialites – was the very antithesis of my own.

Perhaps too preoccupied with these thoughts, and with filling my new Wilkey pipe for what would be its maiden smoke, I was only paying half-attention to the blown whistle as I turned the corner into Montague Street. Even though it was in the quiet of a late afternoon, neither did the two men alighting on to the pavement from a goods growler appear worthy of notice, nor indeed the fact that they wore the same overalls as a third man standing by the horse in the road. It wasn't until I became aware of two sets of footsteps behind me that I realised I was about to be surrounded, but even then it seemed no more than a

normal streets-of-London happenstance. It wasn't until
the men in front blocked the pavement that I realised I
was snared in a trap.

In an instant I knew what had happened. By the
tattoos I saw my assailants were five off-duty guardsmen
from the Second Dragoon Guards and that none was the
one assigned to follow me to and from the Savage Club.
Escape was impossible.

'What do you want?' I asked.

'You've been upsettin' certain parties,' said that largest
one, possibly a Lance Corporal, appointing himself their
spokesman.

'From the Second Dragoons?' I asked as calmly as
circumstances allowed.

I felt a pang of pain as a knee slammed into my right
thigh and at the same time heard: 'Shuddup, no questions.
Now you listen here, boneman, there's a certain ransom
you owe, so pay it!'

'I'm not the person you want—'

This time the stab of pain came from the left ribs as a
short punch hit home. 'Just pay it, that's all we're told to
say. Got it? Pay it!' he shouted in my ear.

'Yes, I believe I have got it. Will you relay a message
back?'

'No! You think you're a right clever messer, don't you?
Well, you're not. Pay what's owed is all you have to do,'
and with that a smashing backhand broke across my face
before I had chance to duck or defend. So much for an
afternoon of boxing practice. With snarling looks and

more abuse the five guardsmen dissolved as deftly as they had formed.

Luckily neither Sara nor Ruby saw me come home and wash clean the blood from my lips and change into fresh clothes, and by the time I arrived at Portland Place, one mile through Fitzrovia in fifteen minutes with the thigh hurting with each step, my lip was still bleeding faster than my attempts to stem the flow. Elizabeth Lewis made an enormous fuss about it, and me, but made no mention of the recent unpleasant postal delivery. By the time George Lewis and I were left alone in his private study we were both ready for our brandy–and–sodas and cigars.

I told him my conclusions about the fourth blackmail note. 'STA, following our own code must be Patsy Cornwallis-West, but that was quite few years ago now, so the blackmailer isn't working chronologically, in other words page by page forwards through the notebook. There are no bank account details; well, they are known by now, I suppose. Now we have "goes to" not "returned to". And why are the outlets all described as "scandal press"? How did Elizabeth take it, their knowing where you live?' I asked.

'Where we live, our address here, is hardly a secret. She entertains constantly and that's all well reported. She's distressed. I never bring my work home, mostly because some of it – ha, most of it – is fairly sordid.'

'May I see the envelope as well?' He retrieved it from his desk and handed it me. 'Now this is interesting; it's addressed to Mrs Elizabeth Lewis and not Mrs George

Lewis as it should be. Then just "At home", not the address. Does the incorrect name usage lessen the odds on Knollys?'

'Unless it's a blind and he's trying to throw us off his scent, perhaps?'

'True, could be a blind. It's interesting, though. Whistler and perhaps Corder probably wouldn't know the correct usage.'

'Well, if that's so, it's that rare event in this case: a clue,' said Lewis.

'I didn't tell you what truly happened to cause my bleeding lip in front of Elizabeth,' I said, then proceeded to explain in detail about the Second Dragoon Guards ambush and their 'pay-up' demands. 'It clearly refers to the blackmail as that's my only case at the moment involving anyone paying up at all,' I explained.

'Do you know who sent them?'

'We know that the Earl of Gifford sent the Savage Club man, so it's a fair supposition he sent these too. He's got nothing against me or you, so it would only have been on Knollys's say-so. Who does Gifford report to?'

'In theory to Bertie, in fact to Alix. Although he and Francis Knollys work closely together. Which brings me to my new problem: Bertie now knows all about it. And of course he wants to know why we don't already know the identity of the blackmailer. He's rattled, as they say in the novels. It's a whole new complication we would both be better off without.'

'Do you know how he found out?' I asked.

'That's even worse news: from his mother. So now we know that the Queen knows too. How she knows, I'm not sure. Maybe Knollys, putting on pressure for a pay-off – if he is the blackmailer. I have to say Bertie couldn't care less about his reputation with the ladies, but these diplomatic and political indiscretions – well, even he can see where that might lead. Then there's having to pay the ransom, now increased to four gold bars. He hasn't got the money. Well he has, he has the wealth of course, but that's different from money. And certainly no gold bars to hand.'

'So the weight is on us to find the blackmailer before he has to pay the ransom?'

'Is an understatement. The Queen will be riding him and he will be riding me every day from now on. I don't know how, but we need to resolve this directly. I've told him about you, by the way.'

'What did he say?'

'He said he'd never heard of you. And are you up to the job? A lot riding on the result of your efforts, et cetera.'

'And what did you say?'

'I said you are a bright young man; thorough, and with a marked capacity for clarity of thought.'

'Thank you. I picked this up on my way over,' I said, 'the latest copy of *Town Talk*.' I handed it to him opened on the second page. He read aloud:

Mrs Langtry's correspondents

There has been lately a rumour that Mrs Langtry was about to appear in the divorce court, with more than

> *one illustrious correspondent. The rumour is, like many others, without the least foundation.*

'Now that is interesting. Let me find the last one. Somewhere on my desk. Here we are:

> *I am informed that Mr Langtry, famous only for being married to the beautiful, iridescent, loose-limbed Mrs Langtry, has announced his intention suing me to libel and if that does not work, then of breaking my neck. For reporting the truth about the divorce, can you imagine such effrontery? And how does clever Mr Langtry imagine* Town Talk *finds out about his machinations? He that consumes the gateau cannot store it. Now, if the brave gentleman wants to go in for neck-breaking, surely he can find plenty of his friends (?) who have injured him more than I have. His wife I might include, to boot or to put in the boot – oh what a fool he has been. Desist, man, desist before it is too late.*

'So what do you make of it, the change of heart?' Lewis asked.

'Maybe he has also had a visit from the Second Dragoon Guards. Maybe the Queen is buying him off through Knollys. Or, as I'm sure Pike or Reynolds would say, it's just good journalism to keep the story alive when the trail has gone quiet.'

'Ask Pike, will you? He will have noticed what's going on.'

I told Lewis about my forthcoming appointment with the graphologist at *Reynolds News*, but he held out as little hope as I that there was much future to be gained there.

He topped up our brandy–and–sodas and we both stared in silence at the empty fireplace for a while. Then George Lewis shook himself together.

'Chin up, Holmes. We've both had bad days; you've been ambushed and injured by some guardsmen and I've been ambushed and tormented by my Queen and her Prince. But I've been on difficult cases for as long as you've been alive. This isn't my usual divorce trial, it's true, but it has a big advantage over these: there is no emotion involved. If there is revenge, it is cold; the worst kind. It's a straightforward intellectual challenge, and I'm convinced the blackmailer isn't cleverer than we, they just happen not to have provided any clues yet. But they'll make a slip soon enough. Maybe this cryptologist will come up trumps after all.'

'Maybe,' I agreed.

'Let's make a move, get on the front foot. It's getting to the point where at four gold bars he couldn't afford to pay it, even if he were minded to. If it goes up to five gold bars, the Queen will have to pay. Then heaven help us. Whatever you're planning to do, you need to do twice as much of it and twice as fast. I don't want to sound over-dramatic, but the future of the monarchy rests on your shoulders. Put another of your announcements in *The Times*. Try to stop these home deliveries. Be brave. There comes a point where the amount of money in prospect is so great that the balance of power moves from their court to ours. Four gold bars is a lot for them to give up.'

The dinner gong rang and Lewis clapped me on the back as he showed me out.

'Keep going, Holmes, we are making more progress than it appears.'

On the short walk home with an aching thigh and a wounded mouth I pondered his parting words and wished I could agree with it. I also still had a nagging feeling about James McNeill Whistler and Rosa Corder, but try as I might to stay with the facts the feeling wouldn't go away.

Back home I composed the next announcement:

Edward's lost notebook. No progress due to misdelivery. Please resend to the office for prompt attention.

CHAPTER 21

Graphology Revisited

THE DAYTIME WALK from Montague Street to Fleet Street is one of the most enjoyable in London, a one-mile stroll right through the core of legal London. On that beautiful mid-summer afternoon I stopped at one of the stalls in Lincoln's Inn Fields for a *citron pressé*, now so popular in London West or East Central that even if you ask for a lemonade they'll give you the more refreshing French equivalent. Approaching down Chancery Lane, there it is from left to right: Fleet Street, the 'street of ink' that never sleeps, the newshounds, editors, researchers, illustrators, typesetters and printers on the streets, the office windows wide open for air, the summer breeze helping the London odours on their way to Essex and the all-pervading excitement of seeing the news gathered, or invented. It was easy to feel as though living at the centre of the known world.

Reynolds News at 147 Fleet Street lies alongside the *Daily Chronicle* building at the Ludgate Circus end and occupies the whole of the second and third floors. George Reynolds's office is on the third floor. He saw me at the entrance and waved me in: me and a constant cast of changing characters as newspapermen rushed in with reports and out with instructions. All the doors and windows were wide open for air. Many of the men were just wearing a vest, and the young boys as runners no tops at all.

'You've caught us at our busiest,' said Reynolds. 'Friday afternoon, thirty-six hours before going to press. Persifor MacDonald is over there,' he said, pointing to no desk in particular. 'Ah, here's Pike.'

In between the comings and goings in George Reynolds's office we discussed *Town Talk*'s new angle on the Langtry divorce. Pike and Reynolds were both convinced the story was still alive, even it had gone quiet, and that it was Rosenberg's way of keeping it so. Of course they didn't know his office had been ransacked, or of Knollys's warning note or Shipley's libel letter. I had the advantage of knowing the Ludgate Circus Building facts and they had the advantage of knowing how Fleet Street works; no conclusion for the reason behind *Town Talk*'s change of tack could be reliably reached.

Reynolds walked me over to meet Persifor MacDonald, who had been given a desk and was preparing his article on graphology for the typesetter and illustrator. He was short, no more than five feet tall, about thirty-five years old, slightly overweight, and like all of us that day perspiring and mopping at the same time. He sported a friendly open face and talked while making wide gestures. He was one of life's enthusiasts. Soon I learned that he was a dentist by profession, with a thriving practice in Pinner in Middlesex, and his interest in graphology had started out of an inkling, had grown into a curiosity and was now, 'I don't mind telling you, Mr Holmes, sometimes I feel it's taking over my life.'

I told him I had read his article on graphology in *New*

Discovery Chronicle and as a result I had ordered *Traité Pratique de Graphologie* by Jules Crépieux-Jamin, but that I found the latter to be no more than an amusement, scientifically.

'*Scientific* is a sore word for a graphologist. The fact that the word graphology ends in "ology" gives an impression of exactitude that we lack at the moment. It is a new field of study, and as such unproven, but I am convinced that the bare bones of it are correct and that this pioneering work that I and a few others are undertaking will be the foundations for something solid in the future.'

'Very well,' I said, 'and I'm sure you are right. I think Reynolds has explained that I'm a consulting detective – and I might say a keen amateur scientist, a chemist – and I would be grateful if you would look at these four envelopes. I handed him the three seemingly identical envelopes addressed to Lewis & Lewis and the other 'At home' one.

George Lewis, Esq
10, Ely Place
London, EC.

Mrs Elizabeth Lewis
At home

After a short while he said: 'It is obvious they were all written by the same person, and that person was trying to disguise their handwriting by not using their natural hand. The question then becomes: is this a naturally left- or right-handed person. For the sake of your investigation, you would hope that it is a naturally left-handed person as only about ten per cent of the population are so inclined.'

'Can we run a partially scientific experiment?' I asked and he agreed immediately. 'If we were to ask all the people within hearing range of where we are sitting now if they are left-handed, and we match that number with right-handed people, and ask them all to write out a sentence containing all the capital letters on the envelope, would that be enough of a sample for you to determine whether or not the author of the envelopes was naturally left or right-handed?'

'Yes, I believe it would,' he said with piqued interest.

'Very well then,' I said, standing on a chair and clapping for our neighbours' attention. 'This is Mr Persifor MacDonald and he is writing an article for Sunday's paper on graphology. I am Sherlock Holmes, a consulting detective with an interest in the subject. Can I please ask if anyone here is left-handed?' From across the press room, four left arms shot up. 'And may I please ask for four right-handed volunteers?' Again four arms were raised, all right ones this time. 'I'm going to pass around a piece of paper and I'd like you all to write it out exactly in your own natural hand and then underneath write the identical sentence with your other, unnatural hand.'

Hoping that MacDonald would agree to such an experiment I had prepared the following sentence in advance. It reflected every capital letter on the envelopes as well as offering a good spread of other letters.

'Great Good Luck Every Evening London Pays 30 Honest Constables Invoices Together'.

Ten minutes and a cup of cold tea later our eight volunteers had finished their exercises. MacDonald laid out the eight pages of paper in front of him.

'In general, the writing of right-handed people slopes forward and that of left-handed people slopes backwards. If you think about the ease or awkwardness of the action, or the opposite, this is only natural, and this is the starting point. Then, because a right-handed person has an easier flow across the page they can and do embellish their writing with loops and flowery embellishments of all kinds, whereas a left-handed person subconsciously wants to get the awkward act of writing over as quickly as possible and therefore the letters are more stark. Another generalisation, but very largely true, is that it's far easier for a right-handed person to keep a horizontal line as they are pulling across the page, whereas a left-handed person is pushing across the page. These are the broad principles before we delve deeper, but you will observe from this experiment that the broad principles yield few exceptions.'

We compared the experiments to the envelopes and it was clear that using these principles the author of the envelope was naturally left-handed.

'Lucky for you,' said Fraser, 'that will narrow it down quite a bit.' And it did: of all the likely suspects that Lewis and I had listed only four complied: Francis Knollys, Christopher Sykes, Rosa Corder and James McNeill Whistler.

From an inside pocket I laid out the writing paper I had taken from Knollys's office on the night of the Marlborough House ball. It contained nothing of significance, beyond of course his handwriting.

'Could you tell me if the person who wrote the envelopes is the same person who wrote these notes? The person is left-handed.'

Persifor MacDonald studied the evidence for a minute, then let out a long sigh and shook his head slowly.

'Put it this way. If you want me to tell you my opinion now, I would say yes, it is the same person. There are enough similarities to justify that conclusion. The way the capital I is not double crossed, the lack of loops on the higher letters, the way the tails are unembellished. If you ask me the same question in court, however, I would have to say no, but from the opposite angle: there aren't enough similarities to justify that conclusion with complete certainty. Sorry, that's probably not very helpful, but if I were a detective building a case, even with inconclusive evidence, I would definitely pursue the approach that this writer and the author of the envelope are one and the same person. And then find more convincing evidence with which to convict them.'

I thanked the helpful MacDonald generously and on the way out thanked Reynolds too for allowing me to interview him. Langdale Pike followed me out.

'Any news on your blackmail case?' he asked.

'No new news, but I might have made some progress today.'

'Yes, all that handwriting; on the blackmail notes I suppose. Listen, I've heard rumours that the Queen is involved. She's had a frightful row with Bertie about some extra-curricular, sudden expense. My palace person thinks it might be to do with gambling, but we know that Bertie doesn't gamble, at least not seriously. Maybe I'm drawing the wrong conclusions, but I reckon the Queen has heard about the blackmail and wants him to pay the ransom.'

'I have heard that he knows but is refusing to pay.'

'I thought you said you didn't have any news. Come on, Holmes, play the game. Have you anything for me?'

'Nothing significant at the moment, but I might have a fraud case coming up at the Gaiety Theatre.'

'To do with Sarah Bernhardt?'

'Probably not directly. But I haven't started yet. When I do, I have a plan to pose as a journalist. I thought I might impersonate you, if you don't mind. Nothing in writing.'

'A journalist with nothing in writing; sounds just like me! Yes, do go ahead as long as you give me the story. You should use *Reynolds News* too. Otherwise Buckingham Palace for the Gaiety Theatre doesn't seem like a very fair exchange of news.'

'Pike, my friend, news is news. We are both waiting at the end of the tap. I'm sure I'm quoting you there. I'm just trying to turn the tap on.'

I can't deny I walked home with a spring in my step.

Although Knollys had been the main suspect from the start, I felt this was the beginning of the net closing in. And there were the other left-handers, or southpaws as we say at the boxing club; James McNeill Whistler, Christopher Sykes and Rosa Corder. Maybe handwriting from one of them would prove more conclusive to Fraser than Knollys's had been. I already had Whistler's from the Oriental Club party, Lewis might well have a way to find Sykes's. Catching Corder's would need a bit of thought, but shouldn't be impossible. On which cheery thought, a smile crossed my lips.

CHAPTER 22

Ricoletti of the Club-foot and his Abominable Wife

AFTER I GAVE Police Sub-inspector Lestrade the Vamberry case on a plate he had told me: 'If I might ever return the favour, Holmes, just let me know'. As I was starting to investigate Ricoletti with the club-foot and what Edward Jarrett had called 'his abominable wife', I thought now would be the time to call in that favour. I had already established that Waifs and Strays had not been registered as a Charity Organisation Society in London. I asked Lestrade if he could find out from his colleagues at the *Sûreté* in Paris what they knew about *Waifs et Errants* and if they had any records for Mr and Mrs Ricoletti.

A surprisingly efficient four days later the report came back. The *Sûreté* had found no evidence that *Waifs et Errants* existed; that Emanuel Ricoletti was registered as a Belgian *citoyen*, and his wife Snežana a Russian *citoyenne*, and that neither of them had police records and both of their *permits domiciles* were in order. 'Sounds like your charity is a phoney,' Lestrade, using the current police slang, had written beneath the French cable.

Readers may have gathered that, as an amateur thespian and a practitioner in the art of disguise I am an enthusiast for the theatre, but I doubt I will ever see again the sort of euphoric reception that Sarah Bernhardt received when she appeared on the Gaiety Theatre stage at the start of the second act of Racine's *Phèdre*. The Prince of Wales, who had been visiting her during rehearsals (and 'just visiting' Lewis had assured me) led the way from the royal box, standing and applauding with almost unseemly gusto. Alongside him Princess Alexandra with their eldest children Prince Albert and Princess Louise, Christopher Sykes, and the lady-in-waiting the Countess of Derby stood and clapped wildly too. In the fifteenth row below the royal box the *Comédie-Française*'s English guests from the Chester Square party were equally enthusiastic. To my left Oscar Wilde said it was 'the most splendid creation' he had ever witnessed, to my right Lady Lonsdale declared herself 'quite overcome with emotion'; I remember it now as the audience being an equal part of the play, and even more so at the final curtain call where 'The Divine Sarah' was so played out that she had to be supported by the two leading men either side of her. The fact that hardly anybody in the audience could understand Racine's mediaeval French only made the bravura of her performance more remarkable.

Edward Jarrett waited for me as the guests were filing out and took me backstage to meet Ricoletti. The cast were being presented to the royal party, and although I didn't hear her myself, I was there when Sarah Bernhardt famously told off the Prince for failing to remove his hat, in accordance with French tradition, when backstage: '*Seigneur, on n'ôte pas sa couronne, mais on ôte son chapeau.*' In the right spirit, Bertie removed his hat with exaggerated aplomb and bowed to her, while Alix clapped and laughed at her husband's riposte.

Jarrett told me that later Sarah Bernhardt was so overcome from her performance that opening night that her travelling doctor from Paris prescribed her too much opium and the next night: 'she acted in a luminous mist, cutting two hundred lines and causing her co-star Croisette to collapse in shock'.

Away from the royal party I recognised Ricoletti as the man in the Rahn & Bodmer bank who I mentioned earlier and who I had dogged to John Brogden, a goldsmith in Henrietta Street, Covent Garden and then to the stage door of the Gaiety Theatre. To my great surprise I also recognised Valentina Kasperskaya, the royal nanny I had come across on the landing when I was disguised as a waiter at the Marlborough House ball. They were both talking with another, younger and slightly thinner woman who looked remarkably like Kasperskaya; her sister no doubt.

Pike had agreed I could masquerade in his guise and so I plunged in.

'Mr Ricoletti, please allow me to introduce myself: Langdale Pike, at your service. I'm a journalist. Miss Bernhardt tells me that you run a charity for homeless children and that you would be interested in my interviewing you for a feature.'

I was watching him closely for a reaction to what must have been an inconvenient development, but it was one that he took in his stride.

'My wife Snežana,' he put his arm around her, 'runs the charity – but she doesn't speak English, do you, dear?' Then back to me: 'I suggest we meet at our lodgings around the corner, 21 Maiden Lane, tomorrow morning at ten o'clock. And this is my sister-in-law Valentina Kasperskaya; Valentina, this is Mr Pike, from the press.'

'Madam,' I said, bowing slightly, only to be met with a snarl and a scowl.

The next morning Cousin Sara and Ruby were agog hearing about their lodger's adventures at the Gaiety Theatre with Sarah Bernhardt and the Prince and Princess of Wales, and I must say I was rather agog as well. It was almost a relief to be taking the walk down Drury Lane to Covent Garden, three quarters of a mile in ten minutes, to re-mix with the more familiar criminal classes in the person of Ricoletti.

As Londoners will know, Maiden Street is particularly narrow, and Number 21 is a three-storey Queen Anne building halfway along it. The Ricolettis had evidently rented the whole house. As I was soon to discover, it had a singular upside-down layout, presumably to catch the air up high. A pageboy let me in and Ricoletti greeted me in the top-floor drawing-room. On the way up I noticed that he and Snežana kept separate bedrooms, and I remembered him saying she didn't speak English; either he spoke Russian or they both spoke French. I also noticed a sports blazer hanging off his wardrobe door. He was an immaculately dressed criminal, with a deep shine on his boots, sharply pressed light grey cotton trousers, a freshly ironed open-neck blouson and tidily tended hair. All the windows were wide open in a vain attempt to counteract the effects of the unremitting heat spell.

As Pike, I pretended to take notes about the charity that he pretended existed. I was only there to observe, and there was something singular about the way he never quite answered the question, but always turned it round to be a question back at me:

'May I ask about the number of homeless children in the different *arrondissements* in Paris?'

'There aren't as many as you would suspect. And in London, how many would you estimate here?'

'I have no idea,' I replied, 'I was hoping you might tell me. Does the French government have any particular policies towards helping charities?'

'The British government's policy on child destitution is something worth studying. I could recommend that for one of your feature articles.'

Apart from clearly knowing absolutely nothing about what he was supposed to know everything, it was equally clear that he had been trained in a conversational art with which I was not familiar, and one I therefore felt increasingly curious about.

With regard to himself and how he became involved with the charity, he said this: he was Anglo-Genovese, with an aristocratic English mother, a Cecil no less, and an Italian father who owned the *Banco di Desio*. He was sent to Lancing College, then to banking school in Zurich, where he met Emile-César-Victor Perrin, who came from a Swiss banking family, also with an aristocratic English mother who knew his own, and who had attended Wellington College. He and Perrin were equal misfits and instant friends: both hated bankers and banking. He went back to Malta to start a children's charity. Perrin's love was the theatre and he went to Paris, eventually joining the *Comédie-Française* and was now of course its *directeur-général*.

Ricoletti visited Perrin in Paris, was appalled by the child poverty and started *Waifs et Errants* and Perrin agreed to make it the official *Comédie-Française* charity and donate a very small take of the box to it. He met and married the Russian girl Snežana Kasperskaya and she now helped him run *Waifs et Errants*.

Remembering the sports blazer hanging off the wardrobe, I asked: 'And away from your charity work, have you any sporting interests?'

'No,' he said, 'because of my club-foot I really have no outside interests at all.'

'And lastly, may I ask what your plans are while you are here in England?'

'I will visit my family in Cheshire, while Snežana carries on the charity work here for the *Comédie-Française* season.'

'And Snežana's sister Valentina Kasperskaya, what does she do?'

'She is married,' he said, 'lives in Highgate, and runs a charity for Russian seamen in London.'

I had heard not a word of truth in any part of the

interview, yet he had given very little of himself away. On my way to New & Lingwood, the blazer outfitters in Jermyn Street, to investigate which club's colours he sported, I reflected on our conversation. He had told lies about all the facts that I knew about, and there was no reason to doubt that what he said of the facts I didn't know about were lies too. What was noticeable was that he told them with such expertise and conviction, with no awkward shifts of the body or sideways glances of the eyes. It was hot and airless in the room, yet he remained precise and calm, immaculately tailored, with no comment or complaint about the conditions. It was all so perfect that it was unnatural.

At New & Lingwood I described the blazer as single-breasted, deep purple with white and yellow alternating one-inch stripes and bronze buttons and asked to which sporting club it belonged. The assistant produced swatches of cloth contenders and from these an exact match was easily identified. He turned the swatch over and read 'Royal Lancers Polo Club.' Before I could ask my next question, he said, 'It's a polo club for current and ex-officers in any of the Lancer regiments, sir.' Ricoletti was becoming more intriguing, an embezzler or blackmailer, but also an ex-officer, or even a serving officer, in one of the cavalry regiments, and sporting a club-foot too; this military aspect would explain to some extent his sangfroid under questioning.

My next stop was Somerset House to look at the current Army List. He didn't take much searching, the main points from which were: Ricoletti, Emanuel Xavier. Reg: Queen's Own Hussars. Rank: Major (1876). Born: Valetta, Malta 1849. Ed: Marlborough College, Cambridge University. M: Snežana Kasperskaya 1875. Ch: 0.

Now the Army List is a matter of record, so Ricoletti's story became even more intriguing: how could a handicapped man, albeit mildly so, of potentially mixed heritage, albeit Empire, become a cavalry officer, with so little obvious progression through the ranks? The answer to that would not become clear until later in the investigation.

My study of criminal cases has shown that wise advice for a detective is to dog the money, and this I set about doing from its very source. On the third night of *Phèdre* I had arranged with Jarrett to drill a small spy hole in the wooden wall of the box office as Snežana Ricoletti was taking her 6 per cent after the performance started. I had asked Jarrett about the logic of 6 per cent, for it seemed an unusually precise figure. He agreed that 5 or 10 per cent would be more natural dividers, but the *Comédie-Française*'s condition was indeed exactly 6 per cent.

I was able to observe Snežana at work through the spy hole at close quarters. She counted out the notes and every time she reached one hundred, she took six off the top and set them aside until there were two piles, one with multiples of 94 notes and the other with the same of six notes. She gave the 94-piles back to the teller. Then she divided the pile of sixes into two equal halves, so instead of having 6 per cent she now had two sets of 3 per cent.

She put each of these smaller piles of notes into their own commonplace white cloth bags. The whole operation took no more than four minutes and was carried out with practised efficiency. I waited for her to leave and dogged her back to her house in Maiden Lane. I couldn't help noticing that she gave short and threatening shrift in Russian to the street arabs she passed on the way.

I have mentioned before that when I need to contact Wiggins I send him a card with an X if he is to report to Montague Street or with an O if to the Diogenes Club, in both cases at nine o'clock the next morning. I also mentioned that, being unable to tell the time, his version of nine o'clock is any time in the morning – and tomorrow I needed him at breakfast time. I was also keen to make sure he'd been keeping out of trouble, so later that evening I took myself off to St Patrick's Benevolent Society in Blackfriars to tell him in person or to make sure the warden, helped by a shilling, gave him the 'early doors' message.

My accomplice wasn't there, but the shilling must have worked because the next morning at 8.15 Wiggins knocked on the door of Montague Street and we set off for Maiden Lane, via an enormous breakfast at Sansom's Café in Drury Lane. That boy can eat, and eat again. Between mouthfuls I gave him instructions: while I was dogging Ricoletti, he was to dog Snežana and we were to meet again outside Muir's coffee shop in Floral Street at one o'clock, and if not both there to try again on every hour; Wiggins would have to work out the time as best he could.

'I'll ask a bloke,' he said.

'Good, but be careful. These aren't nice people. Any trouble, disappear.'

That morning Wiggins had the better of the deal: while Ricoletti stayed indoors all morning, Snežana was commendably busy. Wiggins followed her to St Andrew-by-the-Wardrobe Church in Queen Victoria Street, where he hid in the gloom and saw a handover: she kneeled to pray next to an 'army bloke' and mid-prayer with other eyes closed in prayer all around them, she handed him a small white cloth bag which she took from her bag and he put into his inside pocket.

'How did you know he was an army bloke?' I asked.

'By his ammo boots an' 'aircut,' Wiggins replied. I could accept that for the time being

'Then what did she do?'

'She went to that foreign church with the round tops in Fleet Street,' he replied, meaning without doubt the St Basil Kalika Russian Orthodox church there. 'But they wouldn't let me in, so I hung about and saw 'er leave with another skirt who looked just like 'er, only older and fatter she was. And a big-lookin' bloke, he was wiv 'em too. Right-looking pair of ratbags, they were n'all.'

The next day we combined forces: if Snežana was sufficiently careless or amateur to repeat the pattern we would dog her to St Andrews-in-the-Wardrobe, I would observe the bag swap from a pew close behind her and then Wiggins would dog the 'army bloke' to his destination and I would dog Snežana to hers. Somewhere during the expedition one of us would try to find out if she spoke English or not. Surprisingly, she did repeat the pattern, exactly, and five minutes later I slid silently into a pew three rows and to one side of her and started praying convincingly. Two minutes later a smartly dressed young man with army issue shoes, soles facing me, and neatly pressed trousers kneeled beside her. They appeared to pray. She took one of the white cloth bags I had seen through the spy hole from her handbag and he put it into his jacket. A minute later, the army officer and one of the three-per-cent bags left the church. I saw a movement in the shadows: Wiggins was dogging him. A minute after that Snežana stirred; moments later so did I and we were out in Queen Victoria Street heading for Holborn.

I was far fleeter of foot than Snežana and slipping on a beard and clear spectacles I was praying in the last pew in St Basil Kalika's long before she arrived. She walked down the aisle and kneeled next to an identically dressed and more fully proportioned woman. I walked softly to a pew close behind and slightly offset, and observed as I had in St Andrew's: a white cloth bag was transferred from one petitioner to the other, whereupon the one who had arrived first, Valentina Kasperskaya, rose and left the church. It was she who I decided to dog next. Fifteen minutes later she and her three-per-cent bag walked through the front gates of Marlborough House, but not before I decided my disguise was good enough to try to engage her in conversation. I rushed up behind her waving my fresh handkerchief and asked if she had dropped it. She simply snatched it from me with her right hand, and told me to go away. She also volunteered that I was a 'skinny pig-dog'.

At one o'clock I was outside Muir's coffee shop in Floral Street, and so was a smiling Wiggins. I invited him in, somewhat to the horror of the fellow habitués who were not used to seeing street arabs dining so close to hand. As ever, Wiggins ate like a Trojan, but it was money well spent: he was a good boy and he had good news.

'I dogged the army bloke all the way to the War Office in Horse Guards, Whitehall.'

'Did you, by George? Now that is interesting. Why is one three-per cent white cloth bag in Marlborough House and the other in the War Office?'

'Wotsat?'

'Just thinking aloud. You've been very helpful. Goes to show the value of dogging the oof, as you would say. Even if at this stage its final destinations have yet to be discovered. Another toad in the hole?' He nodded yes with a mouthful of the previous one. I gave him an elementary lesson in the practice of holding a knife and fork correctly, or at least as was the common custom.

'Wot's next?' he asked as we walked back down Floral Street.

'Nothing more for today,' I said, 'but there will be. You enjoy being a detective's assistant, I perceive? You're good at it too.'

'Yeah, fun. I like the oof 'n' all.' I topped his oof up with a few more shillings and disappeared into the throng of Covent Garden.

The new Wilkey pipe wasn't smoked in yet, far from it, and so I repaired to St James's Park to rent a deck-chair, look at the fluttering flamingos and work my way through a pouch of shag. What was known so far? Ricoletti and Perrin were in league to rob the *Comédie-Française* of 6 per cent, or 3 per cent plus 3 per cent, of its takings. Why the very precise 6 per cent and not the more convenient 5 per cent or likely 7½ per cent? A known unknown, as Lewis would say. The extortion had carried over from Paris to London, and Edward Jarrett had said it was a condition of the season. Ricoletti was an international figure, presumably multi-lingual, with a bogus French domicile and a bogus French charity, yet was a serving Queen's cavalry officer and in his current guise not even recognisable as a British subject. The motives seemed to have moved from commonplace crime to international affairs. Although we were not currently at war with France, an intense rivalry existed across empires, and among the people. *Waifs et Errants* and Waifs and Strays were hoax façades and the *Comédie-Française* was, whether knowingly or not, paying money gained dishonestly from the public to the British Army, as seemed most likely. That was known; this was still unknown: was Perrin part of a plot to facilitate this transfer of funds to a rival power, or did he genuinely think he was financing a charity? And why? Why would the *Comédie-Française* be doing so? The only conclusion for now was that Ricoletti was a British spy of unknown description planted in France; a conclusion that admittedly posed as many questions as it provided answers.

Then there was the other 3 per cent, the 3 per cent that

ended up in Marlborough House and not the War Office. It seemed as though when 6 per cent was reached there had been a schoolboy's bargain: half for you, half for me. The obvious question here was: what happened to the 3 per cent when Snežana wasn't in London where she could hide it with her sister Valentina at Marlborough House? The answer must be that in Paris the Ricolettis had their own version of Marlborough House, somewhere totally safe and secure in which to store their takings. That place was of course Rahn & Bodmer bank. Then why not use the London branch, where I had seen Ricoletti? – because Snežana wanted to cut her sister in on the deal while she was in London, for reasons unknown.

There were only two people who could untangle the knot. Ricoletti of course would know everything, but if I were right about the espionage he could only ever admit, if he admitted to anything, to Snežana's 3 per cent. The other person was, unfortunately, Mycroft, who would know nothing about Snežana's 3 per cent, but probably everything about Ricoletti's in the War Office. I knocked out the last of the shag ash from the bowl on the deck-chair, saw the flamingos at their early evening rest and left St James's Park for home, with tomorrow's plans already in place: first Ricoletti, then Mycroft, then Jarrett.

Still posing as Pike, I laid out in front of Ricoletti everything I knew. Practised as he was in the art of deception, the bare facts laid out in quick succession in front of him could not be gainsaid. I made it clear that I had no intention of writing about his spying for our shared country and purpose, but every intention of writing about the dishonest money from a non-existent charity being squirrelled away under his jurisdiction in the royal household of Marlborough House. Surprisingly quickly and with little resistance we reached an accommodation: anxious above all to maintain his espionage façade intact, he agreed that while in London the second three-per-cent extortion, Snežana's and Valentina's, would cease. Mycroft can become almost intolerably patronising and pompous when he wears his well-connected government hat and that morning he was on fine form.

'My dear Sherlock,' he said, 'why didn't you come to me earlier? I know all about it. But what I'm going to tell you is of the utmost national secrecy and so you must promise me that not a word of it will go beyond these walls. In fact, if you weren't my brother, I wouldn't be telling you this at all. You may be finding your way in straightforward criminal cases, but here you are dabbling in the dark arts of treachery and betrayal, of the Great Game, of Empire and influence, of unforeseen consequences, of falsely claiming credit and passing on blame. In other words: Intelligence, military and diplomatic. Learn this different game you have stumbled into well, and other opportunities may fall your way too.

'Now listen to me. The facts are as follows. Emanuel Xavier Ricoletti is Anglo-Maltese, his English mother is a Cecil, so more Anglo than Maltese, thank heavens. His father owns the Bank of M'dina and much else besides. He went to Harrow and Cambridge where, partly because he is multi-lingual and partly because he is a Cecil, he was recruited to work for the Directorate of Military Intelligence, known to us as the DMI, reporting to the War Office. The DMI is a recent invention and purely for reasons of bureaucracy Ricoletti had to be a military officer. With his impediment he could hardly be passed off in the infantry, and as you know he is a keen horseman, and as you don't know his uncle on the Cecil side is Field Marshall Henry Seymour Cecil, Commanding Officer of the Royal Horse Guards. So he was dovetailed painlessly into the cavalry, the Lancers to be precise, though I doubt if he will have to carry a lance in anger.

'Emile-César-Victor Perrin is an Anglo-Swiss aristocrat on both his English and Swiss parentage, if the confederate Swiss might be said to have an aristocracy. He went to Eton and the *Université de Grenoble*, where unsurprisingly he developed a lasting hatred of all things French. His godfather is none other than General Sir Henry Brackenbury, now Commanding Officer of the DMI, then a colonel within it. Brackenbury recruited him and introduced him to Ricoletti.

'Together they came up with a scheme. The French government would give so much money to the *Comédie-Française* that portions of it could go missing without anybody noticing and these missing portions would finance the British spying operation in France. They took it to Brackenbury and he agreed at once. There is something admirably poetic about the few French who pay their taxes indirectly funding British Intelligence, as I'm sure you will agree. A bonus for Ricoletti is that the percentage from the box is rumoured to pay for his ruinously expensive pastime: polo.'

On my way over to the Gaiety Theatre to report to Jarrett, I put the two sides of the puzzle together. In the British interest the DMI were taking 3 per cent of the *Comédie-Française* box. Snežana Ricoletti found out about it and offered Perrin and her husband a proposal they could not reject: either she had equal rights or she would take the whole affair to the *Sûreté*. She was right, they could not reject it, and thus the 3 per cent became 6 per cent.

To Edward Jarrett I could only report half the story, and when I considered it even to report on that aspect would compromise the other, so I had to keep both aspects secret. He had to content himself with the reduction in the extortion from 6 per cent to 3 per cent and although initially a little bewildered he was soon content enough with a compromise that had an element of *force majeure* to it.

There the story ended, or so I thought. A week later a small package arrived at Montague Street and inside was a box and on top of the box a card. The card read: 'Jarrett tells me you have been a good detective. Thank you and I hope you will find a use for these. With affection, Sarah Bernhardt.' Intrigued, I opened the box and inside saw a pair of Persian slippers. One day I hope to find a use for at least one of them.

CHAPTER 23

At Arthur's

I WANTED TO buy Sunday's *Reynolds News*, partly to show George Lewis Persifor MacDonald's article on graphology, but at the Carper & Sons news stand I also saw the latest edition of *Town Talk*. Rosenberg had changed tack again, this time sensationally so.

The Fateful Mrs Langtry

A petition has been filed in the Divorce Court by Mr Langtry. H.R.H. the Prince of Wales and two other gentlemen, whose names up to the time of going to press we have not been enabled to learn, are mentioned as co-respondents. But wait! We have just now been informed that H.R.H. the Prince of Wales has been joined by Lord Lonsdale and Lord Londesborough as the co-respondents in the suit. His poor wife is nothing if not industrious, it must be agreed.

Who is Mrs Langtry?

Mrs Langtry herself cannot assert that there is any modesty in posing to photographic artists in, to say the very least, suggestive attitudes, to leer and wink and simulate smiles that can only be ranked one degree beneath lewdness. The daughter of a family who certainly cannot rank with the old and stable nobility

> *of our country has, by some means, been raised to a fictitious popularity by means of the photographers' camera and lens, and for what purpose? To be exposed in the windows of shops with her name attached to the picture, to have her points criticised as if she were a horse for sale, to give 'Arry and Hedward an opportunity of passing indecent remarks about her, and to disgust all respectable thinking women at the public exhibition she makes of her charms.*

I bought two copies of both papers, the second ones for George Lewis, which I promptly put through his Portland Place letterbox, with a note asking him to confirm a meeting time as presently as possible. Back in Montague Street, as I was about to sit down to Cousin Sara's sumptuous Sunday lunch, Lewis's telegram arrived: TOWNTALK UNFORTUNATE STOP TOMORROW LUNCH 1300 ARTHURS STOP. I folded it away, hoping that Langdale Pike would not be sitting in his customary bay window and so able to observe us both arriving. I really wanted to tell Lewis about MacDonald's left-hander suspects theory more than discuss the *Town Talk* piece, and I didn't want Lewis to know I had been discussing the blackmail case with Pike, even if only minimally. In particular I wanted to find out if Lewis had any ideas how we could find a sample of Christopher Sykes's handwriting, as I already had Jimmy Whistler's and of course Knollys's. On the other hand, Pike was a Portland Place salon regular, Lewis must have known he could easily be at Arthur's at lunchtime and he might have thought a member of the fourth estate could be a useful addition to our armoury.

'Tomorrow lunch' became lunch today and approaching Arthur's at the bottom of St James's Street in the endless heatwave I soon saw Langdale Pike keeping abreast of club-land's comings and goings from his bay window. Inside, over a glass of *fino* sherry I told him I was having lunch with Lewis.

'May I join you? I'm sure I could find a paper to pay for lunch,' Pike asked.

'It's Lewis's lunch, so he'd better decide.'

'Of course. So, then, you'll be discussing the blackmail case?'

'About which you know nothing, please, Pike.'

'About which I know nothing from you, thank you, Holmes.'

'Well, if it comes up, make that clear. Did you see yesterday's *Town Talk*? That's why we are here.'

'Of course I've seen it. And in case you think otherwise, no, I didn't write it. Or even fount it. Have you heard about the Earl of Shrewsbury?'

'No, who's he?' I asked.

'He is Lillie Langtry's new beau. Read all about it in Wednesday's *Vanity Fair*. That will be one of mine.'

'Well, at least *Town Talk* missed that.'

'I only found out on Saturday, after they'd gone to press. I wouldn't have given it to Rosenberg anyway, he's sailing too close to the wind for my founts of gossip.

Shrewsbury is only nineteen, and of course as a recent ex-virgin, thanks to "The Lily", he is madly in love with her. Word I hear is that Gladys and Patsy are encouraging her to hook him, settle down and put all the parties and scandals behind her. He would be a good catch, even if he is five years younger and knows nothing about anything. Anyway, he's off to the Transvaal War next month, so for her it's just a summer fling. Ah, here's Lewis.'

George Lewis arrived ten minutes late, with a recently mopped brow and dusty boots from walking more quickly than usual. The latest copy of *Town Talk* was under his arm. He greeted Pike with 'I thought you might be here', told us both he no longer had time for lunch and suggested we sit in a quiet corner and dissect the latest developments.

Laying the *Town Talk* on the table Lewis said: 'We'll talk about this in a minute, but first, Pike, I hear from Holmes that you've been told about the Queen and Bertie having a big brouhaha about money. You know anything to do about Bertie falls under my purview. So, under Pythic Club rules, what have you heard?'

'Just that: under Pythic Club rules, they've had a big row about money. The Queen is demanding Bertie pays someone a large sum of money, new money outside his allowance and that my palace fount assumes is a large gambling debt that the Queen has suddenly heard about. But I smell a rat, because firstly as we all know he doesn't really gamble properly, and secondly the kind of people he does gamble with, Christopher Sykes and his crew, would never be so demanding over his gambling debts that she would get to hear of it. Look, we all know that she sees his life as useless and as one continuous scandal after another, so my two-plus-two says that one of these scandals has blown up and he is being blackmailed. Now we have these *Town Talk* stories and now he has been named, his enemies in Buckingham Palace, in other words almost anyone and everyone, will make sure that she knows all about it.'

'That makes sense,' said Lewis. 'And beyond that?'

'So all of a sudden the Lillie Langtry scandal is public and, as much as the Queen disdains her Prince personally, she doesn't want the royal train derailed, possibly irreparably, because of him. He, on the other hand, can't or won't pay, hence Holmes here being under the cosh to sort it out pronto before he has to pay. A straight race: Holmes versus time. So the way I read it, the royal money row is somehow connected to what's happening behind the scenes in the *Town Talk* story, and blackmail of some kind looks like the most likely contender.'

Lewis didn't deny the blackmail, and it felt to me and I'm sure to Pike that by not denying it he was admitting it. Instead, Lewis said pointing at the *Town Talk*: 'The first half of this is true; Ned Langtry has filed for divorce. The second half, about milords Lonsdale and Londesborough, may or may not be true – I mean she's not exactly the Virgin Mary. What's your opinion on that?'

'I would say extremely unlikely,' Pike replied. 'Lonsdale's got his hands full with Gladys, who would literally wring his neck if it were true and she found out about it, which she would for sure. Aside from anything else Lillie and Gladys and Patsy are best friends, so no. Definitely not. Londesborough is not really on the social scene and doesn't strike me as the type, although Bertie is, shall we say, friendly with his daughter Lady Edith, as you of all people very well know. But again, no, doesn't make sense at all. To me it's the second half of the story that's more interesting, the public pillorying of Lillie. That's pure editorial, why would Rosenberg do that? She certainly puts it about a bit, but she's hardly the only one in that set. It reads almost like a grudge.'

'Maybe he's carrying the grudge for whoever is feeding him the stories?' asked Lewis.

'I don't think it's the court clerks, as they sell the stories and they haven't contacted me. Let's face it, it could be any number of people. I wouldn't put it past Oscar Wilde. Much as we all love him, since he's become tied up with Bram Stoker and Henry Irving and started writing for *The Theatre* he's rather let his role as a columnist go to his head. He's now a regular in *Vanity Fair* and I know he's feeding gossip to *Sphere* and *Morning Call*. That's all they do at the Lyceum, if you ask me, sit around all day gossiping. But then again he'd never do that to Lillie, who he claims is some kind of protégé.'

I wanted to remind Lewis about Ned Langtry's sly-hand lawyer Lee Shipley and the fact that Langtry had some of Bertie's mildly embarrassing love letters, but couldn't do so in front of Pike. Instead I brought the subject round to something more on my mind and asked Pike:

'You just mentioned Christopher Sykes in connection with gambling. All I know is that he is my family's local MP and Bertie's best friend. What do we know about him?'

'Why do you ask? Is he involved in the blackmail case?'

I waited for Lewis to answer. 'You know I'm not able to comment on that. I have to leave anyway, sorry about lunch. There's no reason why you shouldn't have a chat about it to Holmes, still under Pythic Club rules, please.' As he was leaving, he added: 'It's the most blasted case I've ever come across. I don't know if we are dealing with a Machiavellian genius or a complete simpleton who is too stupid to leave us any clues.'

As Pike had put together the bare bones of the blackmail case, I thought there was no harm, especially with Lewis's blessing, in telling him all I knew so far. I finished with this: 'I am formulating some broad principles of the art of detection that might be applied to all crimes, including this one which is, I'm sure you agree, uncommon singular. I believe there are four principles and no doubt they will be refined. Firstly, there must be a reason to commit the crime, usually if not quite always driven by one of the seven deadly sins. In this case, I would suggest greed, envy and pride as the most likely candidates. Secondly, the perpetrator must have the technique to commit the crime, so for example the physical strength or the ability to use the weapon concerned, which in this case is simply applying pen to paper. Thirdly, the criminal must have the chance to commit the crime, the ability to actually be there when the crime takes place; in this case I would suggest that is when the blackmail note is posted through the Lewis & Lewis letter box. Fourthly, when the detective has ruled out the impossible, whatever is left remains, if only by definition, possible.

'So with Lewis I have narrowed the field down to four: Francis Knollys, James McNeill Whistler, Rosa Corder and Christopher Sykes.'

Pike summoned the waiter and ordered two rounds of devilled herrings and two glasses of Sancerre.

'Yes,' he said slowly, 'I can follow all that. It's interesting for me listening to the logical mind in full flow. Mine is rather the opposite, I'm afraid. Sometimes I think we each have two brains, a north and a south; one for logic and organisation like yours, the other for invention and chaos like mine. So what's next?'

'I have Knollys's and Whistler's handwriting, but not Sykes's or Corder's. I hardly know her, only her reputation, and even that only through Wilde.' I didn't mention the opium den. 'As you say, he is hardly the soul of discretion, so I'd rather not ask him to introduce us. Could you?'

'Why not come with me to the *Comédie-Française*'s Albert Hall fête? They're raising money for a bed at the French Hospital in Leicester Square for visiting French actors who fall ill here. Sarah Bernhardt has talked Bertie into coming and he always brings Alix and Christopher Sykes to these events. Leave Sykes to me, I'll have him write and sign a message for the charity. Wilde will round up the Thames House set for her so Rosa Corder is sure to be there. Wednesday evening, we could meet at the

Arts Club and go on from there. Now last time we met you asked me if you could disguise yourself as me to meet someone called Ricoletti at the Gaiety. Have you anything on that one for me?'

'It's a spurious charity story. Nothing too gossipy. I'll give it to you on Wednesday at the Arts Club.'

Chapter 24

From the Albert Hall to Bethnal Green

THE *COMÉDIE-FRANÇAISE* had made a most impressive set for their London season swansong, the Albert Hall fête to raise money for a new actors' bed at the *Hôpital et Dispensaire Français*, the French hospital in Leicester Square. The stage had been dressed as a dormitory ward, with eight beds occupied by bandaged and stage-blooded actors, while other players acted the parts of physicians and nurses. At the end of the ward was a conspicuously empty new bed, raised slightly on a plinth: the one being funded that day. The papers had been full of the story: one of the Parisian stagehands at the Gaiety Theatre had been taken ill early in the season and there had been no room for him at the French hospital, even though there had been an empty bed – the system being that each bed was underwritten for a particular category of patient. Therefore the fête was to pay for a bed for any member of a visiting French theatre company who fell ill in London. They rather pointedly added that when not in use by one of their kind, it was open for use by any French visitors to London.

There was no doubt that Sarah Bernhardt, 'The Divine Sarah', had been the sensation of the season, and she and Oscar Wilde between them had been encouraging attendance at the fête since it was announced a month ago.

Wilde had been encouraging far more than attendance too, rounding up the Thames House and Arts Club sets to take stalls and sell whatever they wanted to raise charity for the new bed. The Marlborough House set was on full display too, with every newshound worth his salt close by, each looking for an angle that the others would miss. And the famous 'all' of London were there too, well over a thousand supporters paying three pounds each at the box.

The Prince and Princess of Wales led the way, Bertie and Alix leading their five children and their royal nanny Valentina Kasperskaya, followed by his boon companion Christopher Sykes and Alix's lady-in-waiting, the Countess of Derby. They were shown around the stage and stalls by the *Comédie-Française*'s *directeur-general,* Emile-César-Victor Perrin, and where the Prince led, a whole train of camp followers came behind. Even with the high price, the arena was full and the thirty-eight stall holders were busy selling their wares and so taking the visitors' money.

Of course, Wilde was in his element, fussing from here to there, making sure stallholders and public alike were being entertained. The main attraction was Sarah Bernhardt's stall, from where she was auctioning her paintings and sculptures; of course it was all in French, and totally chaotic, and it appeared uncertain that the well-heeled who were bidding and buying had any idea which particular piece they would be taking away, but that only seem to add to the occasion of the affair. Wilde himself had procured a thrust stage, and every fifteen minutes on the quarter would read a villanelle, 'especially constructed for today's charitable interest'. Walking around, I saw other stalls that he had encouraged: Patsy Cornwallis-West was selling signed copies of her Professional Beauty photograph cards for a pound each, Gladys Lonsdale was selling glasses of Pol Roger champagne for the same amount, Frank Miles was giving drawing lessons, Sir John Everett Millais was selling his cartoons, Rosa Corder was sketching pocket portraits for five pounds each and Lillie Langtry was selling cups of tea. I couldn't help noticing that there was not a spouse among them, these preferring the fresh air of the shires to the fetid air of London town, and no doubt the chance to pot a duck or two into the bargain.

As an aside, Langdale Pike told me a few days later that Lillie's cups of tea cost sixpence each, or a shilling if she took the first sip. When Bertie arrived at her stall she gave him a cup that she had already sipped from and asked for a shilling; he said rather stiffly that he'd prefer a clean cup. It could have been viewed as a snub, but as Pike said, with Alix standing right next to him he could hardly be expected to favour a mistress, albeit by now an ex-mistress.

But I had come to meet Rosa Corder and it was to her stall that I repaired. Her talent for pocket portraits justified their £5 price for the occasion. I had not made much use of Lewis's incidentals allowance so far and considered this would be a justifiable extravagance. We each sat on stools a few feet apart, she with a wooden knee-board over her crossed knee, a long charcoal and the paper held in place on the board with clips. I thought back to the time I had seen her smoking opium at the Oriental Club. Behind her on an easel was a lithographic print of James McNeill Whistler's *Arrangement in Brown and Black: Portrait of Miss Rosa Corder.* But it was the paper on her knee-board that caught my first attention: Large Post 10 Quarto halved to give eight by five inches.

'How is Whistler?' I asked. 'Still in Venice?'

'Yes, he's fine. Rebuilding himself. Upsetting everybody there, no doubt. We've met, haven't we?'

'Yes, once at Thames House when Whistler was there too and then at the Oriental Club for his leaving party. Downstairs with Johnny Johnson. We were in the same room, but had no chance to talk.'

'That's right. Johnny J, the sticky O man we call him. Sorry, I can only remember faces. You were looking for Oscar's tie-pin weren't you? Any luck?'

'No, I'm afraid it's in Afghanistan.'

'Oh well. Hold still, will you. Look at my right shoulder.' I held still, although looking at her shoulder rather hampered the more detailed observation I wanted to make of her. With side glances while she sketched, I could tell she was indeed left-handed, a year either side of twenty-five, five feet nine inches tall, nine and a quarter stone. She was undoubtedly very beautiful, but I sensed the kind of beauty fated not to last. She wore a kaftan, rather like Gladys wore only of much greater vintage, and an abundance of necklaces and bracelets, but no rings. At this distance her jewellery appeared to have come from the London markets. Her hair wasn't brushed through and her youthful skin could barely contain her sleep-lost facial features. She licked her lips incessantly, her hangover as undisguised to the observer as it must have been painful to the sufferer. By her complexion I suspected she was a frequent denizen of Johnny Johnson's opium emporia. She fidgeted, except when actually sketching, when she seemed to almost become a different person, physically. She had a certain toughness, a brusqueness about her and I don't think she really cared less when she asked me my name.

'Holmes, Sherlock Holmes,' I said.

'I need it for the heading. Funny name, Sherlock, where did you get it?'

'I've often wondered that myself. My parents must be partly to blame. If you're at the stage of writing the heading, could you please make this a Christmas present to my sister Lottie? Please inscribe: "To my beloved sister Lottie, from her ever-loving brother, Sherlock. Christmas 1879."'

She finished the pocket portrait and inscription and with an ungracious flourish handed it over to me. I must say it was a remarkable likeness and the pocket portrait is now framed in my front room in Montague Street.

'Thank you, that's wonderful,' I said. It looks just like me. And what beautiful paper. Do you mind my asking where you bought it from? I'd like to buy some too.'

She leaned forward and lowered her voice, not that anyone could have heard us anyway with such a throng bargaining and jollifying nearby.

'Actually, I don't buy it as such. It's from a secret source. You remember Princess Louise who comes to Thames House? I give her drawing lessons at Kensington Palace. I borrow the paper from there. By that I mean I borrow it permanently. She doesn't mind. I absolutely love it. The best sketching paper ever. 32 Bond if you can ever find it. But for heaven's sake, don't tell anyone.'

The reader might imagine my bemused thoughts as I looked for Pike to thank him for the invitation and free pass. Finally, with one of the four remaining suspects I had two solid clues: her handwriting, and on the exact, and unique, palace writing paper. However, also a countermanding fact: to the four principles of detection I had outlined to Pike, I now had to add a fifth: competence. Rosa Corder might well have had criminal tendencies, for as Lewis and Wilde claimed she was an accomplished art forger, and although the opium smoking was neither here nor there, legally, I had established she was not above 'borrowing' writing paper from a royal palace, but was she capable of running the complexities of a royal blackmail case? Probably not. At least, not alone; but then who would want her as a partner for the crime? No one capable of masterminding the crime. Except perhaps Whistler. Reluctantly I set Rosa Corder aside for now; not to rule her out, but for now to concentrate more on just one: the constant favourite Francis Knollys, 'the man with no clues' as Lewis had called him.

As I was thanking Pike a strange interlude occurred. Ricoletti limped over to say hello.

'Pike,' he said to me, 'it's very good to see you here supporting our French hospital.'

I replied: 'It's a cause worth supporting. May I introduce my friend Sherlock Holmes? Holmes, this is Mr Ricoletti, he runs the Waifs and Strays charity I was telling you about for the Comédie-Française.'

'It's good to see Pike involving himself in two charities,' Pike said. 'He must've turned over several new leaves.'

Fortunately, at that stage Ricoletti had other fish to fry and left us, only to be replaced by a slightly tipsy Wilde.

'Hello, my two friends in the sleuth department,' he said with an arm round each of our shoulders, 'One for the gossip, one for the crook. I've just been disporting myself at Gladys's champagne stall. I'm beginning to think that pleasure without champagne is purely artificial. Come, Holmes, there's someone I want you to meet.' We weaved our way through the jostling arena to his cries of 'over here' and 'follow me'. Eventually we arrived at the Pol Roger stall. Gladys Lonsdale shouted to him that she was nearly out of stock, and could he be a darling and find some more. 'I can't help feeling charity creates a multitude of sins,' he told me, 'but I suppose we have to enter into the spirit of it. Where is he? Ah, there he is. Adolphus Rosenberg, I'd like you to meet Sherlock Holmes.'

'Sherlock Holmes,' he said, looking me up and down, 'no, doesn't ring a bell. I know most people here, but not you.' If Wilde was slightly tipsy, Rosenberg was well and truly three sheets to the wind, with no immediate prospect of the wind abating.

'There's no reason why you should know me,' I said. 'I'm just one of *Town Talk*'s many devoted readers.'

'How did you know I am *Town Talk*, then?' he asked aggressively.

'Wilde told me on the way over here. That's why I was so keen to meet you.'

'Oh, that Wilde, he's a rare one. I mean that in both senses, if you get me drift? Plays for the other side, know what I mean? Of course, it doesn't worry me who he bats for when no one is looking. Why should it? As long as he's sending me the stories.'

'I see,' I said. 'That's clever of you. So you trade secrecy about his rarity, if I could put it like that, in exchange for *Town Talk* pieces?'

'Well, let's just say we have an arrangement, shall we?' he tapped twice on the side of his nose, while simultaneously taking another glass of Pol Roger from the counter. 'He's not the only one either, I can tell you. One stupid old fool even done himself in. Could have paid, should have paid. What can I say? One of the perquisites of dealing in scandal, know what I mean? Pays me twice, once selling me rag, once in me pocket.'

'The stupid old fool who done himself in – good heavens, who was that?'

'Now you don't expect me to tell you that, do you?' he leered, struggling for balance.

'Go on, you can tell me. I'm just a devoted reader. Read every word of every issue. Won't say a word to anyone, swear on my life.'

'Nah, I can't tell you that. You're not a betting man by the look of you, so it wouldn't mean anything to you anyway. Don't suppose you've got any dark corners in your closet, have you – what's your name again?'

'Holmes, Sherlock Holmes.'

'Name like that, you bloody well should have!' he roared at his own humour.

He was the same age as me; twenty-four, a foot shorter but considerably stockier, muscular with unkempt hair and a stale odour emanating from his body. His eyes never stayed still; and neither did the rest of him. We were all pressed too close together in the arena for me to make a more reasoned observation, but I remember thinking at the time it would be hard to imagine a more revolting specimen of humankind, or anyone who better lived up to their thuggish reputation, an initial opinion that was borne out by forthcoming events.

'I'm following the Langtry divorce case with great interest,' I said. 'You must have wonderful connections in all the right places.'

'Oh, I do. Right at the top. Marlborough House,' he said, looking round for the royal party, then pointing up the royal box where they had landed, he added, 'The perfect sauce-box, if you know what I mean. Good as gold they are. Can't say who they are though. Nod's as good as a wink.'

'Fascinating,' I said. 'And when should we expect the next issue?'

'Tomorrow! I was just putting it to bed when I had to come here. I'm going back there now; do you want to come along? We like our readers to see us at work.'

Of course, I accepted immediately. He downed another glass of champagne, 'one for the gutter', burped shamelessly and beckoned me to follow him. On the way out I was very pleased to see the enterprising Frank Smythson there too, his stall full of beautiful stationery and by the look of his custom the first step on his way to achieving royal warrant status.

Outside Rosenberg staggered on to Kensington Gore, cupped his hands and shouted: 'Negev! Negev! Where are you, you useless imbecile?'

Within moments Negev, a mountain of a man sitting on top of a half-brougham carriage, rode into view and shouted back: 'Right here, boss.'

We clambered into the back and Rosenberg shouted up: 'Paisley's and quick time.' Then to me: 'My office is in Fleet Street,' he said, talking about his room in Ludgate Circus Building. 'I get the stories there, then I typeset and print at Paisley's.'

It was King George II who described the English summer as three fine days and a thunderstorm. London's three days had become three weeks, and more, and the pungent stench of the capital had become almost intolerable; only two days ago Cousin Sara and I had discussed she and Ruby joining the exodus, in their case back to Yorkshire.

But that late afternoon the heavens finally broke and replied proportionately, as it turned out, to the long weeks of heat. Little did we know then that the rest of the summer it would rain incessantly and turn 1879 into the wettest late summer these past twenty years. That afternoon, the rain was so heavy and incessant that the cab and all other traffic had no choice but to pull up. Rosenberg lost his temper, banging on the carriage ceiling and shouting at Negev to press on with increasingly foul oaths. Then the lightning moved directly overhead, the half-brougham rocked as the horse became agitated, Negev tried to steady it and it bolted. Through the window as the carriage shot forward I could only observe unbroken water, a dark grey confusion with a tremendous accompanying tenor; then the carriage stopped as abruptly as it had bolted. The sounds of shouts and neighs were almost drowned out by the ferocious cascade. Rosenberg was exceedingly furious at this new delay.

'Jesus Christ! What the [foul word] hell? What's going on? We're going to be late for press.'

The rainstorm suddenly stopped, the horse and carriage were disentangled from the collision with the side of a goods growler, but with the time lost to the storm and the streets now overwhelmed with floodwater it took an hour and a half to travel the six miles to Bethnal Green. Paisley & Sons was in Carson Street, with other printers either side of them and new, already slum, housing opposite. It was almost part of my patch: Repton Boxing Club was only two streets further on.

Frederick Paisley, the older namesake and owner of Paisley & Sons, was ready and angry.

'You're at least an hour late, Rosenberg. The galleys are ready, I've had three men standing-by to roll and now they'll all want overtime. Quite right too. I've got four other jobs all backed up because of you. You'd better check it right now. Who is this?'

'Never mind who this is – some lucky reader. It's not my fault there's a bloody storm, mate. You'd better watch who you're talking to like that. The customer pays your wage, ever heard of that one, sunshine? Let's see the proofs, then. Come on, you're the one holding it up now.'

I introduced myself properly to Paisley and gave him my card.

With a quick and sobering eye Rosenberg read through the galleys. 'Yeah, they're clean,' he said to Paisley, 'roll the press. Thirteen thousand.'

Then to me: 'Did you hear that? Thirteen thousand copies, not bad, and going up all the time. I only started two months ago. This Langtry story is gold for me. Do you know why *Town Talk*'s a winner?'

'No, but I'm hoping you will tell me.'

'Because we don't do anything regular. You'll have noticed that. All the others come out on a certain day of the week and have a certain number of pages. I only come out when there's something to say. Maybe there is no *Town Talk* for a fortnight. Doesn't matter. Then there'll be three together. Same with the pages; sometimes four, sometimes eight. Doesn't matter. When my readers see a new one, they'll know it's not pap.'

Then he showed me the following, fresh from the galleys and being printed as we spoke:

> **Langtry divorce confirmed behind closed doors**
>
> *No attempt has been made to contradict the statement published in these columns last week as to the Langtry divorce case; and my readers may be assured that it was no invention. I now learn that a few weeks ago an application was made that the case be tried in camera, and I believe the learned judge acceded to the request.*

'This is how we keep the story alive, see. And the rest is true. It will be held behind closed doors. Bloody disgrace if you ask me. Still, if you're the Prince of Wales you can pull a few strings. You and I would be stuffed, that's for sure. Still, I'll get the royal ratbags, don't you worry.'

CHAPTER 25

The Solomons Family

ADOLPHUS ROSENBERG MIGHT have been, and was, a loutish braggart and a brute, and my time spent with him thoroughly unpleasant, but it was at least fruitful. I had learned that he was blackmailing Oscar Wilde and others, and that one of the others had been driven to suicide. Further, this unfortunate had in some way been connected to gambling. I had also learned that the fount of his Langtry divorce stories was someone at Marlborough House and for the time being I was taking all this new information at face value.

From the start it had always seemed reasonable that there would be a relationship between the blackmail attempt and the *Town Talk* stories, for what better way to increase the pressure on Lewis and me than to have a flanking operation playing out in public? All previous efforts to find a connection had come to nothing. Now here was another unexpected strand, that someone connected in some way to the Prince was, inadvertently or not, helping the blackmailer by keeping the Langtry divorce story front page news. Knowing now that Rosenberg was a blackmailer too, on returning home from Paisley's that evening I was sure there were clues lurking somewhere yet to be revealed.

I needed Mycroft's help with Home Office intelligence on the Solomons family and so at nine o'clock the next morning I knocked on the door of Mycroft's Pall Mall rooms. After he had recovered from the shock of this break in his routine, he suggested we walk together to Whitehall. On the short stroll across Trafalgar Square at Mycroft's leisurely state of progress, I laid out what I had learned yesterday and what I planned to do today. We agreed to meet again at six o'clock that evening to see what we had each discovered.

With the Prince hounding Lewis and Lewis hounding me, I felt guilty about spending what might well be the whole of the rest of the day in the British Museum Reading Room going back through each day's copy of *The Times* obituaries, all of this in the uncertain hope that whoever had committed suicide as a result of Rosenberg's blackmail would be noticeable enough to have warranted an obituary. Across the page there were the Deaths columns, but especially in the case of suicide, where an element of shame – and for some even mortal sin – might well be involved, the cause of death is often left vague.

Annoyingly, I had actually come across the obituary of Rosenberg's victim, Sir Hugh Cudmore, fairly early in my investigations that morning, but it wasn't until I read the obituary of the Newmarket and Ascot bookmaker Peter Mould that I connected horse racing with gambling. Sir Hugh had been one of the country's leading racehorse trainers and returning to his obituary I also read that his owners included HRH Prince Alfred, the Duke of Edinburgh; the Earl of Gifford; Sir Peter Moncrief; Mr Peter Solomons; and Mrs Cunliffe-Barrington. By now it was mid-afternoon and I just had time to send a letter to his widow Lady Cudmore, asking for an interview the following day at her home in Lambourn, Berkshire.

As ever, at six o'clock Mycroft was on station at the Diogenes Club and with a big humph and a heave he raised himself out of the green leather Chesterfield and followed me upstairs to the Strangers Room, we in turn followed by one steward and two brandy–and-sodas.

'You are mixing with some murky customers these days, Sherlock,' he said, the armchair plopping as he landed on it.

'You sound almost jealous, brother dearest.'

'There is an element of that, I grant you, but I do have my own excitement on a less murky stage than yours. The Great Game is my sport these days, but friendly wheels within friendly wheels at the Home Office have come up with some useful intelligence for you.'

'About the Solomons family?'

'Exactly so. The patriarch and matriarch, actually the great-grandpatriarch and -matriarch, arrived from St Petersburg in 1829. Their Russian name Solomeynovskova was changed to the more manageable Solomons. In spite of sounding as if they were, they are not Jewish, in fact the current patriarch is a keen adherent for Russian Orthodoxy. They arrived, not penniless like so many others but as legitimate representatives of a Russian trading company based in West India Dock. Yet almost immediately it seems they turned to crime, and by the time Victoria Dock opened they were running rackets all over the Royal Docks, and their gang of thugs became known as the Solly Boys.'

As Mycroft put down one folder and picked up another, I couldn't help but wonder if the 'big bloke' that Wiggins saw with the Kasperskaya sisters with at St Basil Kalika in Fleet Street was somehow connected to the Solomons, all Russian or thereabouts after all. But that was a flight of imagination not logic, so I put the thoughts aside, for now.

Mycroft continued: 'Then it looks like the current generation became more sophisticated, less outright violence and thuggery, more fraud and extortion. Three years ago, they kidnapped a visiting Russian admiral and tried to extort the ransom from the Admiralty. Bit off rather more than they could chew on that occasion when the Royal Marines arrived. What else have they been up to? Protection rackets, smuggling, hijacking, illegal bookmaking and horse-race fixing. Racehorse owners too, Peter Solomons one of the biggest in the country. Now in the third generation, and it looks like your man Adolphus Rosenberg married the second daughter Yelena. No records on him so far. Looks like the younger ones are turning respectable, or at least appearing to do so. We might even recruit young Nikolai ourselves if he continues to show promise.'

'Thank you,' I said, 'that's all very helpful.'

'Helpful to the blackmail case, I presume? How is that progressing?'

'I haven't yet formulated the connection between Rosenberg and the blackmail case. But I'm becoming increasingly sure that there is one. Your suggestion of

Francis Knollys was helpful. We are building our case.'

'Good news. Now some bad news. The cat's out of the bag at Buckingham Palace and the Queen is planning to raise the matter at the Privy Council next week. She's trying to shame the Prince into paying up. And humiliate him publicly. Be a good chap, hurry up and find the blackmailer and put us all out of this misery.'

Chapter 26

At the Garrick Club

'George Lewis, please. He is dining here this evening,' I told the hall porter at the Garrick Club. It was 7.30pm.

I had spent a fruitful day with Lady Cudmore at her home and stables at Lambourn, an initiative I hadn't told Lewis about for fear he wouldn't see the direct connection to the blackmail case and therefore question how I was spending my time, and his money. In truth, when the train had pulled out of Paddington this morning I wasn't sure there was a connection myself. When the train pulled back into Paddington two hours ago I knew the connection was real.

Back at Montague Street the following telegram from Lewis had recently arrived:

NEW BLACKNOTE STOP COURT TOMORROW SO MEET TONIGHT GARRICK CLUB INTERRUPT MY DINNER STOP GL

Hot running water is a wonderful invention and I bathed and changed for club-land, wolfed down some Madeira cake fortified by a glass of Sancerre which Cousin Sara had kindly saved me, and walked along Monmouth Street through Seven Dials to the Garrick Club, six-tenths of a mile quickly dispatched in nine minutes.

Lewis, in black dress suit, open waistcoat and white

neckerchief, hurried out from the Members Dining Room and greeted me.

'Holmes, you got my telegram. Thanks for coming. I'm in court all day tomorrow and should be preparing right now, but I'm on parade at my club here tonight, booked a long time ago.' He beckoned me to follow him into a small private cubicle just off the main hall opposite the Members' Dining Room.

'You're looking very smart,' I complimented him on his formal dress.

'Thank you. Elisabeth says I look like a stuffed ghost. Now this arrived at about five o'clock this afternoon, just as I was leaving to go home to change. He passed me the latest blackmail note – the fifth.

'That's significant,' I said. 'That is the first time a note hasn't been delivered in the middle of the night.' Then I read aloud:

This is the last chance. LL7 is the next and not the last. The Queen is now vilified too. 5 gold bars to R&B. This My final note. You have one day. The book and codes are in an envelope addressed to Reynolds News. Advise in The Times tomorrow or end of Prince. Time to jew up.

'I haven't got time for this now, Holmes, I need to get back in there. Look, I want an end to all this. Enough is enough. Elizabeth is seeing murderers in every corner. Bertie is out of control. We'll pay. We've lost. I'm sorry, but that's it. Put one of your notices in tomorrow's *Times*.'

'But who will pay?'

'It will have to be the Queen, ultimately. Now she's getting the Privy Council involved.'

'I heard.'

'How did you hear? Never mind, haven't got time for that now. We need to stop Langtry and *Town Talk* too. I know it's not your brief, but I want you to buy off Langtry. *I* mustn't be seen to be doing it. At least we'll stop the divorce case and the *Town Talk* stories. Stop Langtry suing *Town Talk* for libel too, that's a hopeless case anyway. And both will have Bertie in the witness box. That really will be the end. Bertie knows as soon as there's a blackmail note now, but thank heavens they're all gadding off to Balmoral on the night train for two weeks.'

'Wait,' I said, 'who will be gadding off to Scotland for two weeks?'

'The whole lot of them. Bertie, Alix, the five children, Gifford and a small army of nannies, maids, valets and grooms, plus Sykes, Lady Derby – the whole shooting match.'

'That's suggestive. More than suggestive, that's informative. And Knollys?'

'No, he stays here. Mans the fort while they're all away. Why do you ask?'

'Because Francis Knollys has finally left us a clue, by leaving no clue at all. The secret is that night train, the one he isn't on. Meanwhile: clues, Lewis, clues. I can't warrant it: none at all, then all at once. One, Bertie now knows as soon as there is a new note. Two, for the first time the note is delivered in the afternoon. Why? Because three, whoever wrote the note is on that night train. Four, the language on the note is slipping. Whoever is writing them is getting slack, or more likely hurried. And five, Knollys has unknowingly disqualified himself.'

'Good thinking, but I'm out of time. We're both out of time. Don't take it badly, you've done your best and we have both lost. I'm due to speak soon. I'm in court all day tomorrow, come to the Café Royal tomorrow evening at six. One of Elizabeth's charities. Donkeys I believe. But first, buy off Langtry. We're fighting on too many fronts.'

The evening was still light and pleasant, and ten minutes after arriving I left the Garrick Club, walked down St Martin's Lane, across Trafalgar Square into Pall Mall and a few minutes later into the peace of the Diogenes Club. Mycroft had long gone. I composed the notice for *The Times*, buying as much time as obeying Lewis's instructions allowed:

Edward's notebook. Payment agreed, will take two to three days to arrange.

Notice despatched, I ordered a glass of Sancerre, took the pipe and pouch to the Garden Room and settled down for a two-piper.

I was pleased that Knollys had inadvertently ruled himself out. In the same way that Rosa Corder lacked the sophistication, I had often intuited that straight-backed Knollys lacked the imagination. I was well into the second pipe and running through the characters on that night train when, for the first time, I started to think the unthinkable. I just needed the proof.

CHAPTER 27

The Negotiation

THE ONE-AND–a-quarter mile, nineteen-minute, early-night walk home from the Diogenes Club through the heart of the West End and up past the full theatres of Shaftesbury Avenue was time enough to devise a plan for the morning. The priority was to put into action Lewis's request to persuade Langtry to cease divorce proceedings against his wife and libel proceedings against *Town Talk*, thereby removing the certain embarrassment of Bertie having to appear in court. Thinking back to the meeting with Langtry at his house in Norfolk Street, I remembered that it was Shipley who kept the letters. They, and he, would clearly be part of the bargaining process. I was also sure that Langtry wouldn't agree to any settlement without Shipley present and therefore my plan was to contact Shipley in the first instance and arrange to meet him and Langtry together later that day.

The Prussian military commander Helmuth von Moltke famously noted that 'No plan of operations reaches with any certainty beyond the first encounter with the enemy's main force', and this was to be the fate of my plan when dealing with Shipley and Langtry. At first light, a quarter past six the next morning, there were loud thumps on our front door along with cries of 'Holmes, Holmes, open up, Holmes, it's me!' I must confess to having no sleepy realisation of who could be stirring us so noisily, though it penetrated my mind that it was already too late to avoid whoever it was waking Sarah and Ruby. I threw on my dressing-gown and rushed down the stairs to open the door. Soon behind me in the hall were Sarah and Ruby in their dressing-gowns too. In front of me, on the doorstep, was a very haggard-looking Ned Langtry. In one hand he held my business card, in the other a silver-topped walking cane. It was a miracle he hadn't been mug-handed on the way here for it.

How haggard? He had clearly been up drinking all night; he hadn't shaved or brushed his hair for four days or washed for two; his breath was rank; his hat was missing; his frock coat stained with a brick dust and London filth; his lower trousers caked with mud and his shoes scuffed all over. He was white, far too pale for a strapping man of his age, with eyes red from tears and lack of sleep – and drink, no doubt. In a word, in a literal word, he looked dreadful.

Cousin Sara, who had been a saint to me, now became a saint to this stranger. Within moments she had Ruby rushing around in all directions: putting on the kettle for 'a nice cup of hot tea', running the bath 'for a nice hot soak' and making up the spare bed for 'a nice long sleep.'

While both the women were out of the room preparing his recuperation, Langtry took out the latest *Town Talk* from his inside pocket, opened it and laid on the table.

He stared blankly at the floor and spoke hoarsely. 'I can't go on. This is killing me. I'm a public laughing-stock. I'm bankrupt from bailiffs, or soon will be. I'll be homeless in a few days. My wife hates me. I have no real friends. Now this,' he said, gesturing to the *Town Talk* piece.

It was yesterday's edition, but I read it again:

Mrs Langtry's Husband Prefers It Behind Closed Doors

I am informed that the Langtry divorce case will be one of the first tried when the Court reopens in November. It has been finally decided to try the case in camera, and so scandal-mongers will be deprived of a fine opportunity. Mrs Langtry has, I understand, filed an answer denying the adultery, and plans to countersue for Mr Langtry's adultery. What a fine mess! What does it say about the morals of our so-called betters? Are we as a nation plummeting to the depths? As far as I can learn the petitioner will find it exceedingly difficult to make good his case. Anyhow at present I will give no opinion either of the petition or the defence. Of course there will be a great outcry against the case being tried privately, but I don't see why anyone need be dissatisfied, especially as the details are not likely to be creditable to us as a nation. But for those who insist on knowing what's going on behind closed, and bedroom, doors – never fear! As ever, Town Talk *has friends in both camps and there are no secrets here. For now though, I don't care about being more explicit.*

I asked gently: 'Is it all true?'

He replied: 'It's worse. It says here she is denying the adultery. That's ridiculous, how can she? She has bedded half of London. Have you heard about the Earl of Shrewsbury? He's a youth for God's sake! But now, now she is threatening to sue me – me! – for adultery too. And she's threatening to hire Lewis to take her case. I'm doomed whichever way you look at it.'

'Well, be assured that she can't use Lewis unless the Prince agrees, which he won't. And she certainly can't afford him. So, don't worry about that. But is the rest true? About your adultery?'

'Yes.' He started sobbing. 'But what can a poor man do with someone like her for a spouse? I was with Agnes Canning and of course that one couldn't wait to tell my wife. In fact she only did it so she could tell my wife, as my wife has bedded her beau. I've been a fool at every turn,' he wailed as Ruby arrived with the cup of tea. Sarah soon followed and in short order, and with no possibility of further words between us, he was refreshed, bathed, changed into some of my looser clothes and asleep in the spare bedroom.

'Is he who I think he is, Sherlock? The famous Lillie Langtry's husband?' Sara asked when we all were back in the kitchen. I confirmed it was so. Ruby was suitably agog. I asked Sara if I could invite his lawyer round for a discussion in my rooms later that afternoon, and borrow a chair. 'Of course,' she replied, 'better than that, use the sitting room. But first we'd better get that nice Mr Latifi round here to spruce Mr Langtry up.' That was another good idea, Latifi being the Persian barber with the hot shave in Museum Street.

All I had to do was telegram Lee Shipley:

LANGTRY HERE UNWELL ASLEEP STOP MEET HERE 3PM 24 MONTAGUE STREET STOP BRING LETTERS STOP HOLMES

and wait, and read more about bees, a current preoccupation.

Latifi came at 2.30pm and a freshly shaven, well-scrubbed and halfway presentable Ned Langtry was ready for the prompt arrival of Lee Shipley at 3.00pm. He hung his coat up in the hall and I noticed a familiar-looking envelope sticking up from the side pocket.

After making them comfortable and with cups of Ruby's tea to hand, I told them: 'I have been asked by George Lewis to take soundings on your giving up the divorce and libel cases. He sends his apologies; he is in court all day today.'

'I'm not going to give it up,' said Langtry immediately. 'I want to see her in court trying to defend herself.'

'I can quite see why you feel that way, but how do you think she's going to react to it?' I asked.

'Badly, I hope. That's what I want to see, her turn to be humiliated for once.'

'I understand, but you told me earlier that she has the same scheme in mind for you. Suing you for your adultery with Agnes Canning.'

Langtry thought for a moment.

'You know, I really don't care any more. I don't care

about money, I haven't got any.' He looked over at Shipley. 'I don't care about love, I haven't got any of that either. I've had it with everything. Just had enough. But I don't see why she should get away with it. Things can't get any worse for me, but they can for her.'

'Things couldn't get worse for you now, but they could get better in the future,' I said. 'In, say, six months' time, what's the best you could wish for?'

Again Langtry talked to the floor. 'I'd like to go back in time, not forwards. Go backwards to three years ago, when we were happy, living in Jersey. I had my yacht, she had her old friends. We were happy then. Truly we were.'

'But it's not going to happen, you have to face that,' said Shipley.

'No, it's not,' Langtry was almost whispering now. 'I need to pay you. I need to pay the rent. She's got a hundred debts run up against my name. I say a hundred, but I've really no idea. I dread the morning post. I dread every minute of the day.'

'So money would help?' I suggested.

'Yes, of course money would help,' he said, looking up.

'If you could only choose one from enough money to pay the debts and start afresh with a new life away from all this, whatever, wherever you like, or a moment of public revenge against your wife in court, which would you take?'

'We'll fight on,' said Shipley. 'What have we got to lose? We're in a winning position.'

'I can't fight on, as you put it,' said Langtry. 'I've had it.'

This was the moment I had been waiting for. 'Look,

I'll leave you two alone for a few minutes,' I said, 'call me when you're ready.' I closed the door and headed straight for the coat rack and Shipley's envelope. Sure enough, it was familiar, identical to the Marlborough House stationery that the blackmail notes were written on. It had already been opened. Inside was a crossed cheque made out to Shipley & Grout Ltd for thirty-three pounds, and signed by the Earl of Gifford. I now knew who had been paying Langtry's legal fees; less clear was why, for now.

Minutes later, Shipley called my name and I rejoined them. If possible, Langtry looked and sounded even worse. 'He can't go on, it must be clear to you,' I said to Shipley. 'Your client is a broken man – for the love of God we need to free him from all this.'

Softly, I asked Langtry how much his debts amounted to; he replied twelve hundred pounds, maybe more, he didn't know exactly. I asked if that included Shipley's fees and he replied that it did. I looked across at Shipley, who nodded back to me once to confirm, not knowing that I knew he was being paid twice over.

I was aware Lewis should have told me what to offer, but in the rush of the Garrick Club he hadn't, and not expecting this discussion today I hadn't had a chance to ask him as planned, but I had read in last week's *Reynolds News* a serialised ransom story and, *faute de mieux*, took my guide from that.

'I am sure there are more bills to come, so let's round up your debts to fifteen hundred pounds. If you received that amount to cover all your debts, and the same amount again, would you give me the Prince's letters to your wife and withdraw the divorce case against her and the libel suit against *Town Talk*?'

'He would if you trebled it,' said Shipley.

Langtry looked at Shipley, then shrugged. 'Yes, then, if you treble it.'

'Very well,' I said, 'as you will understand it's not my money. You will give me a few hours to arrange matters, I trust.'

'We will,' said Shipley. 'In the meantime, I'll keep these letters,' Shipley tapped his attaché case, 'and the divorce case still stands. Agreed?'

'And the libel case. The settlement is to drop both cases,' I said.

'Agreed, and the money is paid into my account?' asked Shipley.

I looked at Langtry for agreement, but he just shrugged hopelessly, lost and defeated by events beyond his comprehension. I nodded to Shipley. Shipley looked wistful, as well he might.

CHAPTER 28

At the Café Royal

IF RUBY WAS agog at Mrs Langtry's husband visiting Montague Street earlier that day, she was equally impressed to hear I was to have cocktails at the Café Royal that evening. I must admit to being rather excited at the prospect too. As Cousin Sara noted, 'It's not every day you are invited there, so make sure you drink up, Sherlock,' – instructions I felt sure I would obey.

Lewis was already there when I arrived promptly at six o'clock. 'What a day I've had, this case drags on, and on,' he said.

'The Duke and Duchess of Salisbury?', I asked referring to the most recent and salacious divorce case, and one reported gleefully in the newspapers day by day.

'The very same. The headlines are a disaster. This afternoon Her Grace described sexual intercourse as a "Hunnish practice". You have to laugh really. Have you seen the *Evening Post*?' I hadn't. "Hunnish practice" was indeed the perfect gift for the headline writers and cartoonists. (Sample: Are you a Hun yet? I hope not, I'm still practising.) 'I saw your notice about settling up in *The Times*. That's good, a relief the blackmail is paid off, even if the aftermath will be catastrophic. I mean the payment question in the royal palaces. Now we need to buy off Langtry, I didn't have a chance to tell you how much to spend doing so. Then Rosenberg; I'll tell you about that later.'

'Well, first I need to tell you about an unexpected development earlier today. You did tell me to dissuade Langtry from the divorce and libel cases, and yesterday at dawn he arrived on my doorstep and without having a chance to check with you, an arrangement seems to have emerged. But I thought at the time I'd better press home whatever advantage lay before me.' Waiters with trays of champagne and canapés came and went; on a plinth, Elizabeth was making an appeal on behalf of maltreated donkeys in the Empire. I told Lewis every detail of today's encounter with Langtry and Shipley.

'Four thousand five hundred pounds. You're a canny bargainer, Holmes. I would have suggested five thousand pounds, so you saved the Prince five hundred. He will be pleased. Less money to borrow.'

'Purely by accident, I assure you. So what happens next?'

'I need to see Shipley and we need to draw up a behind-the-curtains agreement.'

'What's that?'

'It's a short, no more than a page-long secret contract between us that we both keep tucked away in our safes. But it is binding. And then I need to inform Bertie about your deal, well strictly I have to ask Bertie about your deal, but I know he'll agree. I suspect Sykes will do the honours in the lending department. Poor Sykes, he will be bled dry at this rate, but Bertie will agree, for sure. Well done.'

'How do you know he'll agree when he's up in Balmoral?'

'The only secure way is to send the letter up with our own messenger on the night train, the one they took last night. We send correspondence up every night. The next one is at nine o'clock, then Bertie replies directly if he can and the messenger returns on the morning train and delivers it to the office first thing the following morning. So, depending on our luck with the train times and Bertie's engagements it takes between two or three days. Nothing faster, like any of the GPO telegraphs, can be confidential. The royal palaces are just installing these new telephones, but all calls will have prying ears. We are installing a telephone next week.'

'Have you seen this afternoon's *Town Talk*?' I asked. He hadn't and so I unfurled it in front of him, open on the relevant columns.

Langtry Latest: No truth in Truth

The correspondent 'Labby' writes in Truth he read in a 'French paper' that Mr Langtry is petitioning for a divorce from his wife. Why doesn't 'Labby' tell the truth, and say he read it first in Town Talk? He furthermore says there is no truth in the statement. Let me tell him here: there is none in his. If only 'Labby' will take the trouble to go to Somerset House he will be able to see the petition. If he doesn't care to bother himself so much as that, let him ask him a certain Prince and their lordships, Londesborough and Lonsdale.

Elsewhere Mr Jenkins, editor of the Nurdin and Peacock

Review, says he looked through the list of causes set down for hearing in the Divorce Court, and he didn't see the case of 'Langtry v. Langtry.' Of course not, you dunderheaded idiot. The case is to be tried privately, an application for hearing it in camera having been made and consented to as far back as January last. If only these fumblers kept up to date by reading Town Talk.

Lewis shook his head. 'Enough is enough. Bertie has borrowed to pay off Langtry, he'll have to borrow more to pay off Rosenberg. Even if Langtry withdraws the divorce case, Rosenberg can still speculate why. And he will. It's just a question of circulation for him. He'll want compensation, and heaven knows I'm not against compensation. I do it for a living. We know and he knows the libel case hasn't a leg to stand on. He'll be trickier than Langtry and greedier than Shipley, so just find out what he wants and bring it back to me.'

'No offers?'

'No, he will know it's not your money anyway. Now tell me, at the Garrick Club last night you were pretty excited about the clues, but I had to rush back for my speech. Are we any closer?'

'I'm fairly sure, but not wholly so that I know who the blackmailer is. I just need proof.'

'Well, who? Someone now in Scotland?'

The arrival of a waiter gave me a moment to consider. 'Yes, that's my working assumption.'

'That's a shame. I was hoping you were going to say:

yes he is or yes she is, and give me a clue yourself. But I understand you want to have your proof first.'

I nodded then asked a question. 'May I include a sealed letter of my own on your Balmoral delivery tonight?'

'Of course. You know Harris, my secretary?' I did. 'Drop it off with him, tell him what it's for. He's already got one bundle for tonight's train, so you'd better hurry. Go now, in fact.

I'll see you tomorrow evening; I believe the memsahib has invited you to one of her surprise soirées?'

I confirmed; he was referring to Elizabeth Lewis's evening entertainment to which I would rather not have been invited, but which I could hardly decline while working so closely with her husband. She meant well, and on the last occasion was endlessly kind to me, albeit trying to pair me off with some poor woman no doubt as unkeen on the whole idea as I was.

Spurred on by the chase, I covered the one-and-a-half miles to the Lewis & Lewis offices at 10 Ely Place, Holborn in only twenty minutes. Harris found me a quiet corner. I thought for a moment whether to write directly to Alexandra, Princess of Wales or to her cohort, the royal nanny and Mistress of the Bedchamber Valentina Kasperskaya. Then I thought about not writing at all. What if the conclusions were wrong? They would know the letter came from Lewis & Lewis & Co and so my presumptions were at least semi-official. It could rebound disastrously on to Lewis and then badly back to me. Then again, what other conclusions were there? There was no pondering pipe to hand, so I was reduced to looking at a gas street-light through the window. Finally, I wrote to the royal nanny, as the sealed envelope to the old Russian woman was less likely to be opened by a secretarial member of staff. I wrote:

To: Valentina Kasperskaya,

We met in the company of Emanuel Ricoletti at the Gaiety Theatre; I am Sherlock Holmes. Please would you show this note to the Princess of Wales? To eliminate the other, would one of you then please write left-handed on plain palace paper these exact words: "The notebook is found. The game is up". Address the envelope to George Lewis at Lewis & Lewis as you usually do. Return it with the same messenger who brought the Prince of Wales's mail. If you do so, no one will ever know the episode occurred.
Yours truly,

Sherlock Holmes

I sealed it and gave to Harris.

CHAPTER 29

Rosenberg Decides

FLEET STREET IN the middle of the working day is a mass of scurrying souls on missions to fill the morning news, the afternoon news, the evening news, and the wires and cables that find their way around the world. Ludgate Circus Buildings, just around the corner, was where Fleet Street's dependents worked: the freelancers and advertisement bureaux, scandal sheet proprietors and cartoonists that are like moons around the Fleet Street sun. *Town Talk* was where it had been when I broke in before, Number 4 on the ground floor; that was far from a certainty as the occupants of these office cubicles come and go. I had been told that there are no leases, just paid or unpaid rents and changed locks.

That morning Rosenberg was inside, but not alone. He was conferring with another man over a manuscript around a desk and another, a nasty-looking customer, slumped on a chair in the corner. As I knocked and entered Rosenberg looked up and said, 'Yeah? What do you want? We're busy and late.'

The man in the corner glared at me, then picked his nose, looked at his snot, ate it and wiped his hand on his trousers.

'We need to talk, Mr Rosenberg. Preferably alone,' I said.

'Well, we can't. Not now. Haven't I seen you before?' he snarled.

'After the Albert Hall. Afterwards you took me to

Paisley's. I'm one of your readers. In the storm, with Negev.'

'Negev's fired. I got this new one now, Johnson. You all right there, Porky?' Porky grunted back his acknowledgment. 'That's right, you're one of my readers. Hulme, isn't it? I never forget a name.'

'Holmes, Sherlock Holmes. I gave you my card.'

'I'm sure you did, mate. I can't see you right now, will you wait in the Bell & Anchor just up in Fleet Street? I'll only be an hour or so. What do you want anyway?'

'No, it won't wait. I need to see you now. Alone, if you don't mind.'

For the first time since our opening salvo, he looked up. 'This better be worthwhile. Jimbo, go get some fresh air for five minutes and bring me back a pie and a pint.'

'I'll go, boss,' said Porky.

'You'll stay right there, Porky. Jimbo, make that two pies and two pints. Got to feed the brute.' Then to me: 'All right, so you've got a story for me. Sit down and tell me.'

I took Jimbo's chair and looked over the desk at Rosenberg. He looked like he had been up all night, not unusual in his line of work. His eyes were tired, yet darting around all the time, his shirt un-pressed with the sleeves rolled up, and he had a twitch in his jaw. On his table, along with Jimbo's manuscript were two empty teacups without saucers, an empty tumbler, a quarter-bottle of James Eadie X whisky, the remains of a packet of Osborne biscuits, an open packet of Craven A cigarettes and a box of Regal matches.

'I'm a friend of Oscar Wilde's,' I said. 'He doesn't know I'm here. You have a letter compromising him. I want you to give it to me.'

'Oh, you do, do you?' he laughed. 'And why the hell should I do that? What's that simmering molly got to do with anything useful? Anyway, he's in Ireland with his mother, real Mummy's boy, if you ask me.'

'You should do so because it is in your interests to do so. It would be unfortunate if the case of Sir Hugh Cudmore were to become more widely known.'

'That's nothing to do with me, mate.'

'What's nothing to do with you, mate?'

'Cudmore, his death.' He leaned back.

'His suicide. So you know who he is?' I leaned forward.

'Yeah, it was in all the papers. Topped himself.'

'And why did he top himself?'

'I don't know, and you can't bloody ask him. Now then. Get out. Porky!'

I was aware of a stirring from the chair in the corner and spoke quickly.

'Perhaps I can help you. Stop me when I get something wrong. Your in-laws, the Solly Boys, run illegal book-making rackets.' Rosenberg held up his hand to stop Porky advancing. 'The success depends on inside information from the racing stables. This could either be in the form of tips about which horse is under- or over-rated, or by administering a sedative to slow a particular horse down a notch. Sir Hugh Cudmore owns, owned, one of the stables, one of the biggest and one of the best. Your uncle-in-law Peter Solomons keeps his stud there. He either gave or sold you a two-year-old so now you are an owner too; a fine filly called Scandalabra. Am I right so far?'

Rosenberg leaned back in his chair, his eyes narrowing and knuckles whitening on the chair arms. 'Go on.'

'Sir Hugh's stables employ two dozen jockeys, grooms and stable lads. During one of your visits one of the lads mentioned to you that Sir Hugh is having a discreet, but illegal, relationship with one of the grooms. You send Sir Hugh a copy of *Town Talk* and next time you meet him you ask him for money not to break the story. Blackmail, in other words. He paid five times, I have seen the bank records, and then he committed suicide. You had upped the ransom and he could not make the payments or bear the shame. Lady Cudmore could not take her suspicions to the police, as she too fears the scandal and ruin of her husband's reputation. Qualms about which I have none.'

'All right, suppose what you say is on the level. What then?'

'You give me the Oscar Wilde letter and print some news about the Langtry divorce case that I'm about to give you and that's the end of it.'

'Oh, so you're bringing the Langtrys into it now too, are you? And if I don't? If I tell you to [foul word] off out of here?'

'I hear *Reynolds News* is famous for its journalistic investigations. Sir Hugh was a popular figure on the race courses. I don't suppose there is much love lost between *Town Talk* and its rivals. Or *Vanity Fair*. My possibilities seem endless. And I've yet to mention your fellow owner the Earl of Gifford, the noble you have met on at least three occasions in the owners' enclosures.'

'You threaten me, sunshine, now I'm going to threaten you with something far worse. Porky, kill him.'

'You don't mean—' grunted from the corner.

'Yes, Porky, I do mean: kill him. Shut the scumbag up permanently. Then we'll take what's left of him down the docks and Davy Jones's locker.'

Porky heaved himself up and broke into a slow trot over towards me hands and arms outstretched. I knew right then he was a big, strong and stupid kind of boxer, that I would have to stick and move, and smartly too. I took up the standard stance, waited, waited, then sidestepped left and threw a corkscrew as he stumbled past. Back he came, this time roaring too and threw me a haymaker, too hard for a shoulder roll and now I stumbled backwards. On he came again, down I ducked, and a sharp kidney punch doubled him up, then my speciality bolo punch distracted him, I landed an uppercut square on the jaw and he fell slowly, helped down by a rabbit punch, and to complete the illegalities, a sucker punch.

I felt the chair landing on me, rather than saw it flying towards me. Rosenberg was up from behind his desk and heading towards me.

'So, you're a bit of a fighter, are you? Well so am I, we'll see how you like a bit of this.' He opened with two quick jabs, I countered with a check hook, then quickly a combination jab and overhand. Back he came, ducking and weaving, jabbing, jabbing, then he tried an uppercut. I saw it early, sidestepped and landed a hefty overhand on his temple. He winced and in that instant I knew the bout was mine to win. Now quickly, I gave him combinations, left, right, left, right, left, right, then a big left, nothing scientific, just straight brawl boxing and he too was on the floor.

That was when the door opened, Jimbo was back with his pies and pints on a tray. 'Christ, what happened here?' he asked.

'Nothing much, just some local unpleasantness', I replied. I reached past him for my swordstick and unsheathed the sword, as first Porky and then Rosenberg came up on their knees and stood again.

'I think I've made my point,' I said to Rosenberg. 'I'll have that Oscar Wilde letter now if you would be so kind.' Rosenberg tilted up a filing cabinet, took out the letter from underneath it and gave it to me.

'You haven't heard the last of this,' he said.

'And neither have you,' I replied. 'Blackmail is a serious business and one the law does not treat too kindly. You wish to protect your fount the Earl of Gifford, no doubt?' I asked. I saw the merest trickle of blood coming from between his lips; he was a bleeder too.

'Gifford, what about him?'

'In the next issue I want you to print this.' I took a sheet of foolscap from my inside pocket on which was printed:

'I am now informed, on authority which I have no reason to doubt, that Mr Langtry has withdrawn the petition which he had filed in the Divorce Court. The case of Langtry v. Langtry and Others is, therefore, finally disposed of, and we have certainly heard the last of it.'

He read it and shook his head in disbelief. 'You want me to print this?'

I said: 'You are going to print this. And it's true.'

'All right, it keeps the story alive, I suppose. Does Gifford know about this?'

'I don't know; Gifford is your man not mine.'

'When did this happen?'

'It's happening as we speak, certainly before your next issue. You will have the scoop. Langtry is also dropping the libel case against you.'

'That's a shame. This piece,' he said waving my sheet of foolscap, 'I might add a bit to it, give it some spice.'

'Fine, as long as those exact words are in the piece.'

'Very well, Hulme, now get out. Go!'

As I was leaving, Rosenberg looked over his shoulder and said to Porky, 'You're fired! Get out of here too.'

Outside in Ludgate Circus, Porky gave me a sinister glare and I gave him my business card: after all a violent and oversized criminal might well come in useful one day.

CHAPTER 30

The Surprise Social Soirée

IF THERE IS anything I look forward to less than a social soirée, it's a surprise social soirée. Fortunately, Lewis shares my dislike for surprises, and he tipped me off that Elizabeth Lewis had managed to persuade, no doubt under some charitable umbrella, the cast of *Rude Awakening*, the two-hander now playing at the Lyceum, to perform the first act of this new play for her guests. This lightened the load considerably as any part of the theatre is always welcome and being a Lyceum production there was the certainty that Oscar Wilde would be there if he were back from Ireland, and maybe Bram Stoker too. I was also hoping to see Langdale Pike, a Portland Place regular, and at least someone I knew to talk to and so avoid the forced sociability of talking to strangers. The return message from Balmoral wasn't due till tomorrow morning at the earliest, and Lewis had suggested we might even have to wait till the day after that.

As soon as I entered the first-floor drawing-room Lewis hurried over to greet me.

'Holmes, come with me somewhere quieter,' and he steered me into his private study through a connecting door. 'I'm only just back from the office, and guess what? All the train times worked in our favour and our messenger was arriving just as I was leaving. And what did he have with him? This.'

He gave me an unfamiliar envelope with familiar handwriting on it. He said: 'It's addressed to me, so I opened it. But it's clearly meant for you, take a look inside.'

The envelope was already open, so all I had to do was pull out something small and solid inside it. It was a notebook, with a marble-patterned cover, green cloth quarter bound, B5 size, like a household recording book. Inside the pages were ruled, and completely void of any writing. I flipped the pages backwards and forwards, and shook it upside down in case there was an insert, but nothing fell free. It was just a completely blank, brand new notebook.

Lewis and I looked at each other, then we smiled, then we laughed out loud. We both said 'Do you remember...' at the same time, then he finished the sentence: '...you said right from the start that there may not be an incriminating notebook at all, that the whole thing could be an elaborate hoax. And, blow me down, you were right. Keep it, it's yours. It's not worth much, but it has saved us a packet.'

'At least it solves who the blackmailer is, or was,' I said.

'Ah yes, my first question?'

'It had to be someone on that train. I didn't know if it was the royal nanny and Mistress of the Bedchamber Valentina Kasperskaya or the Princess of Wales. Of course they were both in cahoots, but I didn't know who played which part. The message I sent was addressed to the nanny, with instructions for her to show it to Alix, and then send a particular message, which admitted the guilt, back to me with the messenger. Then all would be forgiven and forgotten.'

'Which they have done, but without the message.'

'Exactly. She has clearly shown my note to Alix as instructed, but to send back an empty notebook rather than the exact message shows a certain finesse. Ergo, the notes were Alix's, but actually written by Kasperskaya. With one variation.'

'Go on.'

'The Jew references. Did you notice that they were all at the end of each note, the last few words? I reckon Alix either dictated or wrote out, probably wrote out, each note for the nanny to copy and then off her own bat Kasperskaya added those last few words.'

'That makes sense; the Russians have had more pogroms against the Jews than anyone else. And she is hardly the best educated Russian, let's face it. And the handwriting?' he asked, holding up the new envelope.

'Is the same as all the others. It must be Kasperskaya's as she is the one replying. Which brings me to another point, she is right-handed. All the time we've been looking for someone left-handed on the basis that they were educated and literate and wanted to disguise themselves by writing right-handed. In fact, she is not particularly literate and writing in Roman and not her natural Cyrillic, so this is in fact her best handwriting in a style foreign to her. I don't know if Alix realised this or not, but having the old Russian woman write the notes was clever indeed and led us up many a garden path.'

'I remember saying once I didn't know if the person behind this was a Machiavellian genius or a complete simpleton. I'm still not sure what the answer is. A bit of both, I suppose. Anyway, Holmes, well done.'

'But actually, I think there is yet someone else behind it. There were three of them in on the blackmail. Ever since I knew the plot was hatched inside Marlborough House, ever since the blackmailer had to be on that night train, my suspicion has been that it was all someone else's idea.'

'Such as?'

'Remember that Kasperskaya was the nanny of not just Alix, but her siblings Dagmar and George too? When George came here as the King of Greece, Pike told us that the King couldn't even afford his own crown and Bertie had to find him one.'

'As Knollys confirmed.'

'Yes, and with him was Queen Olga, also Russian, and remember we all thought she was a poor lot. In both senses of the word. We also know from Knollys that all the family including Dagmar's, spend every Christmas together in Copenhagen. It's inconceivable that Queen Olga didn't speak to the royal nanny, who was looking after the children, in Russian. We can only surmise, but knowing what we do about her I strongly suspect Queen Olga planted the seed in Kasperskaya's mind. I know this old Russian woman Kasperskaya in a different context, and she is certainly a petty criminal, but not one capable of imagining something like this. Here in London Alix sees Kasperskaya every day in the royal nursery, even socially when the children are out and about. I'd lay money the nanny talked about it with her childhood charge Alix, and just as Olga had primed Valentina Kasperskaya, Kasperskaya primed Alix.'

Lewis smiled. 'What better revenge for a blackmailer than to have her adulterous husband pay for her brother's crown? It does make sense now you lay it out logically. It's certain the Danish royal family would have a Swiss bank account. And we never knew if the slightly strange English in the notes was a blind or not, turns out they weren't. But one thing is for sure, Holmes, under no circumstances must Bertie ever find out about this. Or Knollys or Gifford. The only four people who will ever know are Alix, the old Russian woman, and you and I.'

'Agreed. I've kept case notes of course, but no one will ever see them and I'll mark them "Private until Prince Edward and Princess Alexandra are dead", just to be double sure.'

'Good, I'll do the same with mine. And Knollys, what of him in all this?'

'Loyal to his Queen and not to her Prince. She was torn between taking at least some pleasure in his public embarrassment and taking responsibility for the future of the monarchy. Luckily, she chose the latter. Knollys arranged the *Town Talk* break-in because she wanted the stories to stop. He never knew Gifford, loyal to a different royal mistress, wanted them to continue.'

'And quickly now, we'll have to go through in a minute, any news on shutting up Rosenberg?'

'I'm sure he now understands our position.'

'So, no more *Town Talk* stories?'

'Nothing speculative.'

'Brilliant, so how much did it cost?'

'Nothing, he was really quite understanding.'

'Come now, Holmes, it can't have been that simple.'

'We men just assumed that Alix either didn't know or didn't care about Bertie's affairs. We couldn't have been more wrong. In public she played the perfect princess, all grace and hauteur, but deep down she not only knew about the affairs, but she wanted revenge for them. She wanted nothing less than to see Bertie humiliated in public in the witness box. She was the one encouraging and paying for the Langtry divorce and the Langtry libel claim. She was also the one behind the *Town Talk* stories.'

'How so?'

'In both cases through the ever-faithful Gifford. She made him track down Shipley and then pay Langtry's fees for the divorce and the libel in return for information on the status of the divorce. She even made him try to scare me off the scent. Then she told Gifford what to send to Rosenberg.'

'How did Gifford know Rosenberg?'

'Through Sir Hugh Cudmore's stables; they both keep racehorses there. Rosenberg blackmailed Sir Hugh to the point of suicide. His widow Lady Cudmore was most forthcoming, but she made me promise not to involve the police.'

'And?'

'I'll keep my promise of course , but I will tell Mycroft.'

The Home Office have deep files on the Solomons family, and one day…'

The connecting door pushed open and Elizabeth Lewis said: 'Ah, what are you two boys doing in here? Come back immediately, the play is about to start.'

I saw Langdale Pike across the room and weaved between the seats to sit next to him.

'Any sign of Oscar Wilde?' I asked.

'Just arrived back in London. Look behind the stage, he's messing around with something or other.'

Rude Awakening wasn't really very well done, or so the first act seemed. The two-hander involved two brothers who hadn't seen each other for five years accidentally meeting on the deck of an Atlantic liner. One was a compulsive liar, a fantasist who kept tripping himself up, the other a doctor of more modest achievements, but real ones. The latter was too polite to point out the former's self-aggrandisements were so obviously false. Act One ended after 26 minutes, we all clapped appreciatively of course and Elizabeth was delighted with the money raised for Distressed Gentlefolk, her *charité du soir*.

'Ah, Holmes, how's my favourite bloodhound? Still sleuthing around to everyone's advantage, I trust?' It was Oscar Wilde, who had appeared suddenly from behind the stage.

'I'm well, thank you, Wilde, very well. I haven't given up on your amethyst tie-pin, in fact I'm hopeful that if and when her husband returns from Afghanistan, a Mrs Rachel Barraclough of Harpenden in Hertfordshire will contact us to negotiate its return and make a tidy profit.'

'Of course she will. By astral travel I have been putting this very thought into her empire wife's brain. With you at the helm, HMS Tie-Pin is certain to find her home port.'

'In the meantime, I have something that may be of more practical use to you,' I said, giving him the blackmail letter which Rosenberg had been good enough to surrender and which I had since deposited in a sealed envelope.

'Oh, I do like surprises,' he said, opening the envelope.

'Don't open it now,' I said, 'someone may see it.'

'So, that settles the surprise, Holmes. It can only be your bill, monstrous no doubt,' at which point someone else pulled him away to join a party of conversations and there the curious case of Oscar Wilde's amethyst tie-pin seemed to have come to an end, of sorts, at least for now.

Unfortunately, just when I thought the case had been settled, the Prince of Wales and Lillie Langtry case had one more nasty twist in the tail, and placed me in a position I care not to be placed in again.

CHAPTER 31

A Difficult Decision

WITH OUR MAIN case behind us, I didn't see George Lewis again for two weeks, not until he arrived unannounced on the Montague Street doorstep; I was on my way to the Albert Hall to hear a selection of Mozart's violin music, climaxing in his Violin Concerto No. 3 performed by the Dresden Staatskapelle, he was on his way home to Portland Place.

'I was hoping to catch you in, Holmes, I thought I'd call on you for a change. I have an important message for you.' He handed me a familiar-looking envelope, which I opened and then read on Marlborough House headed paper:

Dear Mr Holmes

In recent days George Lewis has furnished me with a first-hand account of your exploits and investigative determination in solving a case that would have caused me some inconvenience, and no doubt embarrassment.

Please take this letter as a message of my sincere thanks and appreciation, and one day, and we know not how or when, I hope to be able to assist you in equal measure.

With sincerest regards
Edward P

I thanked Lewis, explained about Mozart at the Albert Hall, and said I'd been expecting him ever since the latest issue of *Town Talk*. He replied with a wry smile.

'So we'll just have time for a quick one in the Museum Tavern and I'll bring you up-to-date with the latest developments.'

Here is what had happened in the meantime with *Town Talk*. Readers will remember Rosenberg agreed to print my prepared paragraph:

> *I am now informed, on authority which I have no reason to doubt, that Mr Langtry has withdrawn the petition which he had filed in the Divorce Court. The case of 'Langtry v. Langtry and Others' is, therefore, finally disposed of, and we have certainly heard the last of it.*

As I suspected Rosenberg was a final-say man and had changed to word 'certainly' to 'probably', so that the paragraph now ended with: 'and we have probably heard the last of it.' He had then added a second paragraph:

> *It is useless for the sixpenny twaddlers to deny that Mr Langtry ever filed a petition. He did, and, as I have said before, an application was made to Sir James Hannen to hear it privately, and he consented. I am told also that it is not at all unlikely that Mr Langtry will shortly be appointed to some diplomatic post abroad. It is not stated whether his beautiful consort*

'No harm done', I thought, and was sure Lewis and Shipley would agree, after all the thrust of our announcement was still made and it would be churlish to deny Rosenberg his small concluding flourish. Then on the back page, as a total surprise was this vicious *ad hominin* attack on Patsy and William Cornwallis-West, headlined 'Mrs Cornwallis-West at Home':

It is an undoubted fact that the most aristocratic portion of English society has done more towards making our British higher classes a byword for scandal and scoffing than all the efforts of demagogues and Republicans put together. To think that a lady of exalted position as Mrs 'Patsy' Cornwallis West should find it worth her while to be photographed for sale, is a disgrace to the upper ten thousand, and I trust that the rumour is true that Her Most Gracious Majesty Queen Victoria herself has issued an express wish that this traffic in the likenesses of photographic beauties shall be discontinued.

It certainly does not make foreign countries and critics think much of our Lord Lieutenant of Denbigh, otherwise styled as Mr William Cornwallis West, that, for the sake of gratifying his wife's stupid vanity and realising a few pounds per sitting, he allows that lady's 'photo' to be exposed for sale at a price ranging from one penny to two shillings and sixpence. Mr Cornwallis West is a dignitary who must certainly uphold his position as a Lord Lieutenant and he does not do so when he allows

Mrs Cornwallis West, the bone of his bone and the flesh of his flesh, to make the public exhibition of herself that is daily seen in our fashionable shop windows. When an official of high rank permits his wife to display her charms side by side with the portraitures of half-naked actresses and entirely naked Zulu women, he can have but little respect for himself, for her, or for his position.

Mrs Cornwallis West lives in the neighbourhood of Eaton Square, in the region known as Belgravia. At the back of the house is a yard, and in this yard are four corners, and in each corner is a photographic studio. In addition to this there is a glass house on the roof and fifteen dark rooms on the various landings.

It is almost impossible to conceive the labour gone through by Mrs Cornwallis West in the course of a day. About 7 o'clock she takes her breakfast, and after reading Town Talk and the Denbigh Daily, she proceeds to her extensive wardrobe and attires herself ready for the first Photographic artist who happens to call. Jane, that is the name of her lady's maid, has strict orders to state that she is not at home to anyone except Fradelle and Marshall or the Stereoscopic Company's young man.

When either of these parties arrive they are taken into the front parlour and treated to a glass of something short, and conducted afterwards into one or other of the photographic studios. Sometimes each of all five of these rooms contains an operator at the same time, and Mrs West rushes from one to the other in various costumes with a rapidity that is something marvellous. Her changes of costume are so quickly manipulated that any quick-change artist is completely 'out of the hunt.' Now in blue satin, now in red, then in green, and next in white, she seems to be as kind of human female chameleon. Sometimes she is taken with a grin, occasionally with a leer; at times with a devotional aspect, and at other times quite 't'other.'

Having been taken about 15 times in as many new positions, the photographers are dismissed for a time and Mrs West rests after her laborious exertions, and having partaken of a light luncheon of hard-boiled eggs, she dresses herself, and the brougham or victoria (according to the state of the weather) is brought round to the door, and she drives round to the various shops to collect her commission on the cartes de visite and the cabinets that have been sold during the previous day. I do not vouch for the truth of the statement, but I am informed that this little commission amounts to thousands annually; and the joke of the whole thing is that these pictures are purchased principally by' cads,' who show the likenesses about to their friends and oftentimes boast that they were given to them by Mrs West herself; and I cannot say that I in any way pity the lady, for she lays herself open to this sort of insult.

A woman must have come indeed to a low estimate of her womanhood when her vanity permits her to do this sort of thing. When actresses get themselves taken it is excusable; when they are sold from the windows of our fashionable shops it is understood that they are as shameless as they are good-looking; but when a woman of position, such as Mrs West, classes herself with the latter, she has only herself to blame if the casual purchaser considers her to be in 'the same street.'

After having received her commission she returns home again to assume fresh positions, put on other costumes, and be taken backwards, full face, and in profile. One of Mrs West's greatest troubles is the fact that she is so out-photographed by Mrs Langtry."

'Cheers!' Lewis and I clinked our glasses of India Pale Ale and found a quiet corner.

'So,' said Lewis, 'after that *Town Talk* blast, as you might expect William Cornwallis-West wants us to sue for libel. I tried to talk him out of it. What's the circulation of *Town Talk*?'

'Thirteen thousand, probably rising.'

'Let's be generous and say the readership is twenty thousand. So, twenty thousand people read about the Cornwallis-Wests and a few days later will have forgotten what they have read. It is in *Town Talk* after all, so not exactly a paper of record. Anyone who actually knows them will realise it's all complete nonsense anyway. But if it goes to court, even we can't keep it out of *The Times*, the *Telegraph*, the *Chronicle,* the *News* – the whole lot of them. Millions of people will read about it. But he's not for turning, family honour and all that. One thing I've learned over the years is that when honour or pride are at stake, no amount of logic will dissuade a wounded party.

'Now at first we thought it wasn't all bad news, the judge is Sir James Hannen, himself named in the *Town Talk* pieces, and along with William Cornwallis-West he is a privy councillor. He is, you might say, on our side.

'Then disaster strikes. In the same way that Rosenberg took revenge on the Society set with his blast against Patsy, Hannen took revenge on Rosenberg by adding Langtry's extant libel case against *Town Talk* on to the new Cornwallis-West one.'

'But what about your behind-the-scenes agreement with Shipley to cease all cases?' I asked.

'You mean behind-the-curtains. What happened was that Shipley and I were so concentrated on the wording of Ned Langtry dropping the divorce case that we forgot about the side-show; writing in the libel case to the behind-the-curtains agreement. Shipley never withdrew it, although it's equally my fault.'

'But it's not libel, it's true. Ned Langtry did file for divorce, as *Town Talk* can claim.'

'Yes, but that was later. When Rosenberg printed the first two pieces about the divorce, Shipley hadn't filed for divorce. So back then it was libel. Since then, with all the other events occurring, it has been forgotten by everyone except our good friend Judge Hannen.'

'So, Rosenberg is clearly out for revenge, and his barrister is sure to call Ned Langtry to the witness stand and—'

'And if he tells the truth about his marriage we are all in trouble, including my most illustrious client. Rosenberg is in big trouble with the Cornwallis-West libel anyway, almost none of the facts are true and the opinions are libellous in themselves. Hannen is a vindictive sort, I reckon he'll give Rosenberg fifteen, maybe eighteen, months inside. Rosenberg has nothing to lose by exposing the whole Langtry marriage saga for the sham and scandal that it is. Let's face it, we'd all do the same in his shoes.'

'And even if he had something to lose, I think he'd still press on with it. At base, he is a scandal-sheet-monger and a successful one, too.'

'Holmes, I'm going to ask you to do something... unusual. Ethically marginal. If you don't want to, I completely understand and will think none the worse of you for turning it down. I'm asking you to see Langtry and persuade him to perjure himself. We can't keep him out of the witness box, so whatever happens he's going to have to face up to that, but if on oath he says his marriage is happy and his wife is faithful it will work out well for all involved – except Rosenberg of course, but he's doomed anyway. I'm not trying to talk you into this, Holmes, but you've bought off Langtry once and you've bought off Rosenberg too, somehow. Neither Shipley nor I can talk to him about this, so I'm asking you. But I'm not expecting you to do it, I want to make that clear.'

'A very timely request,' I said. 'I've just been reading Bentham on analytical jurisprudence. He would suggest that as a practitioner you were more accountable to the concept behind the law than to the realty of the law. With which I disagree, so far.'

I took a sip of the pale ale. 'When I decided on this career there were two forces influencing me. On the one hand there was the intellectual challenge, the logical pursuit of a case, the pitting of wits against the criminal classes, the game if you like. On the other was the nobility, the purity of the law, and the pleasing happenstance that by acting on the former one was serving the latter. I'm not sure if I can do what you're asking.' I looked at my pocket watch. 'Maybe Mozart will enlighten me.'

'Yes, we must both go. Come and see me tomorrow afternoon and we'll talk more.' Outside on parting he said: 'You are young and idealistic, and that's how it should be. I was once. Not that I'm pushing you to be middle-aged and cynical, I'm no great advertisement for that. But as you get older you realise that sometimes the choice isn't between good and bad, or right and wrong, it's between bad and worse, or wrong and calamitous, or in this case tragic. You're bright, the brightest young man I've ever met, so you will decide correctly. Now, you go and hear some Mozart, and I'll go and hear some Elizabeth.'

Mozart didn't enlighten me, in fact the dilemma dulled even Mozart and by the time the rondeau of the Third

Concerto came around I was lost in the whirl of thoughts that only a pipe or two could settle.

Back in Montague Street, the two-piper decreed that the two un-moveables were that Adolphus Rosenberg had clearly slandered the Cornwallis-Wests and will be going to prison, and that Ned Langtry will be going to the witness stand. The first moveable was Langtry. If he perjured himself, everyone would know he had done so and he'd have to leave London, but he did have Ireland to fall back on. He would also have whatever additional amount the royal coffers decided to pay him to live off. On the other hand, if he told the truth, Rosenberg's lawyers would soon have Lillie Langtry on the stand and Bertie wouldn't be far behind her. The second moveable was to some extent procedural and therefore even more unpredictable: Lewis's barristers would no doubt insist that the libel referred only to the filings for divorce reported before they had actually happened, but with the court full of pressmen and public interest aroused it would take a brave judge to agree to limit questioning to this precise point.

My view at bedtime was this: Lewis was right, in this case there were no good choices and now that I knew about the consequences of the choices I had to choose one. I could easily have talked myself into encouraging the perjury as the least bad alternative: Rosenberg would be in prison whatever I did, and it would be best for Langtry and the rest of us if he were living comfortably in Ireland and never seen again. An uncharitable afterthought was that the way he was drinking, he wouldn't last long wherever he was living and in fact the more comfortably he was living the less likely he would be to last much longer. On the other hand, there is such an ideal as right and wrong and the undeniable fact was that it would be wrong for me to promote perjury, that I am an investigator, a discoverer of truth, not a propagator of untruth, and that to comply with Lewis's request would set me on a false path so near the start of my career. Tomorrow morning I would tell Lewis I couldn't do it, and hope that he was as good as his word and not hold it against me.

By the time the trial came up a month later London was changing from summer to autumn. The trial was held at the Old Bailey and reported verbatim in *The Times*, and like all others who knew the Langtrys and the Cornwallis-Wests I followed it verbatim too. There was a late change of judge to Mr Justice Hawkins, which change Lewis thought even worse for Rosenberg. Lewis was in court every day overseeing his barristers and I went to the public gallery on the day Ned Langtry was due to appear. Lewis must have found another way of talking Langtry into perjuring himself and Langtry had learned Lewis's lines by heart to the various questions:

'I am a private gentleman living at 17, Norfolk Street, Park Lane.' 'I am married.' 'I have heard the libels read and there is not one single word of truth in them.' 'I had not presented a petition in the Divorce Court, or even thought of it.' 'I have always lived on terms of affection with my wife. I am living with her at Norfolk Street at the present moment.' 'Yes, I have the honour of knowing His Royal Highness the Prince of Wales and Her Royal Highness the Princess of Wales.' 'No, I do not remember ever having seen Lord Londesborough, and I know that my wife has not.' 'Yes, I have met Lord Lonsdale once at dinner, and I think I spoke two or three words to him.' 'No, my wife does not know him; she met him at dinner, but she was never introduced.' 'I can say there is not one word of truth in my having been offered a diplomatic appointment; it is a tissue of falsehood altogether.'

Two days later Mr Justice Hawkins sentenced Rosenberg to eighteen months in prison and forbade him to name his sources. Two days after that Langtry was dispatched to Ireland, with a no doubt handsome dowry.

And in this roundabout way, a little later than seemed likely when with Lewis at the surprise social soirée at Portland Place, here endeth what I am calling 'The Adventure of the Old Russian Woman'.

S.H.
December 1879

Coda

THROUGHOUT THE FOLLOWING year of 1880 my practice continued to take new cases. In addition to that, my desk at the British Museum Reading Room continued to be well occupied and I reached the semi-finals of the Repton Boxing Club's Gentleman's Middle-Weight tournament. Wiggins I employed a few times and I paid for his Sunday school at St Patrick's so he could at least read and write, somewhat, and tell the time. Latterly I have taken to conducting chemical experiments at St Bartholomew's Hospital where they have been good enough to let me use the laboratory.

I didn't see much more of Lewis, although at one point he was kind enough to say I hadn't let me him down with my decision not to encourage Ned Langtry to perjure himself; quite the contrary, in retrospect he thought better of me for it. He gave me the job of finding the missing funds from Prince Alfred's stud as he had promised to do earlier. Gladys Lonsdale hired me to look into some missing artwork. I did keep in touch with Oscar Wilde, though more through seeing Bram Stoker who asked me to investigate some missing money from the Lyceum Theatre funds where he was the business manager. But over and above these, my main case was what I am calling the Tarleston Murders, a full account of which I will soon write separately.

By the end of last year I was thinking about taking some larger rooms than Montague Street could offer and six weeks ago I met a Dr John Watson who was living in an hotel, and who was also looking for more space. Watson has just returned from the Second Afghan War and is still convalescing, and has yet to meet many people in London. We combined forces and have recently rented a suite in Baker Street that I had my eye on.

After a few days we had unpacked and moved in, and decided to give a small welcoming reception for our few friends. We made the rooms looks as hospitable as possible with candles and a full drinks trolley and both put on our smartest semi-formal wear. I'm not enormously sociable and Watson's friends in town were few as yet, so the guest list, if you could call it that, amounted to no more than can be counted on the fingers of two hands. Young Stamford, who had introduced Watson and I to each other at St Barts was there, plus a few of Watson's regimental friends and cousins. From the Langtry case I invited George and Elizabeth Lewis, Oscar Wilde and Bram Stoker, and I'm pleased to report they all came and toasted our new dwelling. Of course, Wilde arrived just as everyone else was leaving, but once installed he does make up for an awful lot of people.

'Dr Watson, I would like to introduce you to Oscar Wilde. Wilde, please meet Dr John Watson. We only met six weeks ago and here we are sharing a suite together.'

This was a moment I had been waiting for ever since Watson first appeared at our party, and then surprised me enormously. My game now was to see how long it would take Wilde to realise what Watson was wearing. Not long:

Wilde, normally so rapid with his repartee, only stared in complete silence at Watson's cravat. Then he said: 'Good Doctor Watson, that is the most remarkable tie-pin. If it has a brother or sister, I would love to be introduced.'

'Oh this,' replied Watson adjusting it, 'it is beautiful, isn't it? There is an unfortunate story to tell, because I am not the rightful owner.'

'My hopes are rising by the syllable,' said Wilde.

'Eh? Ah well, yes, you see I was an army doctor working in a field hospital in Afghanistan when a young officer sporting this very tie-pin died right before me. With almost his last breath he told me his bride had bought it for him as a farewell gift and begged me to return it to her as his farewell gift to her, as he said. He gave me her name and address which I wrote down in my notebook. Unfortunately, in moving my trunks back here from Afghanistan, I have mislaid the said notebook. Worse, and for which I can never forgive myself, I can't remember his name or I could look him up in the army records and so find her. If you said it I would remember it, but it has completely escaped me.'

'Barraclough?' I suggested.

'By George, Holmes, you are right. Yes, that was the chappy, Barraclough. How on earth did you know that?'

'Rudimentary, my dear Watson. Wilde and I have been looking for this tie-pin. I haven't told you about my profession yet, but I'm a consulting detective. The tie-pin actually belongs to Wilde, although equally it could be said to belong to Mrs Barraclough.'

'But surely it can't belong to both of them,' said Watson.

'Oh, but it does,' said Oscar Wilde. 'It's a family heirloom. But now it's also another family's heirloom too. I have learned to live without it, but young Barraclough didn't live at all. Holmes still has the widow's address, I believe?'

'I do. 14 Bedford Road, Harpenden, Hertfordshire.'

'Then, Dr Watson,' said Oscar Wilde, 'you can fulfil your obligations and pass my amethyst tie-pin on to the widow.'

'This calls for champagne, indeed,' replied Dr Watson. 'You have no idea of the weight you have lifted off my mind.'

And with three clinks and a combined 'Cheers!' the curious case of Oscar Wilde's amethyst tie-pin came to a satisfactory conclusion.

S.H.
February 1881

FINDER'S NOTES

THREE YEARS AGO my wife and I bought Otterwood
Manor, Seaton Ross, Nr. Beverley, Yorkshire, YO42 4LU.
Otterwood is a Queen Anne manor house, perfectly
square with full windows over three decreasing floors:
four large day-rooms and a kitchen on the ground floor,
five sleeping quarters on the first floor and above that a
working attic for extra beds and storage. Outside there
are three outbuildings and four acres of parkland. Lang &
Davies, the local estate agent, described it all as 'Sizable,
yet manageable,' which is I think accurate.

They also added this: 'The property is of historical
interest as it once belonged to the Holmes family when
they were Yorkshire squires. The famous detective
Sherlock Holmes and his brother Mycroft were born and
grew up here. A Yorkshire Society blue plaque beside the
front porch commemorates this fact.' I must say Holmes
meant little to me then and it didn't add or subtract from
the value of the property, but it was an interesting little
touch that visitors always remarked upon. Many a time
the great detective's name was invoked when on leaving
the same guests couldn't find their car keys or similar.

The handover from the old owners to us ended with
the inevitable clear-out rush and with great apologies
they confessed that they hadn't been able to fully clear
out one of the outbuildings, a rather tumbledown small
grange now used for surplus machinery. I wasn't remotely

concerned because the surplus machinery consisted not just of the usual farmyard mechanicals, but an old Velocette motorcycle and an even older Chris Craft speedboat with what looked like a rusty, marinised Chrysler V8 engine, both admirable restoration projects for my retirement years soon ahead.

It wasn't really until the following spring that I started to poke around the old grange to see what could be done with the Velocette and Chris Craft. In a dark corner, underneath what looked like decades of dirt and dust, was an old wooden box about three feet square by two feet tall. Hoping to find some old carburettors or magnetos or anything useful within, I prised open the top and found that instead it contained folders full of papers. They all related back to the time of the Holmes family and they included two large bundles each tied in a ribbon bow. There were no markings on the outside of the bundles, but on top of each inside was a sheet of foolscap with neatly written capitals. One said THE ADVENTURE OF THE OLD RUSSIAN WOMAN and the other THE TARLESTON MURDERS. On top of the former was an added note: 'Private until Prince Edward and Princess Alexandra are dead'. No mention was made of the author's name. At that stage I knew even less about Sherlock Holmes than I do now, and so the titles of the stories meant absolutely nothing to me at all.

I brought them inside, dusted them down and my wife Gillian started reading the one about the old Russian woman. I didn't see much of her for the rest of the day as she became more and more absorbed in the true story about Albert, Prince of Wales, later King Edward VII and the louche and criminal arrangements in his court; Oscar Wilde weaving in and out of the story only added to her interest. By the end of the next day she had one of her many bright ideas: although the handwriting was firm and neat, it was tiring to read pages and pages of script after a while and why didn't we have it transcribed? A few Googles later, after photocopying the foolscap pages locally, the Old Russian Woman bundle was on its way to India where transcribing is done much more economically than here.

A week later I received the following email from Sandeep Naithani in Calcutta: 'The transcription is on time. I'm reading it too. Did you know it contains 3 of the 4 untold Sherlock Holmes cases? *The Adventure of the Old Russian Woman*, *Vamberry the Wine Merchant* and *Ricoletti of the Club-foot and the Abominable Wife*. Only missing now are *The Tarleston Murders*. He must have written these 3 himself before he met Dr Watson.'

Three weeks later the bound volume arrived back from India and when Gillian had finished reading 'The Adventure of the Old Russian Woman', I read it too with equal satisfaction. In the meantime I had been rummaging through the rest of the wooden crate. All the papers there related specifically to Sherlock Holmes and I must say I was rather surprised at his shambolic filing methods. Nevertheless, among the other papers I found a few sheets that were written fourteen months after the main body of the work and I have called this the Coda and added it before this short explanatory note. I have subsequently gifted the manuscripts and all the papers to the Sherlock Holmes Society of London.

The next task was to find a publisher, a notoriously tricky proposition given the dubious nature of the profession but fortunately one of our neighbours owns Affable Media Ltd and he is always game for a gamble. A couple of pints of Black Sheep and a bag of nuts later in the Oddfellows Arms and we had a deal. His only suggestion was to change the title, as the way Holmes describes it, *The Adventure of the Old Russian Woman*, rather gives the game away before it has even started, and so it became *A Case of Royal Blackmail*. It will be a complete miracle if I ever get any royalties out of him, but never mind. If there is any interest in this one, we also have *The Tarleston Murders* from 1880 in the wings. A quick look suggests George Lewis sent Holmes up to Edinburgh to help a Dr. Joseph Bell on a case involving the family of one of his medical students, Arthur Doyle. But one volume at a time is my usually unscrupulous publisher's surprising recommendation.

I.S.

July 2021

ACKNOWLEDGEMENTS

Jon Lellenberg, editorial advisor and inspiration on all matters Sherlockian.

Dea Parkin and Matthew Scarsbrook from Fiction Feedback, editors.

Tim Hurst, Global Licensor from the Conan Doyle Estate.

Helen Molesworth, jewellery advisor.

Peter Bower, paperstock advisor.

Robert Radley, paper and ink advisor.

Tracey Trussell, graphology advisor.

Unicorn Publishing Group LLP, worldwide sales and distribution.

Ian Strathcarron, author and copyright holder.